ALSO BY PHILIP LEE WILLIAMS

The Heart of a Distant Forest
All the Western Stars
Slow Dance in Autumn
The Song of Daniel
Perfect Timing

Final Heat

Final Heat

A novel

PHILIP LEE WILLIAMS

Turtle Bay Books

A DIVISION OF RANDOM HOUSE
NEW YORK   1992

Published in the United States by
Turtle Bay Books, a division of
Random House, Inc., New York,
and simultaneously in Canada by
Random House of Canada Limited,
Toronto.

Library of Congress
Cataloging-in-Publication Data

Williams, Philip Lee.

Final heat : a novel / by Philip Lee
Williams

p.   cm.

ISBN 0-679-40888-6

I. Title.

PS3573.I45535F56   1992

813′.54—dc20   91-75232

Manufactured in the United States
of America

24689753

First Edition

For Marie and Fred Rowley,
who never stopped believing

Final Heat

1

SNAKE RIPLEY STOOD at the fence, watching the thick red moon swing up slowly over the pines. The day lingered in the west, a smudge of pale pink against the clouds, and Snake wondered if the heat would ever break. He'd been up here calling his brother. He never let Leslie stray far because Leslie had been damaged at birth and was not quite right.

Snake had been down in the barn, groaning against the heavy bag with workout gloves, trying to punch himself into forgetfulness. The garage had almost no business these days, and two years before, they'd sold the last of the Herefords. Snake wondered what was happening in New Orleans. A single fly-specked bulb hung on the open rafter of the barn where Snake worked out. Nothing looked real in there.

Leslie was twenty-two, Snake twenty-four, and their father, who was inside now, drunk and singing along with the television, was in his sixties. Snake could hardly bear what was happening these days.

"Leslie!" Snake shouted. "Leslie, come on, it's getting dark!"

From far away, up through the wilting pasture grass and near the pines, a thin voice came back. The air was full of cricket sounds. There was no breeze, and though July was always bad anywhere near Rockton, Mississippi, it was worse this year. The voice came again. To Snake it sounded like someone calling a dog, a voice too high, too harmless, for a man his brother's age.

"Leslie!"

"Coming home," the voice said. Lately, Snake could not get Leslie to make much sense. They'd go to the garage every morning, but Leslie would wander off with a lug wrench, and Snake would find him on the train tracks, talking to a lizard that warmed itself on the sunny rails. Snake would take him back. Leslie was never angry. Snake seemed angry all the time now. In fact, he could barely stand it. He was barely making enough money to keep them alive, much less afloat. The old man didn't go to the garage anymore.

Back in the early eighties, the garage had been making money because it was four miles outside Rockton, where the farmers lived. Farmers planted fields heavy with soybeans and cotton, but then it all fell apart. When the farmers lost their money and their land, few people bothered to drive four miles from Rockton for a mechanic.

People in Rockton thought little of the Ripley family. Harry had never amounted to much. Once, a man had bought three dollars' worth of gas for a lawn mower and given Leslie a five while Snake was in the bathroom at the garage. When Snake came back out, the customer was ready to throttle Leslie, who had gone nearly catatonic, holding the bill and staring at Abraham Lincoln as if he would tell Leslie how much change to give back.

"Come on, before it's all dark," said Snake. He stood on the bottom rung of the barbed wire and held on to a post so he could see farther up the pasture. Leslie, thin and blond, was swinging through the grass, singing to himself, poured through the grass like something liquid.

"It feels like everything is on fire out here," said Leslie. He came down the pasture and stood on the other side of the fence from his brother. Snake climbed off the bottom strand of barbed wire and leaned against the post.

"I can't remember the last time it rained," said Snake. "What were you doing out there?"

"I was out there," said Leslie. His eyes grew vague, and he looked up toward the tree line. The last tint of rose began to fade from the western sky. "It was so hot. I put my face on the ground, and it felt like a fire was going down there." He pointed to the warm earth beneath his feet.

Singing came from the house, as a song would sound if it were being torn in half. Leslie looked back around toward it and saw the lights on, heard the noise.

"Daddy," said Leslie.

"Bastard," said Snake. "I can't stand him much more. He's drunk again."

Leslie knelt and put his hands on the soil, pushing the grass aside. He looked up at Snake and smiled.

"I feel Daddy's song in the dirt," said Leslie, and he

closed his eyes and began to sway gently back and forth. Snake shook his head, clenched his teeth, and cursed softly. He climbed through the fence and took Leslie's arm and helped him up. Snake dusted the dirt from his brother's clothes. Leslie turned sharply back toward the woods.

"What is it?" Snake asked.

"Up there," said Leslie. Snake knew what was up there. At the crest of the hill, the land swept downward toward the swamp, one of the wildest expanses of muck and water in north central Mississippi. "Up there, you can hear the woods singing."

"Leslie, come on now," said Snake. "You just come on. I'm gonna hit the punching bag. You want to watch me hit the punching bag?"

Leslie didn't argue as Snake helped him through the fence. As they moved toward the barn, darkness finally settled completely upon them. Snake felt the familiar, choking helplessness coming again.

Past the house, a car came by fast, its lights leading it west, out of Rockton County.

Truly Crawford lived in Rockton on Wentworth Street in a three-story mansion her father had inherited from his father, O. T. Crawford, who had once farmed cotton on twenty thousand acres of Rockton County soil. Truly had graduated from the University of Mississippi the year before, but she was still home, doing nothing, because she didn't need to. Her father, Oliver Thomas Crawford, Jr., did not farm, but he had cannily bought Xerox stock when it was cheap in the early fifties.

She was small and dark, with firm hips. Her mother, Ada, was a painter, though not much of an artist, doggedly churning out still lifes and landscapes that were usually miserable approximations of the subjects she was trying to capture like a photograph.

Truly didn't want to capture anything. She wanted only to touch things, turn them in her tiny palm and then move on to something else. Her father, whom everyone in Rockton persisted in calling Junior even though he was nearly sixty and wore his silver hair in a leonine mane, couldn't understand her. She should have had either his luck or her mother's fine feelings. As far as he was concerned, she didn't have anything but her looks and a way of getting whatever she wanted.

When she was twelve, Junior had promised her a cherry-red Jaguar on her eighteenth birthday if she would never smoke. She had started smoking at fourteen, but never at home, and when Junior asked at her eighteenth birthday party if she had kept her pact, she swore on the tattered family Bible that she had not smoked, and she got her car.

Her doting grandmother, Junior's mother, had said Truly was going to be president someday, had said that since Truly had taken ballet at the arts center, since she'd won a debating medal in the eighth grade.

Now she stood before the high mirror in her second-floor room on Wentworth Street, naked, a lazily smoking cigarette in one hand and a small tumbler of Jack Daniel's Black in the other. She had felt this way all summer, as if her head would explode if she didn't just do something. She and Snake had gone to Jackson Lake and swum, taking a picnic, but he had been sullen because he didn't have any money and wouldn't take any from Truly, who had all she wanted. We should just take some money, Snake kept saying, but he wouldn't say much more than that. Truly loved the way Snake looked in his swimsuit.

"Screw you," she said to her image. She had met Snake, who was two years older, through Leslie. A combination of disinterest and social promotion had allowed Leslie to make it to Rockton High School, but he needed help, and Truly, who pitied him, often came to the Ripleys' when they were in the tenth grade, the year Leslie finally quit. She would watch Snake working out in the barn. His muscles were all hard planes, sliding and slipping when he moved. He saw her, but then he was going with Gina Marbry, who had later left Snake, married a surveyor, and had a baby down in south Mississippi somewhere.

For a year and a half she had not seen Snake nor Leslie, but the winter before, she had been home for Christmas holidays and on a whim had called Leslie to see how he was. Snake had answered the phone.

She spread her legs apart and looked down them, between them. She blew smoke at her face and pouted, squatting slightly, just like Marilyn Monroe used to do. For four days she hadn't seen Snake because they'd had a fight, and now she wanted to do something, to get out of this dead house. That's how she always thought of the house, dead, because Junior would sit all evening in his study reading *The Wall Street Journal* and sipping sherry, while Ada would retire early to her room to read biographies of artists. She said they inspired her, though Truly thought it was ridiculous.

Lately, all Ada could talk about was Van Gogh, about his passion, about his missionary zeal in the Brabant, about how each of us has the same struggle inside as Van Gogh did, beauty side by side with horror and ugliness. Ada's green eyes had come alive at the supper table as she talked about Arles, about Holland. She tried to paint with violent brush-strokes for a few weeks, but then she had read a biography of Seurat and lately had been experimenting with pointillism.

Truly Crawford stood straight again and blew herself a kiss. She could call Snake and see what was happening out in the boonies. She could drive out there in her Jag, down the old Deerskin Road, which ran straight as the road to hell from Rockton, the fastest road in three counties. She had twice pinned the speedometer going out there, and once she and Snake had drag-raced for a mile, and though she had passed 135, Snake had left her, and she had laughed until she cried at the way he humped over the wheel.

No. She wouldn't call Snake yet. She wanted to feel herself hurt, to wait, bored as hell, for another day. She would stay up far longer than Junior or Ada, stay up until the whole town had settled into its summer snore and she alone was alive, arms spread naked to the dim sound of traffic three blocks away and the minor glory of a few faint stars.

+ + +

"Do you have to listen to that stuff?" asked Snake. His father sat in his deep chair in the living room, listening to scratchy old Glenn Miller records, drunk as Snake had expected, arm swaying, trying to conduct the music. The house always smelled stale, of unwashed dishes, uncleaned toilets. Sometimes it made Snake sick. Harry was just about damn useless now, though only a few people knew it. Snake stared at him and shook his head.

"This is Glenn Miller," said Harry, pumping furiously. "I cried the day he bought it in the Channel. Did I ever tell you that, Henry?" Harry was the only one who called Snake by his proper name, John Henry Ripley, Jr.

"About a million times," said Snake. Harry nodded and took the pint bottle of wine from the TV table, knocking off two copies of *TV Guide*. It was his favorite magazine, and he kept five or six issues out all the time. Snake looked at his father. He was only a few years shy of seventy, but he might have been anything, eighty, a million. His eyes were full of liquid, like the insides of chocolate-covered cherries, viscous, and his lower lids fell away in red rings.

"He fell out of the sky," said Leslie, who sat on the old sofa, listening. "Him and Buddy Holly. Maybe Nazis shot down Buddy Holly." Snake looked at his brother, but it wasn't a joke. Leslie was turning it over in his head, considering it as he considered everything.

"You're drunk," Snake said to his father. Harry looked at Snake and started to smile, but then it went away and his eyes flapped shut.

"And he's a dummy," said Harry, pointing vaguely at Leslie, "and you're puffed up like you fell in a yeller-jacket nest. We're a handsome lot, by God." Then he laughed, a gagging, coughing laugh that ended with Harry Ripley leaning forward and spitting heavily onto the rug beside the old oil stove.

+ + +

Leslie and Snake opened the garage the next morning, and Snake got the cash drawer from the safe, along with the army-issue .45 he kept inside his belt. Then he turned on the radio to a country FM station. They played songs that sometimes got to Snake. But now, *everything* was getting to Snake. If it wasn't cancer, he thought, cancer must be nothing compared to this.

About the only passions Snake had were cars, boxing and weights, women, and guns. By God, he knew guns. Had eighteen rifles, seven handguns, and maybe seven shotguns. His latest pride was a pistol he'd bought in New Orleans. When he'd first shot it into the railroad bank out behind the garage, he'd started laughing as the rounds pattered into the bits of stone and coal, scattering them up into the windless summer air.

Merle Haggard was singing "Kern River" on the radio, and it made Snake feel sad.

"It is not gone rain today," said Leslie. He had this look of unbelievable pleasure on his face. "I heard it on the radio. They said it will be a hundred again. It has been the hottest summer I ever seen."

"Sure has," said Snake. He turned on the air conditioner, and it coughed and clattered to life just as Hal Owens, who had a route for a tool supply company, pulled into the gravel out front by the twin gas pumps. Hal and Snake had graduated the same year, but Hal was married now and had two kids. Snake was one of the few who hadn't married. But he didn't want kids. He wanted money, and working in the garage ensured he'd never have any. That, and having to take care of two of the most helpless human beings ever born, Snake thought.

Hal came into the store carrying a box of oil in quart bottles.

"Snake, me buddy," said Hal. He set the oil down on the counter. Snake glanced at the oil and nodded and then signed the invoice slip.

"Hot as a son of a bitch already," sighed Snake.

"People going crazy," said Hal, who pushed his baseball cap back from his hair. Sweat already covered his arms and his upper lip. "You heard about Bubba O'Dair, I reckon." Leslie picked up the oil and carried it to the shelf.

"Bubba?" said Snake. "What in the hell'd he do?"

"Well, shit, you *didn't* hear," said Hal. "It's just so un-believable that . . ." Hal shook his head and closed his eyes. The air conditioner didn't seem to be cooling much to Snake.

"What?" asked Snake.

"He beat Missy to death yesterday morning," said Hal. Snake backed up two steps into the rack that held old maps of Mississippi. Leslie had started singing "Amazing Grace" while he put up the oil.

"Bullshit," said Snake, but he knew it was true.

"He's in jail," said Hal. "I heard Sam say it was the biggest mess he ever seen in his life." Missy Carillo was a lovely dark girl that Snake had once taken in the backseat when he was in the eleventh grade and she was a senior. She had married Bubba O'Dair two years out of school.

"Bullshit," said Snake. He could see Missy's eyes after they had finished in the broad backseat of his old Chevy, how they were full of love and no fear at all, her black hair a part of the darkness around them, only her face visible in the thin moonlight.

"It's the weather or something, I reckon," said Hal. "Or maybe Bubba's just crazy." Snake sat down on the stool behind the counter. The radio was playing "Help Me Make It

Through the Night." Leslie came swaying back over, and Snake thought it again, how Leslie moved as if there were no bones in his body, like some huge hand had just grabbed his skull and jerked him once and pulled his skeleton out.

"Hal ought to sell bread and fishes," said Leslie. Hal stared at him and smiled weakly and then looked at Snake with some kind of pity.

"They had the funeral yet?" asked Snake.

"Who died?" asked Leslie. God raised people from the dead, Leslie remembered.

"Bubba O'Dair beat Missy to death yesterday," said Snake wearily. Leslie nodded as if it were the most expected news in the world, and then he got a grape NeHi from a cooler they kept and went in the back to read comic books. He kept thousands of them back there, mostly superheroes. Leslie loved the comics.

"He's getting worse, ain't he?" asked Hal.

"Yeah, he's getting worse," said Snake.

"You let me know I can help," Hal said. He opened the door and stood in the doorway for a moment and looked back at Snake. Even though it was early morning, a rush of dry hot air came in, filling Snake's mouth, his throat, his eyes. "Man, this world is getting so messed up you can't believe it." He waited for Snake to say something, but Snake was staring straight ahead into the store, into the wasted icons of Harry's life, the choke collar of a business that held him here. Hal left, and when the truck pulled away, it blew a small cloud of dust that billowed against the window of the store.

"Damn," Snake finally said. He walked through the store, pulling the .45 from his pants as he went, going out the back door. He let the door close behind him, and he held the heavy gun with one hand and fired three times into the railroad bank, and, like an answer, the train whistle sounded, long and faint, toward the west. Snake felt Leslie, and when he turned, Leslie was standing there smiling, holding a comic book rolled into a tube.

"Bang," said Leslie. "Shoot again, Brother."

"No," said Snake. Whatever was in him had receded, but he still felt it there. The trash had not been burned in three days and its rot stank, and Snake wanted to leave forever, leave pitiful Leslie and their father. But he could not leave Leslie. He loved Leslie. He did not love their father.

Leslie smiled. Snake's arm muscles gleamed with sweat, and Leslie wanted to touch them, but he just stood there and smiled.

"I like that smell from guns," Leslie said.

"Yeah," said Snake. He tried to think of Missy, but the one who came to him was Truly Crawford, and he suddenly wanted to see her. He was thinking of Truly when he heard someone inside the store calling his name. He knew who it was: Bob Alexander, who dropped by almost every day.

"I can't get me enough of that smell of guns," smiled Leslie.

But Snake was not thinking of guns. His thoughts rose over the store itself, up over the highway and toward Richards, with its broken heap of old stores, then north to Rockton, with its tree-lined streets, the shining spire of the courthouse in the center of the town square, past the peach orchards and then southwest toward New Orleans, toward anything but this.

He could sell his guns. He would keep three, sell the rest. But that still wouldn't be enough. He could sell the store, but nobody would buy it. His mind came back, and he heard his name again. He slid the gun back into his pants and went inside.

Leslie lingered for a moment, his nose up into the motionless summer air, smelling the gun's stench, not aware until it was nearly upon him that the morning train was again rumbling east out of Rockton County.

2

ADA CRAWFORD LAY propped in bed, her dark hair spilling over the pillow as she read about Vincent van Gogh. She closed her eyes and tried to smell him, to see the blood rushing down into his shirt as he sliced off his ear. She wanted to get to her easel, but she also wanted to wait. Ada loved waiting, loved feeling everything stop at her whim. Junior had not been able to find a way to air-condition their house without either leaving chugging window units hanging out or almost dismantling the walls for a central unit. So he had done what he frequently did, nothing, and the house, even with ten-foot ceilings, was hot all the time, the motionless air scolded from one corner to another by a series of fans. The huge arched window facing east spread the sharp morning light onto Ada's bed.

"You breakfast be ready in a half hour," said a voice from

the partially open door to the second-floor hall. Nova Jernigan, a small black woman who was now only twenty-five, had worked for the Crawfords for two years. Her features were regular, even lovely, though Junior worried about her, and he had once told Ada that he thought he had overheard Nova practicing voodoo in the old visitor's house out back. Junior and his father both called it the visitor's house, but it was a slave house, carefully maintained by the Crawfords and now lavishly praised in tourist manuals, to Ada's great happiness. Ada had told Junior he was being dotty. She had said *dotty*, since she had been reading about Gainsborough and was fond of anglicisms in those days. Nova had two sisters, Lena and Ailene.

"Where is he?" asked Ada, laying the book on the bed and turning to look at Nova's head, which was thrust through the door. Her face was dotted with beads of sweat, and she had that fearful but almost pleasant look that Ada liked.

"Mist' Junior, he be in the shower," said Nova.

"I want her up for breakfast," said Ada languidly, stretching.

"Is you kidding?" asked Nova.

"Please get her up with us," said Ada. "She has slept this entire summer. I want her up for breakfast with us."

"Yes'm," said Nova. She closed the door and went into the hall and walked its length, and then to a room at the other end of the hall, which was Truly's. It had always been her private world, and Junior indulged her whims, letting her buy dozens of dolls that she put in chairs along the walls of the upstairs hall, dolls in the windows, and her room was choked with dolls, smiling, crying, singing, talking dolls. Nova went straight toward Truly's room, which was on the front of the house overlooking the regal silence of Rockton's oldest neighborhood. Out front were the rows of boxwoods Truly's grandfather had planted, a neat garden whose pattern you could see only from the second or third floor of the Crawford house. Beyond the boxwoods was a white picket fence that ran along the street and then came back, enclosing a yard three hundred feet long. Nova opened Truly's door. The smell hit her in the face.

"Jesus wept," said Nova, looking around. The room was nearly out of control, clothes all over the floor and on her dresser. Truly lay sprawled naked on her stomach, the disembodied, thin voice of a radio announcer droning above her. The windows, four of them, two facing north and two east, were closed, and Truly's fan was off. The room smelled like stale cigarettes and whiskey. Nova opened all four windows, hoping a breeze might move the foul air out of Truly's room, but there was no breeze, and the heat poured in, thick as syrup. Truly stirred, pulling one knee up to her chest, turning her head, seeing Nova, her face lined from her sheets, eyes watery and red.

"What is it?" asked Truly. Nova saw the bottle on the floor beside the bed, Jack Daniel's; it had been tipped over and a dark liquid had snaked out three feet across the heart-pine floor, not yet completely dry. The smell of the place nearly made Nova sick.

"You coming to breakfast, Miss Ada say it," said Nova. "You get in the shower, or I drag you." Truly felt mildly sick, but the sweat felt okay, and she wanted a cigarette. She rolled over on her back and her breasts were finely tipped, her legs strong and lean. Nova glanced once at Truly's legs and then picked up the bottle and put it in the trash can. "This stuff be

the death of you." Truly sat up and laughed as
"This place smell terrible. Miss Ada be sick sh

"Everything makes Miss Ada sick," said
walked to the bureau and got a cigarette and lit _ as Nova
went around the room, Truly thought, like a crab, snatching
clothes from the floor and the bed and throwing them in a pile
outside the door in the hall. "Have you heard the weather? Is
it going to rain?"

"Not here nor neither in hell," said Nova, and Truly
laughed brightly and exhaled a cloud of smoke that hung
unmoving until it settled on the floor. Truly yawned and
smiled at Nova as she stood in the door shaking her head.
"Thirty minutes. You be on in the shower and don't be
hacking off Mister Junior. He done be in a bad humor this
morning."

"What's wrong with the king?" asked Truly.

"Hit be something he read in the paper," said Nova.
She squatted and took the great pile of dirty clothes and
headed down the broad stairs toward the laundry room out
back. Truly stood before the window that faced the street,
wishing someone would drive by and see her naked, but she
knew they would not. She hated clothes and loved the feeling of nakedness outdoors. Once, she had gone out to her
car wearing only a raincoat, and had driven out to the in-
terstate, taken it off, and cruised up and down the road with
the top down, waving gaily at truckers, several of whom
nearly wrecked. That would have been the best, Truly
thought, if one of them had taken his eyes off her body to
see disaster coming, and then the cab turning and turning
and turning and silence, the grinding of twisted metal, and
the slick blood upon the wheel.

Truly had her own bathroom adjoining her bedroom, and she adjusted the shower and stepped in, feeling the warm water throb her alive. She washed her hair until it squeaked. And while she was washing it, she was thinking of one thing: Snake Ripley. She had to see him. Today, something would have to happen because she was so bored she could scarcely bear the thought of another day at home in her room. She soaped her body and washed it for a long time.

She got to the table just as Ada did, wearing a pretty green sundress, green flats, and a wide plastic bracelet of the same color. Junior looked up from his seat at the head of the long mahogany table in the dining room and whistled.

"Look at you, and welcome to breakfast for a change," Junior said. He had on his usual outfit: gray slacks, a white shirt, and a striped tie, along with his morning smoking jacket, a burgundy velvet thing with black padded lapels. *I'm not wearing any underwear*, Truly thought as she smiled back at her father.

"It was Mom's doing," said Truly. She came around to his chair and leaned down, and Junior pecked at her cheek. She stood back up and looked down, resisting the urge to giggle at his great white pompadour. "She thinks I've been wasting my life."

"What's that perfume, sweetness?" asked Junior.

"Racy, huh?" said Truly, raising an eyebrow. She saw her father's face fill with blood. "Nova said you were upset about something in the paper." She left his side and sat at the next place setting. Ada was wearing a blue housecoat and smiling loftily, still thinking of Van Gogh's ear and what a lovely gesture it had been.

"The goddamn niggers are trying to keep us from voting to

revoke that holiday for Martin Lucifer Coon," said Junior, his face still flushed. Nova brought their plates in and set them in front of Junior first, then Ada. She went back into the kitchen and got Truly's plate, loaded with scrambled eggs, sausage, bacon, and buttered English muffins. Truly looked at the food and wanted to gag. Junior flipped his cloth napkin open as if he were about to read a parchment declaration. Nova came back in carrying a silver coffeepot, from which she poured coffee into Junior's delft china cup. "Nova, what in the hell is it the niggers want?"

"I be sure I don't know, Mist' Junior," said Nova. She went to Ada's cup.

"Now, you don't think Martin Lucifer Coon's birthday ought to be a holiday, do you, Nova?" asked Junior.

"Nossir," said Nova. She moved to Truly's cup and poured the thick dark liquid, the aroma rising in a lovely cloud to Truly's nostrils. Truly pinched Nova lightly on the leg, teasing, and Nova stepped back sharply without spilling any coffee.

"Well, dammit," said Junior, lifting a steaming forkful of eggs, "that son of a bitch never did a thing but cause trouble. The Citizens' Committee's got a right to see if Rockton wants it or not."

"It's a federal holiday, dear," said Ada. She stared at Junior, knowing as she always had that he was simply a fool, the most unromantic man who ever lived. He would never give his greatest gifts to the woman he loved. Ada, in fact, had never been able to tell if he loved anything but Truly. Junior Crawford adored Truly.

"I'm sorry, but it's true," said Junior. His thick jaws worked on the eggs, and he picked up a link sausage and

21

sucked it between his lips and bit it half off. "Even Nova says it's true. The good colored folks know. I'm not being bad. I've always said you got your colored, and you got your niggers. Nova there is a colored, and Martin Lucifer Coon was a nigger."

"You be needing anything else?" asked Nova. She felt the heat from the coffeepot filling her veins, and her temples hurt. She stared at Junior and could see the scalding coffee from her pot running down his expensive coat, burning red blisters along his fat white skin.

"That's all for now," said Junior, waving the air with his fork. Nova went into the kitchen, where she sat on a stool and looked out the broad back window. A cat was creeping low to the ground, but she couldn't tell if it was being chased by a blue jay or if it was stalking something.

"Really, dear," said Ada.

"It just gets my blood boiling," said Junior, sipping the coffee. Sweat stood out under his eyes.

"I'd like to see that," said Truly, tasting the coffee and finding it good.

"What's that, baby?" asked Junior.

"Blood boiling," said Truly.

The first thing Harry Ripley knew when he awoke that morning was that he was going to die soon. He sat up in bed. He felt light-headed, felt his heart doing odd things, beating in a lightly syncopated rhythm, just like "Sentimental Journey." On the unstressed beats, his heart seemed to be hanging up like a car that wouldn't start in winter.

But it wasn't winter. It was the dead of summer, and

Harry's skin was glistening with sweat. He stood and walked shakily into the kitchen. The boys were gone. Good. He walked out into the yard and sat in the dirt under a pecan tree and stared west toward the garage, even though it was too far away to see. He wanted to see something, maybe the boys, maybe the drifting shade of his wife, because she had always been with him. She told him things. He would talk to her out loud, here in the backyard on mornings when the boys were gone. He would sit naked in the dirt and stare east or west and talk to her, then he would answer for her and in his answers hear her thin whispered voice, so gentle, just like poor Leslie's.

They had met just after the war. Harry Ripley had come home from the Pacific after having seen hell on Okinawa, his only real joy having come when his platoon surprised a lingering foxhole of Japanese, and Harry had shot one in the chest with his .45 pistol. They had been sitting outside sunning themselves when Harry and three of his buddies had surprised them. Harry's hands had shook terribly, but he had pointed his gun at the first man, who stood slowly, utter terror in his eyes. The bullet knocked the man down, a thin young man with poorly cut hair. He sat back up and looked at the huge hole in his lower chest, looked at the blood pouring out like faucet water. He put his hand in the blood and then held the spot as if trying to keep his life inside, but it was useless, and when he knew it, he looked straight at Harry and opened his mouth as if to say something, and then his mouth stayed open and the man hunched over sideways and died. Harry hardly heard the rest of the shooting or noticed the others writhing in their death pains.

"You should forget that now," Harry said.

"I'm trying to, dear," he replied.

"Come with me now," she said.

"This week for sure," Harry said.

He stood and walked into the kitchen and got a new bottle from the counter and opened it and took a long drink. So that was it. He would die this week. What he didn't yet know was how. But he would think of something.

The only thing he hated about leaving was Leslie. Harry loved Leslie as you love a fallen bird, and he knew Leslie would never fly, that he would always need the kind of care Henry couldn't give. Harry saw that Leslie was getting worse, becoming more childlike every day, more openly adoring of his big brother. Harry wished Henry would die with him. The thought did not bother him, but it stayed for only a moment, because Harry thought of Leslie again. Poor Leslie had killed Harry's wife, but it wasn't Leslie's fault. He hadn't known he had killed her until years later.

No, the one who should die with him was Henry, the son of a bitch. Harry and Henry had never gotten along. Harry knew there was something about himself—his helplessness or the unassaultable logic of blood kin—that touched Henry. Harry took a long drink and lit a Camel. He could barely breathe. Yes, he would die very soon. He felt it on his skin like cool dry lips. Probably a heart attack, Harry thought, and he wondered how it would come, just a choking start and then darkness, or maybe it might be pain, grinding, unbelievable pain, and he would touch the pain, try to rub it away. He had seen Owen Flye die that way at a Rockton County football game in '58. Owen had just jumped up and grabbed his chest and started complaining, then groaning, then screaming, his face becoming blue, lying down, shaking, the look of fear and death all over him until two men carried him out to a car. Harry didn't see it, but Owen had died as they put him in the car.

"Oh my God," said Harry, and it was then he decided to shoot himself.

+ + +

Three people came in the garage that morning, two to buy gas and Binnie Holt to buy spark plugs.

It was just before noon, and Snake told Leslie to make some sandwiches, so Leslie got a loaf of bread, some bologna, and mustard and went into the back to slowly make the sandwiches. He did it every day, and it always took him half an hour to make two sandwiches. They had to look just right to him or he wouldn't bring them out.

Snake was listening to the radio and looking out across the field when Truly Crawford was suddenly in front of him, her car crackling over the loose gravel and stopping in a dusty cloud right by the front door. He grinned and went outside. The heat smacked him in the face. She had the top down, and her green sundress was sticking to her with sweat.

"It must be hot out here," said Snake. "I can see your boobs soaked through your dress."

"Go get us some beer," she said. She smiled, and Snake went inside and got a six-pack from the cooler.

"I'll be back directly," he yelled. "I'm going to ride with Truly Crawford."

" 'kay," Leslie shouted from the back. He agreed to anything Snake said. Snake locked the door on the way out and turned the CLOSED sign over. He climbed in beside Truly and opened each of them a beer, setting the others, still stuck in their plastic loops, on the floorboard. Truly put the car in gear and they drove off.

The beer tasted wonderful to Truly, and she drank half of her Budweiser in one gulp. Snake drank all of his in one gulp and threw the can at a stop sign as Truly went through the intersection without looking either way.

"You gone get killed that way one day," said Snake. He opened another beer. She was wearing oversized dark sunglasses, and Snake could not see her eyes. But he didn't mind. Something about Truly made it seem that he was always looking at her from the side, something vague and strange, as if each time he saw her she were a slightly different person.

"That way, some other way," said Truly, and she laughed.

"What you been doing?" Snake asked. "I was going to call you."

"Sure."

"I was," said Snake. "I missed you."

"That's nice," said Truly. She finished her beer and threw the can straight up in the air, and it hit the sticky pavement behind the car and bounced into the ditch.

"It's true," said Snake. "You didn't say what you been doing."

"Listening to my daddy rave and rant about niggers again," said Truly.

"Oh, that," said Snake. "What else?" She turned onto a side road that Snake liked, a long, meandering road that held a couple of dairies and not much else but a long stretch of pine forest.

"Being bored as hell," she said. "Give me another one." He opened a beer and put it in her hand.

"You gone break the damn springs," said Snake, bouncing around the seat. She slid the car to a stop under a canopy of cedars, and when she turned it off, there was no sound but a few idle bird songs some distance off. "Look up there. I'll be damned." Snake pointed up into the branches of two tangled oak trees where a deer stand had been built. Crude steps were nailed to the side of the larger tree. "Damned deer stand."

"I know what it is," Truly said. She finished her second beer just as Snake did. "You climb up there and wait for something to come along, and then you kill it."

"Deer," said Snake.

"Are deer stands good for anything else?" asked Truly in a high, cartoon voice.

"Come on." He climbed out and took her hand, and they climbed the nailed slats, laughing. The platform, fifteen feet over the forest floor, was not sturdy, and felt as if it might fall any moment. "Jesus, we're going to bust our asses."

"Oh, God, isn't it beautiful!" cried Truly, and Snake looked around, expecting to see a deer, but she was looking down upon her car as she slipped the sundress off and lay naked upon it. He got to his knees and took off his shirt and then sat to remove his shoes and pants. Before he rolled over, his left shoe rocked over the edge and fell below them into a carpet of pine needles.

Truly clawed at his back, bit into his shoulder, and finally groaned as he did, and as their breathing subsided, they lay side by side in the deer stand, looking up at the heat and sunlight filtering down upon their shining bodies. For a long time, neither said anything. The guttural grinding of a tractor seemed suddenly close, and Snake sat up and looked around, but Truly did not move, and then it was gone.

"What are you thinking?" she asked. She rolled onto her

flat stomach and leaned on her elbows and looked at his muscled body. She loved the feel of his thick chest on hers.

"That I cain't hardly stand it no more," said Snake.

"What?"

"Everything," he sighed. "I cain't stand the garage or my old man or poor old Leslie. I cain't stand not having any money. I got to get out of this county."

"Leave," said Truly. She rubbed his stomach, swirling the sweat into little circles in the hair around his navel.

"With what?" he said. He sat up and Truly kept her hand on his stomach. "I cain't sell the damn garage, and I'm not selling my guns. I swear to God, Truly, I'm about ready to rob somebody."

"Okay," she said. He turned and stared at her, and her eyes were boring into his. Her hand dropped just enough, and he closed his eyes. In a moment, the deer stand creaked with every thrust, the nails straining against the trees, and Snake knew that if they did not finish soon, the whole thing would come crashing down with them. He had closed his eyes, but now he opened them, and through the limbs of the oaks, above the back of Truly Crawford's head, he could see a hawk lazily circling overhead.

+ + +

Leslie Ripley looked down the blade of the knife and saw the mustard hanging thickly on it. This was his favorite part, and he took the bread and pulled the knife over it, watching the white surface turn yellow. He had been standing in the small back room of the garage for half an hour, looking at the knife and the bread and the mustard. To Leslie, nothing seemed connected anymore.

Harry could remember when Leslie was his sweet boy,

fair and thin, heading off to the first grade with a book satchel and a thick pencil, and though Leslie was uncommonly docile, they'd all said it was because he was a second child. The second child is always the quiet, calm one, and the first is the fighter, combative. It all fit so neatly. It wasn't until the third grade that Leslie's teachers began to know something was really wrong, that Leslie, in fact, wasn't just calm and pleasant, but seemed to be missing something that bound him to this earth. Miss Corinne Bunting, a visiting psychologist the school system used, explained it this way to Harry:

"Suppose," she said, leaning forward and looking over the tops of her glasses, "that there are a series of gears that connect us to everything. There are gears that connect us to our own thoughts, to solving problems, to interacting with other people. There are gears that allow us to walk, to run, to sing, to smile. In most people, those gears mesh neatly. Do you understand that? Well, it seems in Leslie's case, there are some, well, gaps. He will intuitively get ready to perform something, and there is this disengagement, and suddenly Leslie is just staring and smiling pleasantly. We don't exactly know what causes this kind of thing."

Harry hadn't told Leslie what she said. Instead, Harry had told Leslie something he'd been told by his friend Jackie Crown on an LST just before Okinawa. Jackie thought of himself as a poet, and just before they landed, he told Harry that the world was divided into dreamers and movers, and that the dreamers lasted long after the movers had fallen into dust. Jackie had been killed by a stray shot just as the bay opened on the LST, and he died in Harry's arms. So Harry told Leslie that he was a dreamer, and Leslie had always thought of himself as a dreamer.

But lately, his dreams were being filled with images he could not understand. He could go into his dreams at any time, watching Snake hit the heavy bag in the barn, riding to Rockton to see what was happening, sitting on his stool in the small back room of the garage making sandwiches.

He saw birds in his dreams now, had been seeing them since spring, soaring vultures, cardinals, crows, all manner of winged creatures, and they talked to him in his dreams. He looked down at the yellow bread and did not move, thinking now of a parakeet Harry had once brought home, but it had died in a few weeks. Leslie was still staring at the bread when he looked up, and Snake and Truly Crawford were staring at him.

"Do you remember that parakeet Daddy brought home?" Leslie asked.

"Sure," said Snake. He felt better now. He and Truly had finished the six-pack on the way back to the garage, and he was hungry. "Let me." Leslie handed him the knife and the slice of bread, and Snake made three sandwiches.

"Hello, Truly," said Leslie. "I didn't see you. I was just sort of thinking. What you been doing?"

"Not much," she said.

"Are you happy?" Leslie asked.

"Yeah," she said. If Snake was feeling better, Truly wasn't, feeling as always that whatever was good, there wasn't enough of it. There should be more and more and more. They went back out front, where it was cooler, and ate the bologna sandwiches and most of a one-pound bag of rippled potato chips. When they finished, Truly stood and stretched, the thin green sundress coming halfway up her thighs.

"You going?" Snake asked.

"I'm sleepy," she said. "I want to sleep. I'm going home and sleep this afternoon."

"What about tonight?" asked Snake. She smiled at him for the first time since they had come back to the garage. "I work out at eight," he said. He didn't know what in the hell he was doing. "Come over. But don't come in the house. I'll be in the barn. You know where it is. We'll work it up."

"We're going to do it," she said flatly, as if it were an order. "You know we're going to do it."

She didn't say anything else, and a moment later the only thing left of her was the blowing dust from where the car had scratched off and the lingering scent of her body in Snake's nostrils.

"I saw a hawk," Snake said to no one in particular as he looked at the sunbrowned field of grain sorghum across the road.

"I know," said Leslie.

3

SERGEANT SLAUGHTER HAD just thrown Kamala, the Ugandan Giant, halfway across the ring, and Harry Ripley sat in the frayed comfort of his chair and laughed and cheered. He had spent most of the afternoon reading the *TV Guide* for the week of January 11–17, 1958, but now he was watching wrestling. Harry was drunk, but pleasantly so, and he had decided to live a while longer.

Harry often read thirty-three-year-old magazines. He would sit in the sweltering gloom of his house and try to hang his life on details from those years, who he had been, what he had been doing. He no longer knew who he was, though. He had decided to live at least a couple of weeks longer. He had a few things to tidy up, then he would shoot himself.

Or maybe he could have his heart attack. He had napped just after noon in his chair and dreamed that he was running down the road in front of his house, naked arms up to God, and then the heart attack came, but it was sweet and healing, the brief flicker of pain and the sensation of being swept up to a forgiving God. Except when Harry had awakened, he thought of something he wanted to do before he died, something for which God likely would not forgive him.

The sun was almost gone in the west, another one of his last days spent. Snake and Leslie had come home late in the afternoon and hung around outside, working on Snake's car. Harry had toddled around them for a while, holding his bottle by the neck.

"You afraid that thing's gonna escape?" asked Snake. "You're about to choke it to death."

"What are you doing, boy?" Harry asked. He was naked except for a nasty pair of old boxer shorts, and Snake could barely stand his presence.

"Go inside before I puke looking at you," said Snake.

"What's he doing, Leslie?" Harry asked. Leslie was staring intently at Snake's strong fingers.

"Carburetor," said Leslie.

"New plugs," said Snake softly, leaning low under the hood. "Would you please drag yourself inside?"

Harry had walked instead to the fence and looked through his thick watery eyes at the pasture where the Herefords had been. They had been part of his blasted life, of the person who was soon to be lying under the sod of the Shiloh Baptist Church. Harry saw himself lying in a coffin and rain falling hard upon his face in winter. He wondered if he could hear the rain and the wind and the nearby vibrations of a plow.

He had not seen Leslie until the boy was right next to him. Leslie had lately taken to wearing Western clothes, and he had on his pointed boots, pearl-button shirt, and tight jeans. Leslie was nice-looking until you saw his eyes, then you knew that it was true, he had been damaged.

"Sonny boy, we had some cattle, didn't we?" asked Harry Ripley.

"Cattle," repeated Leslie.

"They would come up here with their big moon eyes and wouldn't know they'd wind up as steaks and hamburgers," said Harry. He had spat onto the hard red clay soil.

"Moon eyes," said Leslie. He had turned and smiled broadly at Harry. "We saw a hawk today. It was the biggest thing I ever saw. And I smelled the smell of guns shooting."

"Life," said Harry, and he had had a coughing fit and went back inside, where the sun did not flame his scalp, leaving Leslie to watch the field where the Herefords had been. Except now Leslie and Snake were out there somewhere, having eaten and piled the dishes with all the others, out there while Harry watched wrestling. Kamala surprised Sergeant Slaughter and hit him in the throat with some mysterious punch.

"That's one mean fella," allowed Harry, but soon the Sergeant was back, and he threw Kamala across the ring and pinned him as the crowd howled and stamped. Harry was staring at the ring so hard he did not see the car pull around the house and stop out back near the barn.

Truly Crawford had slept most of the afternoon in her own bed, feeling the lazy, full sensation of having made love twice with Snake in the deer stand. When she had awakened, she had put on a new sundress, this one blue and yellow, and gone out back where Nova Jernigan was sitting in the visitor's house watching her small black-and-white TV. Nova didn't live there, but Ada Crawford had allowed her to buy a TV so she could escape the house for periods during the day. Nova had been watching a soap opera when Truly came in.

"Hush up," Nova said. Truly was still half asleep, barefoot, thinking of what she and Snake were going to plan that night. "Tommy, he be the one there, done got his sister-in-law pregnant."

"Pregnant," said Truly. She sat on the cool floorboards next to Nova's rocker. She and Nova were nearly the same age, and Nova looked lovely in this light. They would often sit out here and talk, and though Ada did not care, Junior despised Nova for her time with Truly.

"That his sister-in-law, Désirée," said Nova, leaning forward. "What in the hell he be doing now? Law', to get his sister-in-law pregnant. He coulda kept the thang in his pants, wouldn't be no trouble. Thang is, Désirée don't care no more than he do."

"That Désirée?" asked Truly, staring at the small black-and-white image that flickered in the heat of the small house.

"You miss her," said Nova. "That his wife, Kelley. She be good as God ever made a woman, and he be running around on her." A commercial came on, and Nova leaned back and shook her head in disgust at Désirée. "Désirée be a tramp."

"I'm sorry for what Daddy said this morning," Truly blurted. She did not know she would say it, didn't, in fact, have any plans to come out here at all.

"You mean 'bou' niggers?" asked Nova. She turned, eyes wide, staring at Truly. "Shit." Truly smiled with delight, never having heard Nova swear before.

"He's a son of a bitch," said Truly. "A goddamn son of a bitch."

"Well, you say it," Nova said, looking out the open, screenless window at the perfectly manicured backyard. Truly looked at Nova, at her hands and her face.

"You know he's scared of you," said Truly. She sat on the floor next to Nova's chair and rested her arm on Nova's leg, looking up into her eyes. Nova flinched and did not notice when the soap came back on.

"I know that," Nova said carefully. She wasn't sure what to make of Truly. But she wasn't the monster that Mister Junior Crawford was.

She did not notice until a full minute later that Truly was gently stroking her calf, her ankle. To Truly, Nova's leg felt strangely wonderful.

"Does that feel good?" Truly asked.

"You ain' turning into no fairy godmother, is you?" asked Nova. They both laughed so loud that Ada, who was in her studio back at the house, stopped and listened, thinking she had heard dogs barking. When she was sure there were no dogs, she went back to her painting, a landscape with what she believed to be an eagle soaring above it.

Ada Crawford was terrified of dogs.

"You just don't take any crap off him," said Truly as she stood. Nova was trembling and she looked up at Truly, who was beautiful, her dark skin and hair, the even features and the smile lighting them all up. Nova tried not to think of how she had looked on the bed that morning, but the image burrowed into her eyes, and she reached for Truly, who took her hand.

"You be good to talk to me," said Nova. Truly looked at

Nova and felt something surge up in her throat and break, a scream of terror and disgust and hate and passion, that feeling she courted and caressed nearly every day. She pulled Nova up, and they stood in the late-afternoon motes that filtered through the window. The television droned in the background.

"Yes," said Truly. She took Nova Jernigan in her arms and kissed her on the lips. Nova pushed at Truly as they kissed, but it was the faint effort of failed resistance, and they both trembled as Truly backed off, arms on arms, trembling, eyes moist and staring.

"Jesus wept," whispered Nova. Truly looked into her eyes. Junior stepped onto the back porch and called Truly, yelling "Sweetness!" in his thin sibilance. For a moment, they hung, suspended in the unmoving heat of the visitor's house.

"Gotta go," whispered Truly. And before Nova could answer, Truly had almost evaporated, Nova thought, and was running across the lawn, waving gaily at Junior as if he were the man she loved most in this world.

Now, Truly was climbing out of her car and peeking into the barn. The sun was gone in a red mass of fire toward Dallas, but the light hung, fireflies undulating out over the fields around the house and barn. From inside the house, she could see the dim flicker of a television. Inside the barn, she first saw Leslie, sitting on the backless chair, looking as if his mind had been let out like old oil from Snake's car. She did not see Snake at first, but she heard him grunting, heard the chugging smacks of his gloves on the heavy bag. She went inside and saw him leaning into it, sweat coating his lovely body and his hair matted against his forehead. Snake saw

Truly and stared at her for a moment, but he said nothing and did not acknowledge her presence. When Snake worked out, he was different. That was why he did it. He told Leslie that all the time: you become somebody different, the person who is inside you. When you work out, you become what's inside, all gut.

Truly sat on Snake's barbell bench and watched until he finished with the bag and sank to his knees, chest heaving.

"Hey, babe," Snake finally said.

"You'll die," she said. She lit a cigarette, and the smell of sulfur from the match drifted through the barn.

"That's the thing gone kill *you*," he said, pointing at the match.

"Hey, Leslie," said Truly.

"Hi, Truly," said Leslie. "He's coming out of his skin." He pointed proudly at Snake and looked back and forth between them, nodding. "A little more and his muscles will come out. They pop out when he works out."

"They surely do that," said Truly. Snake slowly struggled to his feet under the dim glow of the single light. Snake lifted weights, shadowboxed, danced around the speed bag, ducking invisible punches, snapping his head while Truly and Leslie watched. It lasted another forty minutes, but Truly did not mind. She loved watching him leap like a spring around the musty barn, loved the smell of him and the sound of his bag gloves, his grunt when he pressed the barbell over his wet hair.

Leslie stared at Snake, mouth hanging halfway open. He could not stop thinking of the hawk or the smell of guns, and somehow they had become so swirled in Leslie that as he watched Snake, he felt with them a monstrous bird that flapped gun smoke from its broad wings.

Snake had done ten presses when he dropped the barbell. It bounced once on the dusty floor and then rolled a
few feet. Snake sat down, breathing hard, dissolved in
sweat. He looked at Truly, who was staring at him with a
hard smile.

"Leslie, you go on in the house," said Snake.

"Okay," said Leslie. He liked doing what Snake asked
him to do. He walked out of the barn into the darkness, and
he went halfway to the house and then veered out under the
heavy pecan trees to the edge of the pasture, where he looked
up at the sky.

"God," said Truly.

"What?" asked Snake.

"I was just thinking how it would be if blood came out
instead of sweat," she said. She stared at Snake and lit another cigarette.

"Sometimes you're so full of shit it's scary," said Snake.
He stood shakily and went to her, jerked the smoke from her
lips and threw it on the floor, where he stamped it out with his
sneaker. "You'll burn my gym down."

"Gym," said Truly. "Didn't you have chickens in here
one time?"

"Yeah," said Snake. He sat down next to her on the
barbell bench. "When I was a boy I'd come out here and get
the eggs." His voice suddenly fell off and there was only the
cricket-laced silence for a moment. "I'm gone do it."

"I know," she said. "When?"

"Tomorrow night," said Snake. "Hell, she lives there by
herself. I know for a fact she's got it there, that's what I
always heard. Didn't you always hear that?"

"Everybody always heard that," said Truly. "I'm going
with you."

"Bullshit."

"I am. You better let me or I'll do something."

"What?"

"Something."

"Shit."

"You have masks?"

"We'll have to wear stockings," Snake said. "I've seen it on TV. You can't tell who you are. It makes your face flat and mean."

"Would we have to kill her if she sees us?" asked Truly.

"You are one crazy bitch," said Snake, shaking his head.

"Then make the plans," Truly said.

Snake stared at the light bulb. His head hurt from the workout on the heavy bag.

"I keep thinking about Missy O'Dair," Snake said. "You hear about that?"

"Oh yeah," said Truly. "I heard Bubba just went stark, raving mad. That was so sad." She said it as if she were speaking of something that had happened in another country, many years ago. Snake stared at her and decided to drop it. But he had been thinking about Missy all day, and he could almost see her misshapen skull as she lay in some satin coffin. "Funeral's tomorrow. You going?"

"Nah," said Snake. "Nah. Just wanted to know if you heard."

"I heard," said Truly.

Her name was Agnes Longley and she was seventy-eight, a tall skinny old lady who had been deaf for years. She lived by herself on Wentworth Street, down from the Crawfords in an old mansion she had inherited from her father, Richard S. Longley. He, in turn, had inherited it from his father and grandfather, the latter of whom was shot at Petersburg and died on the field of battle. The house was a huge square Greek Revival structure with six great Doric columns across the front over a wide porch. Hundred-year-old water oaks always kept the yard cool. Agnes had never married, and when Truly and others in the neighborhood had been children, she would never let any of them in her yard, often standing in a window where she could see them. But that was before she went deaf. She went to the Rockton Baptist Church like Truly's family, and now, on the Sundays Truly bothered to go, Agnes Longley would sing loudly in spite of her deafness and the sound was terrible.

They would go to her house the following night after midnight and break in one of the windows off the back porch. For all the house's glamour out front, the back porch had been added in the thirties and looked as if it had been slapped on with chewing gum. The yard stretched out a hundred yards behind the house, and her gardener, who worked only one day a week now, tried to keep it one step from wildness but had lately been losing the battle.

People in Rockton had always said she had money hidden in the house, in coffee cans that were rolled in newspaper and kept in the fireplace. Nobody knew just which fireplace, though.

"You're right, Snake," said Truly. "It's as safe a thing as we can do."

"What is it with you?" he asked. "You got money. Why are you even out here? You're the one who even suggested this."

"You know," she said. She could not take her eyes off his

knotted body. She had the feeling it might just explode any minute, spattering the barn with blood and bone.

"Yeah, I know," he laughed. He stood and walked to her and she stood and both were sweating heavily in the low-ceilinged barn. He took her, and they kissed as she gently squeezed his arms as if trying somehow to make him bigger. Snake's back was to the door, and so he didn't understand when Truly backed up, her eyes unmoving as the sockets of a corpse, and said, "Oh my God." Snake turned and Harry Ripley was standing there in the doorway, completely naked, holding a bottle of MD 20-20 in one of his scabrous claws.

Truly had never seen anything quite so horrible in her life. His entire upper body seemed to sag down to his waist. His mouth was open, showing he had taken his teeth out, and his eyes drooped more than ever. He brought a stale odor of death with him.

"Jesus Christ," said Snake.

"That's who I am," cackled Harry. "I know you," he said to Truly, squinting. He took a long pull from the bottle. "You must be the Virgin Mary." Snake thought he might vomit. "That'd make you my mother."

"Jesus Christ," Snake said.

"I just come out to tell you something," said Harry. He sucked in his stomach and for a moment his chest went out, his eyes closed, and he almost looked human. But then the wheezed breath fell from him and the stomach came out and he opened his eyes. They were red and terrible.

"Get in the house," Snake said, and he started toward his father.

"Try to make me and I'll kill you," said Harry with such fierce intensity Snake completely stopped. "I just come out to tell you something amazing is gonna happen within a week."

"What, you gone put on clothes?" Snake tried to sound sarcastic, but his voice was trembling.

"Darkness," whispered Harry, and he took another drink and turned and tottered off back toward the house. Snake stood still for nearly a minute, and Truly didn't move either. She felt like running after the old man and seeing his penis again. It had amazed her. Finally Snake took one step back and kicked a wide board on the wall of the barn, kicked it with such unspoken fury that it splintered and fell into the dust just as Leslie, looking for all the world to Truly like an angel, walked into the barn with his hands in his pockets.

"Who was that man?" asked Leslie, turning and looking at the house where the back screen door had finally quit flapping after Harry went in.

"The Lone Ranger," said Snake bitterly. "Who in the hell you think it was?"

"Daddy," said Leslie. "Our father." He looked at the house. Truly still didn't move, and Snake's foot hurt terribly from where he had kicked the board. "Truly, I just saw a great bird in the field. It was God in his clothing come to see where our cattle have gone."

"Wouldn't surprise me a bit," said Snake. He slid on his bag gloves and went after the heavy bag again, feeling better at the swishing sound of his blows landing one after another.

The pasture stretched for hundreds of yards behind the house, up toward the second night of a heavy red moon, and if Snake had come out there, had stood long enough for his eyes to adjust to the night, he might have seen the buck, sturdy and silent, standing there as if waiting for daylight or rain.

+ + +

Truly and Snake did not make love, though she wanted to. Leslie would not leave, and Snake could not bear to send him away again. Truly had stayed until nearly midnight, until they had gone back into the house and found Harry asleep in his chair, still naked, snoring raggedly, a late-night boxing show playing before nobody.

Snake had sat down to watch. Two welterweights were pounding each other's skulls apart, and Snake loved to watch it. He had heard about the TV bout when Emile Griffith had fought Benny "Kid" Paret. He had seen "Boom Boom" Mancini's fatal fight with Duk-Koo Kim, and he knew that if he watched long enough, something else terrible would happen.

Truly had stood there watching Harry snoring, Leslie staring at Snake with unashamed adoration, and Snake, temples pulsing as he watched the fight. She had walked slowly back through the kitchen, noticing the smells, some of them pleasant, some acrid and rank. Then she had walked out the back door and driven home. Snake heard her go but did not move. He stared at Harry and wondered what the old man meant. He felt as if he were a thread holding his family to this earth, but the thread was breaking now, and he didn't know how long he could remain.

A long driveway went from one side of the Crawford house to the back, where Truly usually parked next to Junior's Cadillac, and she drove slowly around, wishing she were drunk. She had not touched a drink all evening, and she could barely wait until the following night. As she turned the car off, she tried to think of Missy O'Dair, face clubbed into the shape of another animal. She was still in the car when she saw the woman standing in the moonlight not twenty feet from her. She felt the usual thrill of delight, hoping it might be some madwoman come to wreck the careful order of the Crawford home. If Truly hated one thing, it was order. She wanted all things unmoored to float freely and find their own order: trees, weeds, winds. She got out of the car and walked toward the shape.

Before she got to it, she could tell it was Nova Jernigan, standing unsteadily and holding a small bottle. Without hesitating, Truly came up to Nova and stood so close each could feel the other's breath as they spoke.

"I was thinking you never come home," said Nova, her voice hard and raspy.

"What are you doing here?" asked Truly. She did not feel tired. Truly never felt tired once darkness came. "Is something wrong?"

"I wanted to . . . I wisht I could . . . Miss Truly, I . . ." Nova stammered. She looked down and then reached out and put her hand on Truly's shoulder.

"Yes," said Truly. She took Nova's hand and they walked across the deep green lawn that Junior kept watered, up the old stone steps, and into the visitor's house. Moonlight poured across the floor, and Truly sat in the light and pulled Nova down to her. She took the bottle from Nova's hand and drank from it, not stopping to see what it was. Bourbon filled her mouth and she swallowed, loving the fiery plunge of the liquid. The patch of moonlight was like a bath on the floor, and Truly held her hand toward the window as if she could touch the air like water.

"I be thinking about you since this afternoon," choked Nova. Her voice sounded like it had been crushed. Truly looked at her and saw Nova was crying, drops large as summer rain coming down her cheeks and landing on her poor cotton dress. "I had me men, but I ain't never . . ." She licked her lips, and Truly touched her hair. Truly did not know what this meant. She did not feel much of anything for Nova, but she would lie with anything that gave her pleasure. She could feel the power pouring into her hands as she stroked Nova's hair, and she loved it. "I feeled like I was on fire, Miss Truly! I mean absolute on fire when you touched me!"

"Does this feel good?" asked Truly. She touched Nova's face, and it felt like the skin of ripe fruit. Nova's mouth was slightly open, and the tears gleamed on her teeth.

"Yes'm, it sure do," whispered Nova. Truly let her hand fall and she rubbed Nova's shoulder and took another drink. Truly moved closer. She looked at Nova and tried to imagine how it would be by flashlight the following night when they were breaking into the house down the street, and it excited her. She felt relaxed from the bourbon, so she slid right up to Nova.

Nova was breathing so hard she thought she might die any minute. This was against God, a twisting of nature, but she could not stop. It was going to happen now. It was like rain. When it started falling you could stand there and get wet or move inside. You couldn't stop anything like rain or these feelings.

"Something is going to happen," whispered Truly.

"I know that," gasped Nova. She touched Truly's hair and looked into her eyes. "Hit be that red moon do it. You see a red moon rise in July, Ailene tell me all manner of mischief float up from the mouth of hell."

"This is from hell," said Truly, and she leaned down and put her face on Nova's chest.

"Jesus wept," said Nova Jernigan. "I cain't stop the pleasure of the Devil." She wailed out loud one time before Truly pulled away and smiled, not making any motion to quiet her.

+   +   +

In the house, in the four-poster with the swirled walnut uprights, Ada Crawford sat up, not quite knowing why. She looked down at Junior, who was snoring peacefully on his back, his huge white stomach rising and falling in the moonlight. All she heard now was the dull drone of the fan in their room, but she waited for it again. When it did not come, Ada stared at Junior with absolute fury, wishing more than anything that he would simply dissolve, that rain would fall on him and he would melt like Dorothy's witch. He would never cut off his ear for her. He would never show his love for anyone.

Once a month he would crush the breath from her, and he would ask all the while if it was good, and she would say *yes*, but he was as empty of poetry as his house, and the best course was to ignore him. She was an artist, wasn't she? And artists can act eccentrically. She looked at his massive white stomach now, and she could almost see it like a beef carcass, split, hung up like a Rembrandt etching to drip and cool.

She got up and floated down the stairs and into the kitchen, which was larger than many houses in Rockton. The antique clock's hands lingered at 1 A.M. while she got a glass from the cupboard and took a bottle of wine out of the refrigerator, poured it, turned out the light, and sat at the table. It seemed completely dark to Ada for a minute, but then the moonlight was seeping in the windows, around the curtains, into her eyes, her mouth. She looked at the way it lit the room and wanted to paint it that way, a different room in this light and this time of night.

She listened for the sound again. It might be a dog. When Ada had been seven, a Doberman had attacked her on the sidewalk in front of her own house, holding her leg until it bled, and when she saw the dog's mouth full of blood, she had started screaming until her father ran out and beat the dog. And even then the dog would not let go, and her father had run back inside, come out with his old Colt Woodsman pistol, and shot it. Since then, Ada had been terrified of dogs, all of them, and the barking of a solitary dog in the darkness could awaken her, fill her with dread that she could never tell Junior about. It might be another Doberman. Lately she had been thinking of painting it, a little girl standing on a sunny sidewalk, a dog's bared teeth on her leg, blood streaming everywhere. She drank all the wine and refilled her glass and listened.

The cry came again, sharp, almost like a sob.

+ + +

"Lord, no," said Nova. She stood and reached out for Truly, but Truly gently pushed her hand away as she dressed. "Please, Truly. Please, please. Don't leave me." Truly looked at her in the moonlight. "Please. Oh sweet Jesus, don't leave me now."

"Well, now," Truly said as she finished dressing. Nova saw Truly smiling broadly, then Truly turned and went out the door, and Nova sat on the floor, which was suddenly cold, and wept.

Truly could take what she wanted. Softly now, so softly she was not sure at all she was doing it, she began to bark, almost like the sound of some distant regret. Inside, Ada did not move. Instead, she only nodded and wondered if the animal was whispering for more blood or only crying for rain.

4

S U N E D G E D I N from the east, plowing over the
rolling fields of Rockton County, dragging with it another
rainless day. The county had once been planted fence row to
fence row with cotton. When Snake was a boy, he could stand
on the roof of the garage and see whiteness all around, an
ocean of cotton in endless waves. Now, less than eight hundred acres of cotton were planted in the entire county.

As the sun rose, it came over fields of soybeans, grain
sorghum, over pastures of gently gnawing Holsteins. It came
over the wasted small towns like Herter and Scottown and
Bear Knoll, towns that had been happy and flourishing until
paved roads and the boll weevil had killed them. It came first
on the spire of the courthouse on the square in the center of
Rockton, casting the shadow of its tip across the First Na-
tional Bank. The sun also brought with it streamers of red

clouds like swollen fingers pointing west. Leslie Ripley had already been up for an hour when he first saw the clouds and loved them.

He and Snake slept in the same room as they always had, and each morning Leslie was the first to rise, creeping from the room with his boots and clothes in his hand to go outside and watch the sun rise. When he had come through the living room, he saw Harry lying on the frayed sofa, naked and snoring. Leslie smiled at his father and dressed in the kitchen and went outside.

He loved the morning, the first bird sounds, the gentle moving air in the pasture, and the way light changed in the pines. On some benevolent mornings, he felt as if he would rise with the earth's swelling heat into the clouds, just like Jesus rose after he had died and come back to life. There was a picture of it in his Bible, Jesus standing on this hill, arms up, light in his face, just before he rose into heaven. That was death, Leslie thought, an arm extended toward the stars and a light upon the face.

Leslie stood by the fence line as the sun came up and looked into the sky. First he saw a crow, and then a lone buzzard gliding south. There were a few songbirds, but he was waiting for the hawk. The night before, safe in his bed with Snake ten feet away, Leslie had dreamed of the hawk, dreamed it had landed early in the morning in their pasture, and it had spoken to him with what he imagined to be his mother's voice. He had always loved his mother, loved the faded photographs with the scalloped edges. Her face was plain, but her eyes had a kind of light that Leslie loved. His favorite, which he kept beside his bed, was the last photograph Harry Ripley had ever taken, his wife standing on the front porch, eight months pregnant with Leslie, only three weeks before she died pushing Leslie into this world. Leslie had dreamed that the hawk had landed near him and had spoken to him.

"Leslie, you are so beautiful . . ." it had said, and then he could not remember anything else, except, perhaps, an odor, something burning, acrid but pleasant. This morning, he felt beautiful and he waited for the hawk to come down.

Inside, the sound of Snake's shower awoke Harry Ripley, who sat up on the couch, felt for a moment like dying, and then grinned broadly, remembering. This was going to be great. He threw his legs over the edge of the sofa and started coughing violently, spitting finally on the floor and standing and cursing his chest. The cough had been getting much worse. It had been that way with his own father, who had died at forty-nine from a heart attack. Coughing for weeks, clutching at his chest, then one day coughing in a high-pitched wheeze and falling over flat on his face, dead. Harry Ripley knew he would last long enough to do what he wanted to do now. He just knew it.

Snake came out of the shower feeling choked, scared. His black hair was combed but still wet as he watched Harry spit on the floor again.

"I'm gone to kick your ass if you do that again," said Snake. "It's not fit to live here."

"This?" asked Harry, and he spit again on the floor. Snake did not have time to worry about his father; he was running late and needed to get to the garage, needed to get Leslie inside and ready. Snake had to get Leslie ready like a child for school.

"Clean it up," pleaded Snake. His temples throbbed. The

air outside was unmoving again, hot and damp, but it was better than being in that house. Snake did not know if he could ever go back. At first he did not see Leslie. Snake walked out into the yard and called him. It was eight forty-five.

Snake looked into the pasture, and there was Leslie, arms up into the morning sun, standing silently like a medicine man. Snake screamed his name, but Leslie did not answer or turn.

"Leslie!" screamed Snake. Leslie finally lowered his arms and turned, and when he did, Snake could see, even this far away, that he had been crying, and Snake thought only of one thing: *I love my brother and he will never really know it.*

+   +   +

It was Saturday. Junior Crawford sat in his smoking jacket at the head of the table, forking an oozing slice of fried egg between his thick lips. Ada watched him in disgust and fascination, but Truly ignored them both, instead looking at Nova's shaking hands as she poured Truly's coffee.

"Thank you," said Truly. She looked up at Nova, who glanced down, face pulled back in anguish. All night Nova had slept fitfully at her house, crying out until Lena had shaken her awake and told her stories about the moon. Nova had finally slipped into dreams.

"You welcome," Nova whispered. She shuttled out of the dining room and back into the kitchen, the door flapping back and forth. Truly felt Nova's presence still beside her and decided then to do it again. She was thinking of Nova as she sipped the coffee.

"I'm joining the damn Citizens' Committee," said Junior,

bringing his palm down lightly on the tabletop. Ada stared at him.

"Why?" asked Truly.

"Because the niggers think they're going to rule the world," said Junior. "They think they should get what it took white folks two hundred years to earn. They've not earned shit as far as I'm concerned."

"Please," said Ada. She lifted a rasher of bacon and bit a dainty flake from its end.

"It's not just this Martin Lucifer Coon thing, either," Junior said. "It's the whole thing. Nova! Get in here!" He leaned back in his chair, his face red and unhealthy looking as Nova came creeping into the room like a terrified mouse. She stopped by Junior's chair.

"Yessir," she said. She looked at Truly, who was smiling broadly, thinking of many wonderful things.

"I want your opinion on something, Nova," said Junior. He folded his arms over his chest. "Do the niggers in this town think they ought to have overnight what it took white people two hundred years to earn?" Nova held her hands at waist level and squeezed them together as if she held a lemon and were trying to drain its juice. Her knuckles went white under her dark skin.

"I don't hardly know," said Nova softly.

"Oh, come now, Nova," said Junior grandly. "This town's full of niggers who think they ought to get something for nothing. They sit around on their lazy asses flashing their huge white teeth, and once a month they go down to the welfare office to pick up their checks so they can drive their Cadillacs to the liquor store. I'm joining the Rockton Citizens' Committee. I think we have the duty to make sure that we are all equal in the eyes of the law. What do you think about that?"

"I don't think nothing about that," said Nova.

"You must have some opinion," said Junior.

"Nossir, I ain't never had no opinion," said Nova.

Junior laughed, and pieces of egg flew out onto his maroon smoking jacket. Truly stared at her father, and when Nova looked at Truly, Ada cleared her throat.

"My God," Ada said. "Don't you have any pride?"

"Are you talking to me?" asked Junior. "Pride? What are you talking about? I was just asking this little colored gal what she thought about niggers." He started giggling and took a bite of toast smeared thickly with grape jelly.

"I want a dog," said Ada. She looked with fierce hatred at Junior. Truly's attention was suddenly on her mother, and Nova seemed to have almost forgotten her fear. The only sound in the room was the ticking of the clock Junior's grandfather had bought in Europe years before.

"You want a dog?" said Junior. "Did you just say you wanted a dog, Ada?"

"That what she say," said Nova. Junior glared at her, and Nova started, surprised she had spoken.

"But honey, you—"

"I want a dog," said Ada. Her voice was shaking and angry. "I want a dog, and I want it here today. I want you to get me a Doberman."

"Oh, come on now, baby," said Junior, all bluster, "you don't really mean that."

"Get her a dog," said Truly, gesturing with a piece of toast. "Get her a Doberman."

"But baby, you are afraid of dogs," said Junior. His face

had gone from red to purple, and he suspected he was being mocked, but he could never deny anything to Ada, who rarely asked for anything. He had always wanted to be her hero.

"Get me a damn Doberman today, or you'll regret it, I promise you," hissed Ada. Junior looked at Truly for help.

"Sweetness, talk to your mama and—"

"Get her a damn Doberman," Truly said.

"Don't swear, sweetness," Junior said.

"Is it one of them dogs with the pointy ears?" asked Nova. Truly howled with laughter, but Ada stared straight at Junior, eyes hard, mouth tight.

"If it's what you really want," said Junior, "I could ask Charlie Davis. He raises them things, I think. Maybe he's got a pup."

"I don't want a puppy," said Ada. "I want a grown dog. I want the biggest one you can find."

"Baby, you have to train them and—"

"Daddy, shut up and do it," said Truly. Nova started moving slowly backward toward the kitchen, her eyes all the time on Truly. Lord, thought Nova, she is pretty, but it's like watching a person on fire. Nova had a boyfriend, Elder Robert Thomas III, but he had these huge soft hands, and he was going to Morehouse in Atlanta and wanted to be a preacher.

"Sounds crazy," said Junior absently. He slid his chair back and stood, his massive stomach coming up over the tablecloth like some horrible surprise. "But I'll get at it. I'm going to talk to Jimmy Ray Caldwell about the Citizens' Committee anyway. I'll go by Charlie's while I'm out." He smiled this agonizing phony smile that made Truly's anger rise. "Okay, honey?" Ada stared at him but did not answer. He nodded, licked his lips, and left the room. Truly and her mother sat in silence until they heard his car start and roll over the gravel driveway.

"Where you going to keep it?" asked Truly.

"There are men," said Ada, staring at the sun pouring through the window, "who would die for the woman they love. They would bring them suns and moons, paint beautiful pictures for them, or write the most beautiful poems, words that make your very heart ache."

"Where are you going to keep it?" Truly repeated.

"I could just die," said Ada, and she stood and drifted out of the room. Truly thought about it for a moment and began to cry, the tears surprising and uncontrollable. She walked upstairs and sat on her bed until she felt calm again. She turned on the radio and waited until the weather came on. There was a 30 percent chance of thundershowers that afternoon, but Truly didn't believe it.

+ + +

It was nearly ten-thirty, and Snake Ripley was staring out the broad front window of the garage, barely breathing, thinking of being rich. He did not give a damn about Harry, but it hurt Snake to think what might happen to Leslie. He often daydreamed, and now he saw Leslie on his hands and knees speaking to the rotted corpse of their father, not knowing of death, of what to do. Snake was afraid Leslie would never be able to understand again how things connected.

Snake was thinking of Leslie when he heard the old car, asthmatic, sputtering, coming from his left, and as soon as he saw it, he knew it was his father.

"What in the hell," muttered Snake. When the car, Harry's 1968 Bel Air, came even with the garage, Snake saw him, hunched over the wheel as if trying to see five feet in front of the car as he drove. "Leslie!" There was no answer, and when Snake called again, Leslie came from the back, where he had been reading about Batman and Robin.

"Hello," said Leslie pleasantly.

"Daddy just drove by," said Snake. "Did he say anything about going anywhere?"

"Daddy?" Leslie said.

"In the Bel Air. Did he say anything about going any-where?"

"The Bel Air," said Leslie. He tried to think, but instead of cars, he saw air, and in the air, birds, a hawk, and he turned to Snake and smiled broadly. "Yes."

"What did he say?" asked Snake. He wanted to follow Harry, but Leslie was not being much help. "Where was he going?" Leslie looked at Snake. He knew the answer. It always made him feel wonderful when he knew an answer.

"Into the air," said Leslie. "On wings."

"Jesus Christ," said Snake. "I'm locking the door. You go out back and read your comics. I'm going after him."

"Will you come over the garage?" asked Leslie. Snake felt like he wanted to cry, but he merely walked out the door, locked it, leapt into his old Chevy, and scratched off toward Rockton, cursing, feeling the swelling power beneath his foot. He could not believe it had been Harry. His father had not been out of the yard in a year. *Maybe I'm wrong*, thought Snake, stretching to see the car.

But he wasn't wrong. That morning, after Snake and Leslie had finally left, Harry had taken a shower, his first in eight months, shaved, and put on a white shirt, dark pants, socks, his old black wing tips. He had shaved and combed his white hair back from his brow. Except for his eyes and the color of his skin, he might have been the same man who had lived there a few years back. He had to jump-start the Bel Air from an old marine battery Snake had gotten from a friend, but the car finally started.

Harry let the car run for a while as he sat inside at the kitchen table having only one glass of bourbon. The clothes felt strange to Harry, like some new skin that had grown overnight, or something he had long ago shed. He wanted to walk behind the barn and dig his own grave and lie in it, to feel the earth closing in. But first there was this other thing, and he could barely wait.

He had been middleweight boxing champ of his division. He had been the one who had taught Snake to box, taking him as far as the regional Golden Gloves in New Orleans, where Snake had been knocked flat by a gangling redhead from Baton Rouge. Harry had wanted the boy to bounce back, but Snake had never gotten over it. Harry had been thinking about boxing that morning, wondering how it would feel to beat the everloving shit out of Snake. And by God, he could still do it. He just knew he could sucker punch the little son of a bitch. But Harry would never get the chance to do that. He had this other thing to do, and he felt so damn good about it he could barely sit still on the seat of the Bel Air when he left.

He could feel it in his chest like some dark star, growing blindly. It might be a week or a month, but when it came, it would be no stranger. He would touch it, and it would welcome him warmly.

Snake didn't have any trouble catching sight of Harry. Harry drove as if his wheels were partially glued to the asphalt, wandering over the centerline and back. Snake decided to hang back and see if the old man killed himself, but after ten miles, it was clear Harry was going to make it all the way to Rockton. Snake was casually watching the rear of the Bel Air when he noticed that the car was moving oddly, almost like it was getting away. Snake didn't think that was possible, so he waited until it was too late, until Harry's car was far ahead, turning down Pine Street on the left. Snake stomped the accelerator and the car leapt once and roared toward Pine, but when he turned, the tires squealing like some dying animal, Harry's car was no longer in sight.

"Son of a bitch," Snake muttered. He drove fast down the length of the street, but there were four or five ways Harry could have gone. Snake decided to drive into town, but after hanging around there for half an hour and not seeing his father, he drove back toward the garage, figuring that by now Leslie had likely wandered off or something worse. Maybe, thought Snake, Harry was driving toward some distant line of a new county or state, toward the sunset, sunrise—anywhere but rotting any longer in their home.

Harry, in fact, had not gone anywhere. He had been looking steadily in his mirror. After turning onto Pine, he had raced down to Oak, turning right, and tucked in behind the Rockton Baptist Church. He sat there for a long time, laughing, looking up ahead of him at the sunlight, hot and wet along the beams of a cross.

5

JUNIOR CRAWFORD HELD the leash tight as the dog strained against it. The Doberman was grown, weighed one hundred and eight pounds, and now it was regarding him with its neck pulled down and a low guttural growling that sounded to Junior like something being torn.

"Hit's a good dog," said Charlie Davis. He was tall as a basketball player and slightly deaf. This dog was the only grown one he had now for sale, because its left foreleg had been flattened when Charlie's wife, Pearline, had backed over it when it was a puppy. Charlie had told Junior the dog was mild as May, but that wasn't entirely true, since it had once nearly torn the leg off the rural mail carrier, who had gotten out to see if his tire was low. "Hit's name is Butch. But you could name it anything. You can take a dog and name him anything and he'll come. Hell, you can even kick a old dog and hit'll come slobbering after you a-crawling." Charlie laughed and began coughing and then spit into the grass.

"You said you wanted how much?" asked Junior. Butch was still growling idly, and Junior held the leash as if he were pushing away his own death.

"Well, Mr. Crawford," whined Charlie, "hit's worth least seventy-five dollars, I'd say."

"For this damn dog?" shouted Junior. He was used to having his way. He had found out early that most people are losers waiting to be intimidated.

"Well, he's a good thang," said Charlie. "How about sixty dollars?"

"I'll give you forty," said Junior. Charlie looked down, feeling good despite the heaving in his chest. He had been going to give the dog to his brother-in-law, but forty dollars was much better.

"I'll let you have him out of respect for your daddy," said Charlie. Junior swore and handed the leash back to Charlie, reached into his hip pocket, and took out the billfold, from which he peeled two twenties and handed them to Charlie.

"I've lost my mind," said Junior.

"Hit's just the weather," said Charlie.

Junior Crawford took the dog and put it in the backseat and drove down the road back toward Rockton, eight miles away. Charlie lived out in the country, and as he pulled away, Junior could hear Butch howling as he looked out the back window at the only home he'd ever had disappearing behind him.

"Shut up, dammit!" screamed Junior. He felt anger swelling, then falling, swelling, falling. He didn't know how much longer he could stand her damn painting and whining about

how Junior did nothing around the house. Well, he was going
to do something. He was going to join the Rockton Citizens'
Committee, and then he'd see who had the power over things
in this county, which family could make people jump.

He could not make any sense out of why Ada had wanted
a Doberman, except to irritate him. Everything she did was to
irritate him; it had been three weeks since they had made
love, and she refused him all the time now. He had thought
of leaving her, but that wouldn't work. What might work was
this other idea he had: bedding down with Nova Jernigan.

Junior could let Ada paint and play with her damn dog,
and he could crawl all over little Nova out in the visitor's
house. That's how those people are, he thought, all feelings,
no brains. That's why you always see them singing and dancing and you never see any of them doing real work. They live
in the senses. Junior was thinking about how black people
live within their senses when he looked into the rearview
mirror. Standing just behind him, lip pulled back tight and
showing a row of wet teeth, was his wife's new friend, Butch.

Night would come to Rockton with the dust. The air was
heavy with water, and if you stood on the corner of Jackson
and Pierce you could see Hank Hardy closing his pharmacy,
nodding to Merry Lang, who owned Sew What, the fabric
shop next door. You could see them smile and nod, while
next to them Richard James came out stretching, looking up
at the heavy red clouds, the sun still high now. Richard was
a lawyer, who was defending Big Bob Douglas on charges of
assault and battery. Big Bob was guilty, of course, but a few
days later, Richard would get him off. And it went on, the

doors closing up, the store lights left on against the night, Rockton folding into itself for the weekend. And already, kids were roaring around town drunk, laughing, touching, feeling the cool joy of automobile air-conditioning. They would consume gallons of beer and liquor. Jonas Watson was late closing his funeral home.

He had been busy for two days with the burial of Missy O'Dair, whose husband had beaten her to death, everyone now knew, with a plaster statue of the Pietà her sister had sent them from Jacksonville for Christmas. He was in jail, and Missy was under the warm sod of Rockton County. Richard James was going to defend him, already laying groundwork for an insanity plea. The funeral was one of the best Jonas Watson had ever handled, and though he tried to look sad, Missy's family had money and the profit looked to be enormous.

The sun lingered until well after the shops were closed, and ten miles south, past the darkened window of the garage, lights were already on in the home of Harry Ripley. Snake had made french fries in deep fat, heated fish sticks in the oven, and he, Leslie, and Harry sat at the kitchen table buttering thick slices of bread.

Harry had drunk only a half bottle of bourbon that Saturday because he was making plans. He had gone about checking things and was now feeling much better. When you stay at home for a time, the world can turn, even slightly, and when you look again it has changed color or shape. But Harry was satisfied now. When he had come home, he read the *TV Guide* for the week of October 16–22, 1965, as he drank slowly and watched boxing.

Harry's hands shook terribly as he shoved a piece of fish coated in ketchup between his lips.

"You're getting it all over your face," said Snake. By the next morning, he would be rich, and after a decent interval he would leave this wretched town and head west or north.

"You saw me, didn't you?" asked Harry, his eyes glazed and gleaming, a dog's eyes, Leslie thought. He stared at his father and tried to place them, and it came back, their old dog, Cassius Clay, who had taken sick and died in about two weeks. Harry refused to spend money on a vet, and Cassius Clay had curled up behind the barn and died. Harry's eyes reminded him of Cassius Clay's.

"What the hell," said Snake.

"You saw me driving," said Harry. He grinned broadly.

"You're crazy," said Snake. He ate a slice of bread. Snake was thinking of going to California.

"You *know*," said Harry, laughing.

"Where did you go?" asked Snake.

"You know!" cackled Harry.

"It's too bad you didn't wreck that piece of crap and kill yourself," said Snake. Leslie smiled and drank from his sweating glass of water.

"Can we shoot the gun after supper?" Leslie asked. "I like its smell."

"I don't know," said Snake. He turned on Harry. "I asked where you went."

"I was just making sure," said Harry. "You'll see. Something big's going to happen."

"What happened to Cassius Clay?" asked Leslie. He tried to remember, but all he could see were the dog's red eyes as it tottered along the fence row behind the barn.

"He lost," said Harry. "Was it George Foreman? Frazier was the Thrilla in Manila . . . hell, I don't remember."

"It's a wonder you remember anything," said Snake.

Harry laughed and ate a small piece of fish. Leslie looked at the fish and the bread and suddenly realized it would last forever. It was a miracle.

"His eyes are all I remember," said Leslie.

"Right," said Snake. "I don't know what you're up to," he said to Harry, "but I hope it's nothing involving me. You'll be sorry."

"It involves everybody," said Harry. He leaned forward and his shirt came into the plate and the front was smeared with ketchup. "*Everybody*."

"Snake?" said Leslie.

"Come on," said Snake. They got up and went into the front room where Snake kept his weapons. This was his favorite room, and he looked lovingly at the Colt AR-15, the Mossberg Model 402 Palamino, the old Winchester 270 slide action, the Universal Model 100 Carbine. God, they were wonderful. He picked up the Harrington and Richardson .30-30, set it down, then lifted the High Standard Flite-King Brush Pump-Action shotgun, the .12-gauge bore with a 28-inch barrel, full choke. Snake loved the grain and the smell, but he put it down and went for the handguns.

On one wall, he had made a pegboard and hung the pistols, all sizes and calibers. He loved pistols more than rifles or shotguns. He had lots of them, from a beat-up Ruger Blackhawk .357 Magnum to the Browning Medalist .22. He looked slowly over them, a Browning Nomad, his old Colt Buntline Scout, his cowboy gun, then to the Colt Python .357 with the six-inch barrel.

He took the Python off the wall, feeling its familiar heft. He took a box of cartridges from the ammo cabinet and motioned with his head for Leslie to follow him. They walked out the front door, which hardly anyone ever used, down into the yard, across the road, through a fence, and into a large field. The sun was nearly gone. Snake was to pick up Truly at the cemetery at eleven, and already he was worried that he would be caught, that he could wind up in jail instead of rich. But he would have to take that chance.

"Explode it," said Leslie joyfully. Snake looked at him as they walked a hundred yards into the field. "Explode it, Brother."

"*Shoot* it," said Snake, stopping. Leslie's blond hair was dirty and sweaty, stuck to his forehead, and his eyes had an almost unbearable opalescence. "You don't say *explode* it, Leslie."

"I don't remember sometimes how to say things," Leslie said.

"I know," said Snake softly.

"I remember our Lord," said Leslie. "We will have fishes to eat forever."

"Leslie, try to think," said Snake. He gestured back toward the house with the Colt. "You need to know what things are really like around here. You don't know what Daddy's up to, do you?"

"He's up to?" asked Leslie. He glanced around and then into the air.

"Harry," sighed Snake. Leslie looked back toward the house. "Do you know what he's up to?" Leslie kept staring at the house. "Never mind." He wheeled and aimed the gun at the dead oak that stood in the middle of the pasture. When he fired, the sound left their ears ringing, but Leslie could not have been happier. A small cloud of gun smoke drifted in the still air and Leslie ran for it, thrust his nose up into it, and inhaled.

"It's that smell," said Leslie. "Do it again, Brother."

Snake looked at his brother and held the gun over his head and fired it five times, his arm jerking hard, the sound rolling down the field to a row of pines and back. Leslie whooped and ran about in the dying light, trying to smell the powder.

"I have to leave this place," Snake said, but so softly Snake barely heard his own words, and he knew even if Leslie had, he would not have understood.

+ + +

Truly and Ada were sitting in the huge living room watching television when Junior came struggling in the room with Butch at the end of a short chain. The dog was breathing raggedly, and its pointed ears were turning, trying to catch the sounds. Truly saw it immediately, the dog dragging Junior across the floor toward Ada, and she wanted to laugh. Instead, she opened her purse and took out a cigarette and lit it.

"Sweetness!" said Junior when he saw the cigarette. "You said you wouldn't!" Ada turned and saw the dog, and her muscles went icy and numb, and her mouth became sour with fear. The dog was straining at the short chain, eyes bulging.

"That was before now," Truly said. Ada looked at Truly's cigarette. It looked positively beautiful next to the dog. She wondered if the dog might kill her, and she tried to see it romantically, the artist dying by her greatest fear, and there was heroism in it, she admitted.

"Here's the dog," said Junior, trying to smile and looking, Ada thought, embarrassingly foolish. "It's the biggest Doberman Charlie had. He tried to rob me, but I jewed him down to forty bucks." Ada did not notice that the dog was looking at her and wagging its tail.

"It's beautiful," Ada said. "Let it go."

Junior leaned backward against the weight of the dog and stared at her, trying to think of what might have gone wrong in her head.

"It's artistic temperament," said Junior. "I know that. You told me that a hundred times, Ada, but let it go? It'll roam the house." Nova Jernigan came in to tell them that supper was ready, but when she saw the dog, she backed up toward Truly.

"Jesus wept!" yelled Nova. "Hit'll rip your throat out!"

"Yes," said Ada softly, and Truly smiled and stood beside Nova. For a moment, Nova did not notice, then she felt Truly beside her and looked into her eyes.

"It will not," said Junior, who was sweating heavily despite the fans. "I'm going to tie it up out by the visitor's house."

"I said let it go," said Ada, her voice harsh and high. Junior felt disgust for her, for the house, for everything. He dropped the chain, and the dog went around the room sniffing, then it turned and ran up the stairs, its toenails tapping on the hardwood floors.

"This is crazy," said Junior, trying to laugh.

"What do you know about crazy?" said Ada. "Nova, is dinner ready?"

"If that animal ain't done ate it up," said Nova, looking toward the hall.

Ada walked past them, her knees trembling, her stomach knotted with a sharp pain, toward the dining room, and Junior followed, jabbering about how they really must, honey, tie the dog up outside. Nova did not move and neither did Truly. They were so close they were touching. Nova wanted to move.

This is not natural, she thought, but then nothing about this house was natural. She knew only what she felt. Truly did not want to move. She put her face close to Nova's.

"Truly," said Nova. "I want . . . can we . . ." She choked on the words. Truly smiled.

"What is it, sweetness?" asked Truly.

"That his name for you," said Nova. "You call me that name he have for you." From the dining room, Junior called Nova's name. "Mist' Junior, he want his supper."

"What were you going to say?" asked Truly. Their faces were only two inches apart. Nova's mouth was slightly open, and she licked her lips, her tongue looking pale against the full dark lips.

"I need you," choked Nova. "God hisself help me, but I need to lie with you again. It's like what I'm feeling is . . . it's like love or something."

"No," said Truly. "It isn't like love." She kissed Nova on the lips.

"I'm sorry," said Nova, and tears came down her cheeks. She stumbled backward, blinded by the salty tears. "You right. Hit's not like love or nothing. Hit's like being pulled into hell itself. God, I don't want to feel none. Feel this way about a white girl. A girl! Hit's the Devil work."

"No," said Truly. Junior Crawford called Nova again, louder this time. He was very hungry and angry about Ada and that damn limping Doberman. "There is no such thing as love. The only thing we have is how we feel. Take how you feel, Nova. It's a gift."

They stood and stared at each other for a long time, not noticing Junior until he was behind them. When he came into the room, he thought he smelled something exciting, like the odor of a woman, but it might be the dog, he thought.

"What in the hell are you two doing in here?" asked Junior. "Sweetness, come on to the table. I'm starving. Nova, you getting deaf?"

"May be," she said absently. "Blind. Struck by God, maybe." Nova turned, and Junior walked with her. He knew it was the lovely Nova he smelled, a musky sweat that made him feel weak, and he decided as they walked back toward the dining room that he would take her soon.

Truly walked slowly into the hallway. She thought about laughing or screaming. *Love.* To hear Nova Jernigan talk about love. It was so perverse, so pitiful, that it almost seemed real, as if there were such a thing. Truly stopped at the foot of the stairs, and when she looked up, the dog was sitting halfway up, unmoving, staring at her down the broad, worn steps.

+ + +

By 10 P.M., clouds had thickened over Rockton, but they did not yet promise rain. For three nights clouds had swollen over the county, shepherding thunder and great twisting streaks of lightning, but it had not rained. Over in Carver County, rain had come, soaking pastures from one town to another, but not here. The air began to move, not a wind really, but one solid moving wall of air, and Snake felt it as he stood by his Chevy at the edge of the Rockton City Cemetery. It had been all he could do to stop Leslie from coming.

Snake wore his old moccasins. A brief shield of lightning came, and Snake could see a marble shaft in the cemetery. It was now after eleven.

Already, Truly was late, but Snake wasn't surprised. She was always late. He should just leave her anyway. It was madness to let her come along. Snake looked into the car and saw that the flashlight and the pistol were still on the seat. He had settled on a .38 Police Special. It didn't have much knockdown power, not like a .45, but he was only going to rob an old lady. He could probably knock her down with a whisper if she even woke up.

It was Saturday night, and all day Snake had imagined the coffee can in the coal-grate fireplace, stuffed full of hundred-dollar bills, untraceable, the best thing you'd want. He thought he'd wait a couple of weeks before he left. He was standing there looking at the marble shaft and thinking of the money when he felt someone near him. He turned and saw Truly Crawford's face in the dim aura of a streetlight fifteen feet away.

"Dammit," said Snake, "it's a good thing I didn't have my gun."

"Would you have shot me?" asked Truly. She was smiling easily. She wore a pair of dark shorts and a T-shirt, and she was barefoot.

"Maybe," said Snake. "Come on." She got in the car, and they drove across the railroad tracks.

"Here?" she asked. "It's a mile back to her house."

"Here," Snake said. "We don't want anyone to see us." They got out, and Snake snugged the .38 inside the back of his pants. It hurt as he walked, but he felt somehow invincible, in control now, not afraid. Truly was never afraid. They walked back toward the railroad tracks and could hear the rising arc of the train's whistle. Snake stopped under a water oak to wait for the train to pass.

"My mother got a dog," said Truly. Snake stared at her for a long time until the train was finally gone, the air again full of slowly moving wind and silence.

"She got a dog?" asked Snake. Truly could say anything at any time. He liked that about her, that she often made about as much sense as Leslie. It was easier to deal with someone who didn't make sense. "You mean a real dog?"

"A Doberman," said Truly. "It's loose up there in the house. I think she's going crazy. It's my father. She asked him for it, and now it's up there in the house running loose. My mother is more scared of dogs than dying."

"Then why'd she ask for one?" Snake said.

"Something she felt," said Truly. "I guess she couldn't rub it raw enough."

They went through the backyard of a mansion, then behind the church. They stayed out of the streetlights, creeping down the edges of yards until they came to Agnes Longley's house, which sat back thirty yards from the street behind six shady columns. They moved deep into the shadows and around the back of the house. A sheet of lightning lit the yard, and they could see the dog not five feet from them, huge mouth open, and Snake leapt backward into Truly. They stood, motionless, until another, longer flash came, and they saw it was a statue, paws buried in the neat green lawn.

"Good Lord," Snake whispered. Truly giggled softly. The back steps were wooden, going up to a shaky porch. It had a wooden screen door. Snake took two stockings out of his pocket and shook them out and handed one to Truly. Neither of them spoke as they pulled the stockings down over their faces, flattening their noses. Snake felt as if he might never breathe again, but he would not stop this now. It was almost a righteousness. "Stay right with me."

"Okay," said Truly. He could feel her near him, smell her body. They walked slowly up the porch, and Snake pulled on the screen door, but it was locked, so he took out his large case knife, slit the screen, and flipped the latch. They were on the porch. A light was on in the kitchen, which was the next room, and when their eyes adjusted, they could see mounds of old newspapers and magazines scattered everywhere, falling off an old glider, stacked in the corners, everywhere. Snake tried the door to the kitchen. He knew it would be locked, but there were two windows they might go in, windows that had once been on the outside of the house before the porch had been added. But Snake was wrong. The door swung back as if the hinges had just been oiled, and they were both suddenly in the kitchen.

It was a large room, full of the odors of coffee and trash that had been left inside too long. A table with heavy curving legs squatted in the middle of the room, and the ceilings went up high and were lost in darkness. The counters were littered with old dishes, stacks and stacks of them. Truly could not see well, so she put her hand in the back of Snake's pants to hold on to him and felt the cold grip of the gun.

"Careful," Snake whispered. Truly realized as they walked across the room that she was struggling to breathe, that the floor was filthy, covered with dirt and what seemed to be small stones that hurt her bare feet.

"Okay," she said. They came out of the kitchen into the dining room. It was also large, and was nearly stuffed with a long oval table that was polished so highly it seemed to glow from the small light that was on in the kitchen. The rest of the room was cluttered with newspapers and what appeared to be old rags. The smell was enough to gag Snake, but Truly didn't mind. Every smell fascinated her, every taste, every touch.

They saw it at the same time, an old fireplace filled with newspapers.

"There," whispered Snake. The other rooms out ahead of them were only darkness, and Snake felt his throat swelling, felt as if he should run now before someone found them. But if he ran, he would have nothing. He knelt by the fireplace, and Truly came down beside him. He began to pull the paper out, and the noise seemed deafening, and Snake stopped and waited, then kept pulling. Soot was suddenly in the room, in their eyes, but Snake tugged until the paper was all out and he could hear, up the chimney, the first roll of thunder from the west.

"Empty?" asked Truly. Snake felt through the papers, and he knew nothing was there. It meant moving on into the living room. He didn't answer her. He stood and turned on the small flashlight he had brought, and she stayed behind him as they moved into the next room. He moved the beam around the room, and they saw it was full of old heavy furniture with tattered throws, and the curtains were slightly torn and musty. A room to one side might be a bedroom, but Snake didn't know. The fireplace was on the wall to their right.

"There," whispered Snake. He handed the light to her and she squatted as he began to pull the paper out of this fireplace. His heart was beating so fast he thought it would bounce out of his chest, but it was just like he'd always heard, a fireplace full of newspaper. He pulled out a large piece, and when he set it on the floor, he could see by the beam from the flashlight that it said PRESIDENT SHOT in huge letters. He kept pulling until a metal coffee can fell heavily onto the floor. "Turn it off!" Truly flicked off the flashlight, and they squatted there for a long time until the only sound was the distant threat of the thunder. They stood and Snake held the can. It wasn't as heavy as he thought it would be, but he felt suddenly wonderful, and they went back through the dining room and had just come into the kitchen when they saw the old woman standing there staring at them, holding a pistol level with Snake Ripley's chest.

Truly knew her, had known her for years, but this was something different. Her face was the color of ash, her teeth out, lips shrunken inside her face. Her gown could not hide the pitiful thinness of her arms and chest, and flesh sagged from her elbow under her arm, trembling as she held the gun out.

"Oh my God," Snake said weakly. He took a step backward. He moved the coffee can to his left hand and with his right felt for the gun in his waistband. The stocking over his face was suffocating him. He felt a manic urge to rip the nylon off, to say it was all a joke, that she had found them out. Then they would make coffee and talk about antebellum days in Rockton.

"Don't move another step," she said. Her voice was raspy with fear. Truly thought it was like a scene from a movie, and though she thought Snake might get shot, she knew she wouldn't. Snake took another step back, almost into the darkness of the dining room. "Don't . . . I said . . ." The old woman's voice was unearthly now, deep and terrified. Snake pulled the gun out slowly.

"Put it down," he said, and he brought his own gun around slowly.

A grunting clap of thunder broke with the flash from the window, and the old woman squinted her eyes and shot Snake

Ripley. Snake was standing there oddly, looking at the gun, a
.22 pistol, not much range or knockdown power, when he realized she had fired. He stumbled back a foot, the bullet having entered just under his right collarbone. His arm felt weak,
and he heard Truly make a high-pitched moan. The woman
was still holding the gun out toward him, and now she was
squinting again, so Snake shot her in the middle of the chest.

She jumped up from her aged limbs, jerked backward
like a marionette, and fell heavily onto the kitchen floor.

"You're shot," said Truly. She did not recognize her own
voice and looked to see from where it had come. Snake felt as
if he would vomit. She was trying to look at his shoulder,
where blood was pumping all over his shirt, but he pushed
her away. He came further into the kitchen, where the smell
hung heavily. His shoulder was just now starting to hurt.
Truly was suddenly crying, heaving sobs, shaking uncontrollably.

"Don't!" said Snake. "Quiet down, dammit! Just quiet
down!" He saw that Agnes's small pistol had skittered across
the tile. He leaned over her and blood was everywhere, already snaking out three feet from her body. He had hit her
square in the chest, and her body was jerking as if mildly
shocked. Her eyes were open and blinking, mouth moving as
if she were trying to say something. She raised her right hand,
the bony finger pointing almost but not quite at Snake, then
it slowly went down, and she was dead.

"We've got to get out of here," said Truly. "Dear sweet
Jesus. Is she dead?"

"Oh my God," said Snake.

"Dear sweet Jesus," said Truly. A wind was coming up
outside, but it still wasn't raining. "This is bad."

Snake looked at her as he stood up. He felt giddy and weak from the loss of blood, then he was crying, and Truly pushed him out onto the porch. The numbness of his wound was beginning to wear off and a searing pain shot from his shoulder down his right side. They came down the steps and went through the yard toward the cemetery.

The night sky was lit by sheets of electricity, and a strong wind was bending the old oaks all over Rockton. Rain. You could almost smell it rising over the county, gathering to soak the farmland. But it never fell, not in Rockton. The next day, Rocktonians found that Carver County had been soaked, three inches, but not one drop was recorded in Rockton County.

Truly and Snake got back to his car, climbed in. They closed the doors, and then Snake immediately cracked his door and vomited on the ground a few feet from the tombstone of Thomas Follett Shaw, who had been minister of the Rockton Methodist Church in the early twentieth century.

"Are you all right?" asked Truly. He had gotten the stocking off his face just before he was sick, and now Truly took the stocking from her own face. Snake choked the bile back into his mouth.

"Shine it on my shoulder," Snake said, handing the flashlight to Truly. She clicked it on, looking around for cars, but there were none. He wiped the blood off. The hole was neat, clean, and he took a towel from under the seat and held it to his shoulder. It felt better.

"Are you going to die?" asked Truly.

"I'm scared," he said, looking through the window.

"I love you," said Truly.

"Don't say that," said Snake.

"Please," she said.

"Hold this," he said, pointing toward the bloody towel with his left hand. She reached out and pressed the towel hard to him, and he lifted the coffee can. He took the plastic top off the can and looked inside. He pulled out the porcelain head of a doll, eyes gone, sockets empty, a benign smile creasing its face.

"It's a baby," said Truly.

"A baby boy," said Snake. He held the doll's head in his thick hand. Truly shifted the flashlight, and the beam came up through the head. Its eyes glowed. Snake could not bear it. He brought it down on the dash, and it shattered, shards cutting his palm until it bled.

6

S U N D A Y   R O S E   I N   a tangle of red clouds. Harry
Ripley was still asleep at 8 A.M. and so was Snake, but Leslie
was dressed and sitting in the middle of the old fescue pasture behind the house. He had tried to wait up for Snake, but
some time after midnight he had fallen asleep reading the
Bible.

When Snake had gotten home, he had spent an hour in
the bathroom pouring iodine and Mercurochrome on his
wound. The bleeding had stopped quickly in the hard muscle, and he could tell, turning and looking in the mirror, that
the slug had gone straight through, clean. He had taped it up
and lay down, but he slept very little.

Harry had been asleep in his chair when Snake had gotten home, content because he had made a list. He had spent
an hour thinking, and he had made the list, three names. The

first name was Dr. Owen Smith, the second was Billy Homer, and the third was John Henry Ripley, Jr. Harry had tried to think of another, but there should be only three.

Truly had walked home and stood for a moment in the front hallway, feeling sick and scared. She could not stop seeing the ceramic doll's head, its eyes lighting up before Snake crushed it. She was going to jail now, she had thought. She had gone into the dark dining room and stood there for a while, taking a bottle of wine from the liquor cabinet and drinking from the neck. Her hands had been shaking. It wasn't just the blood. *She had liked it.* Liked the fear in the old woman's eyes and the smell of the gunfire, and Snake's torment and blood, liked it all. *Something,* she had thought, *is terribly wrong with me.* That was when she had seen Butch sitting in the kitchen door, tongue lolling out, eyes electric.

Leslie Ripley could swear feathers were growing along his arms. He sat in the middle of the pasture and touched his arms, looking at them, thinking of rising into the light. His brother had been the first, Leslie thought, to see the hawk of the Lord as it came down toward Rockton. Wonderful things were going to happen. If you had enough faith, the kind of faith that changes one fish into thousands, that changes water into wine, you could believe one day you might rise up and fly.

"I will rise up," said Leslie out loud. He tried to think of the things he loved. He loved this place, his house, the garage, loved Snake, and God bless Harry. He loved the feathers growing along his arms and the smell of the earth. He loved rain when it came and the hardness of the soil when it did not. He loved his Mommy, who had gone to live with God when Leslie had been born. If he could see God, he could see his Mommy. She would look like she did in the picture, stomach swollen with a baby, eyes tired but full of light.

"I will see her face," Leslie said.

Leslie wondered how Jesus had cured things. He had touched a lame man and the man walked again. He had made a blind man's eyes clear as a river up in the mountains. Jesus could have turned a man into a hawk if he had wanted to, Leslie thought, turned into a hawk himself, and the two of them could soar over the farmland, the towns, like superheroes, looking for things to heal.

"I could heal," said Leslie.

He could take the anger out of Snake, the old age from Harry. He could take it all into his own wings and then scatter it like fertilizer over the earth. What did Jesus do to save the ones he loved? Leslie tried to remember what it was that Jesus had done. He had read the story before.

Leslie looked down toward the house. It was looking bad, shingles loose and falling. The barn sagged in the middle. The yard was grown up. It was like nobody lived there, but Leslie lived there. Maybe Jesus would come down and touch the yard and heal it and bring the animals back, because Leslie missed the animals.

The day they had come and taken the Herefords, Leslie had stood by the truck and watched their eyes. They all had asked him with their eyes where they were going, what would happen to them, and Leslie had kept saying as they passed, *I don't know, I don't know*, to the annoyance of the men who'd come for them. When the truck had driven off, they had all been crying for Leslie, and he had run after the truck, crying, nose running. He had run for a mile before Snake caught up with him in the car and took him home.

But now, Leslie felt peaceful and light. The storms had missed the county the night before, but they had left a few stray breezes, and now one seemed to catch under Leslie's feathers as he stood and lifted himself higher into the light.

That was when he remembered what Jesus had done for those he loved. He had died for them. He had been nailed to a tree, and then he had died for them. Leslie walked slowly back down toward the house, and before he got there, he saw his hawk coming over the tree line, its eye planted like a nail on Leslie's feathered arms. Leslie stopped and flapped his arms, and he felt himself rise a few inches off the ground as the hawk soared past, and he thought of wonderful things he might do for the love of his family.

Nova Jernigan stood over the stove, lifting rashers of bacon with silvered tongs, turning them in their own hot grease. She had come early as she always did, and when she got there, Butch had been sitting in the kitchen. She was not afraid of him now, talking quietly as she cleaned up after him. Butch limped to Nova and lifted his great nose to her, tail wagging.

"You done come to a crazy house," Nova said out loud. Junior and Ada were still in bed. It was Sunday morning, and there was no use thinking Truly would be up before noon. When Nova had first started to work for the Crawfords, they had gone to church together each Sunday, starched and neat, but now they never went at all. "I bet you being hungry, crazy old dog." Nova opened the refrigerator and took out a new pack of bologna, sliced it open, and handed it to Butch. He limped to a corner and ate it with four jerks of his head.

Nova had wanted to talk to Ailene the night before, but she had gone out, and Nova had spent the evening lying on her bed thinking of Truly, wondering how it would feel to lie in her arms again. She thought of how it would feel to kill Junior Crawford. Except she did not hate him as much as she loved Truly. Butch came back over, and Nova squatted by him and scratched his head. She was looking at Butch when she saw the footprint on the floor, a smeared footprint in something that looked like blackberry jelly.

"Miss Ada step in something," said Nova. She got the washcloth from the sink and wiped it up, but the stain would not completely fade. "Done stain the floor. She done stain the floor."

The kitchen filled with fine smells of bacon and perking coffee. Sunlight streamed through the curtained windows, and Nova felt the heat on her face. She was standing at the stove when she heard a rustling behind her. She did not turn, but a fragrance came with the sound, and she knew it was Truly. Nova turned, smiling, to see Junior Crawford standing there in a red bathrobe, opened to his waist, his massive stomach pushing it out. His hair was combed neatly, flowing back in a white wave, and he was smiling at her, smiling, she thought, like a Halloween face.

"Mist' Junior," Nova said. "I give that dog a hunk of baloney. You best let him out." Junior looked at the dog with disgust.

"Mrs. Crawford is not well," he said. "But I've got to humor her."

"I understand that," said Nova. Junior stared at Nova. She was wearing a thin blue dress, and through it he could see her panties riding high along her hips. He had been thinking of her that morning, having dreamed of her. He had tried to make love to Ada, but she had slapped him so hard he had slapped her back, and she'd cried herself to sleep, sobbing about cut-off ears and paintings. Then Junior had gone to sleep dreaming of Nova, of her shining eyes. He'd awakened filled with blood and lust for her, for the idea of his smooth white skin along her black limbs.

"You don't understand," Junior said. He came closer to Nova, thinking of how the men at the seed store talked about the old days when their fathers had all had black mistresses. It was just something every man did those years ago, something that proved a man's worth to himself. You could never count on a wife for love, only on a woman who knew sex was her duty. "That dog's just a thing from her mind. She's terrified of dogs. She's trying to look into the eye of hell."

"Hell," said Nova. He was now only two feet from her. The odor of cologne suddenly turned into a stench in Nova's nostrils, his sagging white face and red eyes only inches from her. "I understands hell."

"I bet you do," said Junior. He would take her out to the visitor's house. She wouldn't mind. Hell, she'd probably been waiting for it since she'd come to work, would go home that evening and tell her sisters it finally happened, wondering what took the old man so long to avail himself of her body. "You look so pretty this morning."

"I don', " said Nova. She turned and lifted the last of the rashers of bacon from the frying pan and put them on folded paper towels to drain. She turned off the burner and wiped her hands on a soft towel, wondering what was happening. When she turned back, Junior had pulled the waist tie on his robe and it was hanging open, revealing himself. "Jesus wept."

"It's okay now," said Junior, smiling as if he were giving

her something of great value. "You come on out to the visitor's house with me now, Nova. I just need me a little love. They ain't enough love in this house to spit into a thimble."

"I ain't gone let you," she said, backing up into the counter. The tone in her voice made Butch stand and come close to them. Junior was sweating heavily, his face now red, eyes widening.

"Come on, Nova," he pleaded. "I need you. It would be so good." He grabbed her and pulled her to him and hugged her, and then he kissed her hard on her lips, and he tasted to her like toothpaste and salt, something terrible. She felt him pushing up along her leg, thrusting into the blue cloth of her dress, between her legs. She felt the breath going out of her lungs, and it was like death coming over her.

"Don' hurt me, Mist' Junior," she said. "You hurtin' me. Don' hurt me." But Junior Crawford was no longer listening. He couldn't wait to get out to the visitor's house. It was too late for that. He grabbed the front of her dress and pulled it up, looking once over his shoulder and seeing nothing. Then he grabbed the corner of her worn and tattered panties and ripped them off her body.

Junior was grunting and thrusting, sweating now, sweat streaming down his flushed face, sweat rising in all his pores like blood, salt coming to the surface as he groaned, begging Nova to stand still in some inarticulate gargle. Nova tried to shout, but one of Junior's heavy hands came across her face, trying not to hurt her but to keep the sounds inside her.

It was then that Butch began to bark. The sound was deafening, and Junior fell back a step. Nova and Junior looked at the dog, which was hopping up and down, barking, snarling, nape flared into heavy bristles.

"God in heaven," said Junior. He took a step back toward the window, and Butch came toward him. He tied the bathrobe back around his stomach. The mutt was going to kill him in his own house. "Nova, get my pistol from the bedroom. He's done gone mad. Got the hydrophobia."

"Don' you shoot Miss Ada dog!" she gasped. She squatted and picked up the frayed remains of her panties and hugged them into a ball against her breast. "You shoot that dog, I tell you try to rape me." She looked hard at Junior, who was trying to smile, his face soaked with sweat, mouth a weak, trembling line.

"I didn't try to rape you," he whispered. Butch had quit barking but was growling. "I was just needing a little love. You know how it gets, a man needs a little love. Nova." He looked at her. "Nova."

"Don' you touch Miss Ada dog," she said, and she knelt and Butch came to her, licking her face, tail waving the still hot air of the kitchen.

"Okay," Junior said. "It likes you. Why don't you tie it up outside somewhere? Find some rope out back. It likes you." He began to edge out of the room, wondering if he should go get his gun and shoot them both. He could say the dog was attacking her, that he shot and hit her. No, he'd seen on the TV how they could find out with science any lie you told now.

"Miss Ada want him in the house," said Nova.

"You're not going to tell, are you?" said Junior. "It was just love, Nova. I needed to feel it. It's been so long."

"Yeah, it is," she said. Junior waited for her promise that she would say nothing about it, but Nova said nothing else audible, only nuzzled the dog. Junior was in the hallway when the phone rang.

Upstairs, Truly Crawford sat straight up in bed. She looked at the phone and then fell back down. Someone had answered it. She had slept with her clothes on. When she realized it, she remembered, felt her stomach heave, and walked into the bathroom. After that she felt better, but she wondered what she should do first. First, she would take a shower.

She could do anything. She could be president or be a whore. She could win an Academy Award and then cut sugarcane in Cuba. She could climb the Matterhorn or fly off the steeple of the Rockton Baptist Church. She lay naked on her bed, sweating, the windows open, the fan whirring, but with no air moving anywhere at all. Sweat blossomed along her limbs. Someone knocked on the door.

"Who is it?" she asked. She jumped up and got her robe off the back of the bathroom door.

"Daddy," a voice said. "Can I come in?"

Truly opened the door, and Junior was standing there looking shaken, his skin mottled in red and white patches. My God, she thought, he is going to die soon.

"What's wrong?" she asked. He looked away from her, down the hall, then back.

"Oh, sweetness," he said, "something terrible has happened."

"What?" She felt the excitement lift her again.

"Something so terrible," said Junior, "that you just would not believe it."

Agnes Longley had been found by her nephew, who came to pick her up each Sunday morning for the early service. In less than half an hour, all three of Rockton's police cars, the four Rockton County Sheriff's cars, and six Mississippi state patrolmen were on the scene. Men and women stood up and down the placid street in their robes, staring in horror at the antebellum mansion where Agnes had lived alone. Besides the killing of Missy O'Dair, it was the first murder in Rockton in four years, and the first one not tied to a drunken family quarrel since Arnie Salinger had been found shot to death in his house in 1964. Arnie was an agent for Farm Mutual, well liked by nearly everyone, but he'd been shot in the head with a pistol. No one was ever arrested, no suspect was even found. It was still a source of darkness to many of Rockton's older citizens that a man could work all his life and suddenly be killed, and nobody would ever know why or who had done it.

Rockton's police chief, Erwin "Monk" Reubens, took charge. He had been the third one on the scene, and he had never seen anything quite this bad. They had found her in the kitchen, attached to a twenty-foot rope of blood that had run across the kitchen and then under the stove. Her mouth was open. A gun was lying under the kitchen table. Her eyes were wide, opalescent, staring at the ceiling, face frozen in something like pain or terror.

Miss Agnes had taught music to half of Rockton, including Truly Crawford. For years she had been the only piano teacher in town, and she played for assemblies at the elementary school until she had retired in 1981, when she was nearly eighty. Everyone loved Agnes Longley, and as the word spread, no one could believe anyone would kill her, not for money or anything. But money was the first thing Monk Reubens suspected, and when he found the paper pulled out of the fireplaces, he knew it was money. They'd all heard the stories.

Monk was tall and heavy, his features thick but not un-
pleasant, a wide nose flaring over a heavy mustache. He had
been chief for ten years now, and in the past week, two
women had been killed in Rockton. He felt sick and angry as
they began to take pictures, measure the rooms. They called
the state crime lab, but it would be three hours before anyone
could get to Rockton. Monk would have to wait at the house
with Agnes.

At least he knew who had killed Missy O'Dair. This was
much worse. Agnes Longley's house stank of death.

Snake finally awoke at ten-fifteen. All morning he had
been dreaming of the garage, the floating dream, one that
came regularly. In it, all the boxes of nuts and bolts—
everything slowly began to float up into the air, and Snake
was trying to grab them all and put them back onto the
shelves. But it was hopeless, and then everything was moving
circularly, as if running around a track, faster and then even
faster, and Snake went outside the garage and the debris
broke through the window and floated off, and then Snake
found that he was floating, too, feet at first barely touching the
ground, no matter how hard he tried to stay down. Then he
was tipping higher, over the fields of grain sorghum in a
tornado of debris from the store.

When he awoke he was in the middle of a formation of oil
filters, possibly flying north for cooler weather, he thought.
He sat up and remembered what had happened the night
before. The skin on his shoulder had drawn into a tight
wound, and he could scarcely lift his arm.

"Oh my God," he said. He lay in bed and trembled for a

long time. He had to leave. He could get to Mexico and then disappear. He could do something in Mexico for money, maybe sell his guns or be a bodyguard or something. He wondered what evidence he had left in Agnes Longley's house, if Truly would tell. My God, she might be telling everything she knew right now, saying Snake had kidnapped her. She could do anything. She could say she had been forced to witness the entire thing, that Snake had killed Agnes out of simple meanness just as Bubba had killed Missy. Snake jumped out of bed and slid into his jeans and sneakers, then went into the bathroom. He would have to leave. There wasn't any choice. "But if I leave, they'll know," he said to the mirror. And there was Leslie.

He groaned and cried and looked at the wound in the mirror. The clean small hole was dark, and he poured iodine on it again, knees going rubbery from the pain. Then he taped it back up and went into the kitchen, where he found Harry Ripley, Sr., drinking a sweating bottle of Coke and eating a Twinkie. Snake had pulled a T-shirt over his muscles, but he could barely move his arm.

"Where you been, boy?" asked Harry.

"Shut up," said Snake. He got five aspirins from the bottle in the middle of the table and took them, cupping water into his palm from the sink.

"Not a very friendly greeting on this fine Sunday morning," laughed Harry. "I was thinking that you might wake up full of the Holy Ghost or something, like Leslie." As if on cue, Leslie came walking into the kitchen from the back steps, face full of light, arms drifting up over his waist.

"Just shut up and don't bother me this morning," said Snake.

"In the sky, there are signs," said Leslie. Harry started giggling, and Snake opened the refrigerator and took out a cold Budweiser and then sat at the kitchen table. Harry's lips were covered with Twinkie crumbs. He was nearly naked, and the stubble was already growing back.

"Damn," said Snake when he tried to lift the beer with his right hand. He switched it to his left.

"Do something to your arm, son?" asked Harry.

"Don't ever call me that," said Snake sourly.

"What?" said Harry. "What did I call you?"

"Son," said Leslie. "You have a father and then you have a son. Unless the father is the son. The father dies first unless the father and the son are the same fella." He smiled in shock at his own brilliance.

"What in the hell are you talking about?" asked Harry. "Never mind. Henry, what did you do to your arm?"

"None of your damn business," said Snake.

"Well it don't matter none to me," said Harry. "Because today is number one."

"What in the hell are *you* talking about?" asked Snake.

"Number one," whispered Harry. "That's all."

"Oh," said Leslie, eyes brightening. "Number one!"

"What in the hell are you up to?" asked Snake. "I'm getting so tired of people jerking me around. I can't stand much more of this."

"Sure you can," said Harry, laughing. "You have to. We all have to stand everything that comes toward us. You can't just pick and choose, son. That's where I was wrong all these years. You just have to stand it, but when you get to a certain place, you don't have to stand it."

"You're making shit for sense," Snake said. He finished the beer and got another one.

"Anyway, today is number one," said Harry. He finished the Twinkie and threw the paper on the floor. Snake had given up trying to keep the place sanitary or even neat, and he could think of only one thing: he had to get out of this house or it would kill him. They had not really noticed Leslie standing and spreading his arms, his right toward Snake, the left toward Harry. They looked up at him only when he began to speak. Tears were slowly coming down his smooth white cheeks. Snake felt the sickness rising.

"I am going to do something for you because I love you both so very much," said Leslie. He held his arms straight out to his sides and looked lovingly from Harry to Snake and back again. "I could fly if I wanted to. But now I will do it for you."

Harry's eyes were merry as he looked at Snake, waiting for him to react. Snake felt only a deep sadness for Leslie. When the phone rang, none of them moved until the fourth ring, and Snake got up for it. He knew it would be that way. He would answer it.

His head was full of darkness.

+ + +

He met Truly at the deer stand up the road. She was wearing a pair of tight blue short shorts, a T-shirt from Panama City, and sandals that laced up her ankles. She had carefully put on her makeup, blue shadow over her eyes, liner, then a liberal spraying of cologne. She had not worn a bra, and Snake knew it as soon as she got out of her car and came toward him, smiling and waving happily.

"Are you crazy?" asked Snake. He got out of the old Chevy. His hands were shaking and he lit a cigarette and looked around him warily. The woods were hot and still. "You look like some yuppie going to the beach."

"What did you want me to wear?" she asked. She stood only a few inches from him, and he felt it, the absolute power she had over him, and he hated the power, hated himself. "A black crêpe dress?"

"You're worse off than Leslie," said Snake. He took five or six long steps down into the woods, under the deer stand and toward the wilderness. She came after him slowly, knowing he would not go far away. He stopped, leaned against a tree, and held his thick arms over his chest.

"What have you heard?" he asked.

"I drove by there on my way," said Truly. "I never saw so many cop cars in my life. State patrol, sheriff, even city cops."

"My God," said Snake Ripley. "It was an accident!"

"They had the whole yard blocked off," Truly said. "It was a sight."

"I didn't mean to kill her," said Snake. "It was self-defense." He stopped and looked at her. She didn't seem to be listening. Instead, she was standing very still and staring into his eyes. Her T-shirt was getting very wet from her perspiration, and Snake felt as if he were drowning. "You think I'm crazy, don't you?"

"I think you've got the best body in Rockton County," she said softly.

"Don't you even care?" he cried. He backed up from her, but she came with him, staying the same distance away. "I killed that old woman last night, Truly. I killed her! I never hurt a thing in my life. I just wanted to get out of this hole. I just . . ." The words strangled in his throat, and he slid down the trunk of a stalk-straight pine.

"They'll never find out who did it," Truly said. She smiled

brilliantly. "Besides, her life was over anyway. Our life is just beginning. We need to take it."

"I've got to get out of here," Snake said. "I think Leslie's losing his mind. And my daddy's making me crazy."

"They'll never find out," said Truly. She stood over Snake, and he felt her, a swirling mixture of sweat and musk, the echo of violence that seemed to play off her like lightning.

"Come here." She smiled again. Snake threw the cigarette butt away and tried to gather some feeling in his lips. He felt numb all over, as if he had been shocked, and the color seemed bleached from the world. She stood over him, her tight legs spread wide. She raised her arms and stretched, and when she had finished she grabbed the hem of her T-shirt and pulled it over her head. Truly squatted, legs astride Snake's lap, and came down on him without taking off her shorts.

"How is this?" she asked.

"Jesus," said Snake. "I'm going to die."

"Yes," Truly said. "It's all right if you die."

"What the hell does that mean?" Snake asked. He felt himself near some irretrievable point in his body chemistry.

"I'd rather die than be my mother," said Truly.

"At least you have a mother," he said.

"I got you," she said. "This is what I am. This here."

Snake knew that no death was different from any other.

7

HARRY PARKED BEHIND the Rockton Baptist Church an hour after services had ended. All anyone could talk about that morning was Agnes Longley, the horror of it all. Harry didn't know about Agnes, and if he had, he would not have cared.

When he was a boy, the Ripleys were real men, growing cotton, making money. Now the Ripley name was only a dusty memory, and Harry's two sons were nothing a man would want to bear his name.

The times were right for a Ripley to do something heroic. The land was going idle, farmers nearly gone in Rockton County, and everything was changing into filth, waste. A man could live his entire life without knowing if he was a coward. Henry, Harry was sure, was a coward. Leslie was like something you collect and pin to Sheetrock, a set of wings to take out twice a year and look at, marvel over. It had not been Leslie's fault that he had been damaged, but Harry knew whose fault it had been.

Harry sat in his car looking at the church. A block away Dr. Owen Smith's house squatted behind a hundred yards of still-green lawn, its automatic sprinklers coming on each evening when it was obvious the rains again would not come. Harry closed his eyes and remembered how it had been.

Harry had been working late at the garage when she had called and said it was time to go. When Harry got home, she was groaning and pale, face covered with a fine layer of sweat, but she had managed to smile. This would be Harry's daughter, she just knew it. They had talked about it for weeks. Harry's father was still alive, and he said it would be a girl. They all said it would be.

They had gathered up Henry, taken him to his grandmother's house, and then Harry had taken his fainting wife to Smith Hospital, built in the early fifties two miles from town. Harry could remember what had happened now, how Owen Smith could not be found for nearly three hours. Harry had been paralyzed with fear and would not say anything.

An hour later, Owen Smith had thrust his thin head out of the door and asked Harry to come inside. Owen was nearly as tiny as a midget, five feet four and thin, very ugly. But he was Rockton's only doctor, had been since the forties.

"Sit down, Harry," Owen had said, taking Harry into his office. Harry had not been able to breathe, and he had held his old brown felt hat in his lap, wrenching it into some new shape.

"What is it?" Harry had asked flatly. Owen had lit a

cigarette and leaned back in his chair. "What is it? Tell me what it is."

"A tragedy has happened," sighed Owen. He had looked uninterestedly at the ceiling.

"A tragedy," said Harry.

"There was nothing that could be done," said Owen. "Nothing at all. The baby had the cord wrapped around its neck, and while I was trying to unwrap it, Mary's blood pressure suddenly shot up. I couldn't do a thing. You want a cigarette?"

"What are you saying?" asked Harry. He had felt as if his brain had been frozen, and everything in the room had seemed horrible. On one corner of the desk there had been a human appendix in alcohol.

"Harry, Mary's gone," he said.

"Lord God in heaven," cried Harry. He had stared at his hands. They were rough, cracked open from work. Mary had been rubbing corn oil into them each evening. "The child?"

"It's going to live," said Owen Smith, "but I've got to warn you, there's a problem. It's damaged. I tried my best, but in the delivery, it got damaged. I can't tell you how sorry I am."

Harry had stood and crushed his hat to his chest, tears filling his eyes. He had turned, not knowing where to go or what to do.

"What was it?" he asked, turning back.

"Another little boy," said Owen.

Harry sat in his car now, holding the Magic Marker and carefully drawing a mustache across his upper lip. Another little boy, he thought. He looked at his face in the mirror and chuckled. Then he lifted the gun and whirled the cylinder to make sure it was filled.

It was time for a Ripley to do something important. It was just after Harry had covered his chin with black Magic Marker that the first pain hit him squarely in the middle of the chest.

+ + +

Ada had been sleeping earlier that morning, dreaming about Van Gogh and how it would feel to pose naked for him. She would do nearly anything for a man who understood her artistic feelings. Except the dream had changed, and Van Gogh's head had turned into a dog's, a snarling bloody-fanged dog that started chasing Ada, and she had fled the house and run naked through town. And people were laughing at her. She felt her folds of flesh flopping as she ran, but the dog was gaining, and then it had her by the arm, shaking her.

She awoke and found that Junior had her arm, trying to shake her awake. She pulled her arm back and sat up.

"Get away from me!" she said angrily. He stepped back, wanting to hit her but knowing it would do no good.

"I'm sorry," he said bitterly. "I just thought you might want to know somebody shot Miss Agnes Longley to death last night." Ada felt as if someone had squeezed the breath out of her.

"My God," she said, clearing the dreams and sleep from her eyes. "Do they know who . . ."

"Nothing, I understand," said Junior.

"My God," said Ada. And then she began to cry uncontrollably, and Junior tried to sit by her and put his fat arm around her, but she pushed him away, knowing immediately what she must do: paint "The Death of Miss Agnes Longley." She stopped crying. She remembered about her dog, but she would not give Junior the pleasure of seeing her fear. She would do even more. She would caress her fear, pull it into her skin.

"Baby, oh baby," said Junior. He tried to remember how pretty she had been twenty years before.

"Bring my dog to me," said Ada. Junior stared at her.

"It tried to eat me up this morning, baby," he said.

"Now," said Ada. "Do it." Junior shrugged and turned, promising to himself that he would get immersed in the Rockton Citizens' Committee and see as little of Ada as possible.

"One day, you're going to see what you've done to this family," Junior said.

"God damn your soul to hell," said Ada Crawford.

She had never before wished another person pain, but her loveless life had broken something inside. It had been running for years, but then it had exploded in a shower of gears and springs. Now Agnes Longley was dead, just like that precious Missy O'Dair was dead, beaten to death by her husband. Junior Crawford was a hopeless fool. And then there was Truly.

Once, Truly had been such a lovely little girl, but when she was in the tenth grade, something had happened to her. Her breasts had begun to grow, and she had become tough and inflexible, saccharine. When she was a junior, she had come to Ada one night in the studio. Truly had been smiling, showing her straight white teeth when she had told Ada she thought she was pregnant, but she had no idea who the father was. Ada had sat down and cried while Truly comforted her, cried for innocence and wedding linens, for all dreams broken. Then at breakfast the next morning, Truly had announced that she had started her period after all, and Ada had wept and immediately taken her to a gynecologist and put her on birth control pills. Junior never knew, but after that, Truly had sex at least twice a week and began to drink. She could not get enough of anything.

Ada put on her robe and stood shivering in a corner. She turned the fan off. The sun made the entire room hot to the touch, and she waited until she heard Junior struggling back toward the bedroom with Butch. Ada blinked and clenched her teeth as Junior came into the room trying to hold Butch, but the dog pulled its leash away and in one leap jumped into the middle of their bed and began growling and playfully tearing at the sheets.

"Get off the damn bed!" yelled Junior. He grabbed the dog's leash and dragged it off, and it limped over toward Ada. "He's got a limp foot."

"A limp foot," said Ada. She felt beyond fear, on the verge of collapse. "Get out of here."

"But sweetness, I —"

"Get the hell out of here!" she screamed.

"I might just do that permanently," said Junior. "This whole damn house has gone absolutely crazy. I think you need to get some new pills."

"I don't care what you do," said Ada. "Just get out." Junior laughed harshly and dropped the leash and walked out of the room, out the front door, and into the yard where he could breathe. Ada and Butch were only two feet apart. Butch was idly wagging his tail, holding up his injured foot, and she huddled in the corner, trembling.

She knelt slowly, slowly, and reached out, and Butch sniffed her hand and then abruptly bolted back out into the hall. Ada followed him and found him in a patch of sunlight that was oozing down the hall. She made a cricket noise with her teeth and walked down the hall to her studio, and Butch followed her. They both went inside, and she closed the door and locked it. The dog ran wildly about the room, headlong into her easel, on which a still life was propped. The painting fell off flat on the floor. Ada stood in front of the full-length mirror and pulled the sash on her robe. Butch was running into things, knocking them over. Tubes of paint fell from her worktable, and Ada looked up in time to see Butch step on a new tube of black, saw the paint squirt out in a thick stream.

She turned back to the mirror and let the robe shrug from her shoulders, and she was naked. She felt very old, and her body was lumpy, all wrong, loveless. She wanted to be as beautiful as a painting by Degas, wanted her lover to see her at her toilet, so beautiful she would make his jaws ache. Then she let her eyes wander again and saw the dog, standing at her heel in the mirror, breathing heavily. She could feel its breath on the back of her legs.

After lunch, Nova Jernigan had gone out to the visitor's house, where she was trying to think. She didn't know what to do, except that she wanted to talk to Truly. That was too much. Her father was evil, but she could not do anything about that.

Ailene had told her life was like that for black women. She had said that it was like having a razor at your throat all the time, and half the time you hoped it would leave you alone and half the time you hoped it would spill every drop of blood God gave you.

She was thinking of things that came in threes when Truly's car came roaring into the backyard. Nova did not wait to think. She came running out of the visitor's house and went straight to the car. Truly had on very dark sunglasses, and she looked at Nova without a hint of expression on her face.

But she felt something. She felt as if Nova were a sheet of sandpaper that was trying to rub her bones bloody and raw, unlovely, dull as the Southern summer. Truly got out of the car and Nova stood close, her eyes and face twisted deeply back into her face.

Nova had heard on the radio about Agnes Longley. It sounded like more work of the Devil. In fact, she was sure the Devil was living in Rockton, that he had spread his dark wings over the entire town. Nova looked at Truly and saw her own face reflected in the glasses.

"Miss Truly, that dog up there with you mama," said Nova.

"How about stopping the nigger imitation," said Truly.

"What's that?"

"Jesus, Nova," said Truly. "You're not that stupid. Just stop acting like a shuffling, head-scratching nigger. I can't bear it." Nova tried to smile, put her hands on the backs of her hips.

"Okay," Nova said. "But that dog be up there with you mama. I'm afraid one gone kill the other, and you daddy, he . . ." Nova remembered what Junior had done and her mouth went dry.

"What did he do?" asked Truly.

"He said he gone shoot Miss Ada dog," said Nova. "He about gone crazy."

"It's the whole town," said Truly.

"You hear Miss Longley got murder?" asked Nova. "Devil done rose up and took this town by the throat."

"They know who did it yet?" asked Truly.

"I ain't hear nothing," said Nova. "It's hot out here, Truly. Let's us go inside in the visitor's house and get us some ice water."

"Is that what you really want?" Truly did not smile, had no expression on her face at all.

"No," whispered Nova.

"I'm going to see my mother," said Truly, and she turned and did not look back, feeling her power over Nova growing like a magnet. She could do anything she wanted with Nova, humiliate her, raise her up to ecstasy, anytime she wished. Truly walked into the house, through the kitchen, into the dining room, and then upstairs into the hall. The doors were open, and a breeze was trying to crawl its length. On one side was Ada's study, and when Truly got to it, the door was closed. Truly did not knock. Instead, she walked straight into the room, where Ada was sitting on the old rattan sofa with a beret tilted on her hair. Butch was sitting on the window seat looking out over the broad west lawn. When he saw Truly he stared at her, tail thumping a couple of times, then he calmed down and looked out the window again.

"I'm leaving your father," Ada said before Truly could say anything. Truly sat down next to her mother.

"Where in the hell did you get that hat?" she asked.

"He is a fool, and I am going to leave him," said Ada. "Or I will force him to leave. I will not live with him another week."

"Of course he's a fool," said Truly. She had not taken off her sunglasses. Ada stared straight ahead and shook her head as she talked.

"He does not have any fine feelings, Truly," said Ada. "I

did not know what fine feelings were when I married your father. I knew only what it was like to be afraid. I felt afraid of nearly everything, of being left behind, of not being loved, of being childless. He was so full of himself, with an opinion on everything, and I didn't have opinions about anything.

"I didn't know about the French Impressionists then, Truly. I didn't know how Vincent van Gogh had suffered for his art, how all of us who are artists must suffer for our art. We must keep an eye on it with all the passion of eternity. Did you know that is what art is, having an eye on eternity? I didn't read that, either. It just came into my head while I was painting last week. It was an illumination."

"You hear about Miss Longley?" asked Truly. Her upper lip was trembling visibly beneath the rim of her glasses, but Ada was not looking at her.

"Awful," said Ada. "Anyway, I have found that suffering tempers us, Truly. In that respect, I should be thankful for your father's incompetence. He has taught me that my life is designed for love, not for art." She turned and looked at Truly. It had been a long time since she had really seen her daughter, and she was sure she no longer knew her, perhaps had never known her. "Do you understand any of what I am saying?"

"About suffering?" asked Truly. She took off her sunglasses and looked at her mother. "Mother, you've suffered about as much as the Queen of England."

"I will not end up like Agnes," said Ada.

"Sure you will," said Truly. "You mean dead? Death is just tomorrow, that's all. Today is being alive, death is what happens to you tomorrow. If you aren't alive today, you might as well have died yesterday."

"I don't know what you mean," said Ada. "You are such a strange child."

"I *am* a strange child," said Truly, nodding and smiling. "And I'm the only hope you have, and it's no hope at all. You have to do it now, by yourself, without me. I'm lost already."

"Why do you say that, honey bear?" asked Ada. Truly could not remember the last time her mother had used the pet name from her girlhood. "You aren't lost. You have a good life. You've graduated college, have your whole life in front of you."

"I don't know what there is left to feel," said Truly. "I've felt all I could."

"Love," said Ada. "We have love left to feel, both of us. I have never loved your father."

"I know that," said Truly.

"So we both have love left to feel in what is left of our lives," said Ada. "You think you've loved, but that's just what you feel when you are a girl. Love is something else, something full and dark and then light, then dark again, then light again. I have died for love, honey bear. I did not even know I had lost it until I started to read about the lives of the artists."

"You found out about love in a book," said Truly.

"Yes," said Ada, "and for it, I am leaving your father. There is someone out there who would die for me."

Truly wanted a drink more than anything. She rose and drifted out of the room, hearing Ada call her name but not stopping. Love, thought Truly. Jesus. Ada was as big a fool as Junior.

+ + +

Harry Ripley thought he had suffered a heart attack, but he did not care. The pain had gone away after a minute or so. Maybe it wasn't a heart attack, he thought; maybe it was just a reminder, a sign or something. He could not be bent from his heroic deed. He got out of the car, his facial skin feeling taut from the marker beard and mustache, and walked to the shade of some pecan trees a hundred yards away. The gun was in his pocket. As he walked, he felt better and better, and he wondered if he would make it to Owen Smith's house before collapsing and feeling his soul jerked out of his body. He came across the grove of pecan trees, down behind houses in the next block under the steamy, eerie quietness of Sunday afternoon. His clothes hung on him limply, and his left arm felt heavy, as if it would detach and fall off.

Dr. Owen Smith's house was just ahead, and Harry, sweating in thick streams now, walked slowly around back and came up the broad rear steps of the house, opened the screen door, and came inside. He could hear voices. He stopped and listened, and there was Mrs. Smith, there was somebody he did not know, there was Owen. He knew his voice. It was like a nail file on the rim of a crystal goblet. Harry took the gun out of his pocket and thumbed the hammer back. He walked into the hall and took three soft steps down it and saw himself in an ornate mirror on the wall, saw his wild red-lidded stare, the blackened face, saw that sweat had made the marker run and that great black streams were going off his face all over his white shirt.

Harry held the gun out and walked into the dining room. Owen was there, still in his Sunday clothes, and his wife, Ellen, and at the end of the table a man Harry had never seen, but he looked enough like a weasel to be Owen's brother. When they saw Harry, they stopped eating and somebody cursed softly.

None of them recognized Harry. There was not much left of him to recognize. Owen Smith fleetingly thought he'd seen corpses that looked better, and in that same instant, he knew that he was going to die, and even after the apparition began speaking, Owen felt only death huddled around his face.

"I know I wasn't invited," said Harry. He grinned and licked his lips and his tongue came away black. "I just want to damage the doctor a little bit." Owen knew immediately. It had never left him, never gone from his heart, and after that night with Leslie he had stopped drinking. But this was not the agonized Harry Ripley he remembered. This was not a man at all, simply something dead that had not yet been buried. Owen stood slowly, and when Harry pulled the trigger, the slug knocked Owen back down into his chair. Ellen Smith screamed and the other man jumped up, shouting and cursing.

Owen Smith looked down at his chest. He was starting to have trouble breathing. The bullet had gone through his lung, and he knew the wound was fatal. He looked up at Harry and opened his mouth to call his name, but blood bubbled up and poured out and Owen felt tired, then he felt nothing at all, falling out of his chair and onto the floor, convulsing, then dying. Ellen screamed again, and Harry shot her in the head. The other man tried to run, but Harry shot him three times in the back, and he fell down on the opulent Oriental rug in the dining room, unmoving.

"I am a hero," said Harry out loud. "I killed all of them." Blood was everywhere. Harry walked calmly out of the house and back toward his car. Nobody was on the streets, nobody saw him. No one, not even in the nearest house, had heard the gunfire. Harry didn't care if they had. There was nothing anyone could do to him but kill him, and he was going to die soon anyway.

He got back into the car and then drove slowly toward home, whistling, thinking of the next name on his list, and the next.

Snake's shoulder was killing him. During the morning and early afternoon, it had only stung, but now it ached, so he drove to the garage with Leslie and found the pills he kept there, blues that Truly had stolen from her mother. Neither of them knew exactly what they were, but they made you feel like you were drifting. Snake took two and he turned on the air conditioner, leaving the lights off. If he turned the lights on, somebody would think he was open and would stop.

"It's dark," said Leslie. "What did you do to your shoulder?"

"I fell down and hurt it," said Snake.

"I'm sorry, Brother," said Leslie. They sat in the darkness and felt the cool air rush over them.

"I'm thinking about leaving," said Snake.

"Okay," said Leslie. "Can I go?"

"I don't know what to do," said Snake.

"Can you fly?" asked Leslie.

"I could," said Snake, "but they'd be able to follow me."

"I could fly," nodded Leslie. He smiled. It would be wonderful, he and Brother flying low over the pastures, the towns.

"I don't know what to do with you," said Snake. He didn't

really know what to say to him either, but he had to try. The pills started to work quickly, and he felt dreamy and scared.

"Do with me?" said Leslie. Snake had this dream that came back, that Leslie was normal and was talking and thinking like other boys, but he always woke up and found Leslie the same. "You can take me with you. We will fly away. We could come back in the spring. I will follow you. Just fly away."

"I'm in trouble, Leslie," said Snake.

"What?"

"It's too terrible to say. Something terrible has happened. It wasn't my fault. Christ Jesus."

"Christ Jesus," said Leslie. "I will take your trouble away, Brother."

"Nobody can take this away from me now," Snake said. The pills did make him float, but his shoulder still hurt, and when he touched it, rubbed it, blood soaked through the bandage and through his shirt. "Oh, God, I'm bleeding."

"It's blood," said Leslie, and he thought of the Bible story of the children of Israel putting blood over their doors so death would pass over them. It was one of his favorite stories.

"Go get me the gauze," said Snake. Leslie did not move, instead stood staring at Snake's shoulder, which was leaking blood heavily now. "Get me gauze, Leslie." Snake's voice was soft and sad. But Leslie wanted to do only one thing, so he walked toward Snake, rubbed his hand in the blood, and then smeared it over his own face. "Jesus Christ, Leslie!" Snake floated to Leslie and hit him hard with his good left hand, and Leslie fell to the floor. "Death will pass over this house now," said Leslie, looking up at his brother. Snake nearly wept and then found the gauze and took five or six pads and pressed them under his shirt where the blood ran. Soon, the bleeding stopped, but the pain didn't. Leslie lay on the floor, smiling. He no longer needed to fly away. This house was safe from death. "I'm going to do something wonderful for you and Daddy."

"What," asked Snake sourly, "save me from all this?"

"Something wonderful," said Leslie.

Snake felt as if he would be sick. He was staring at Leslie when he saw the old Bel Air roll up to the front door in a cloud of dust, and he knew it was his father. Snake wanted to kill him. Maybe, he thought, he was made only for killing things. Nothing had ever been alive in his family, in this garage, this county. It was all acting, all death, deaths. Harry got out, saw Snake's old Chevy, and then peeked in the door. Snake could see Harry's face shimmering in the heat, and it was like the Devil's, smeared black, thin white hair sticking up everywhere. Harry turned the door handle, but Snake had locked it.

"Dammit, Henry, open the door!" he shouted.

"Go to hell!" yelled Snake, but Leslie was up, still smiling, and before Snake could stop him, he had pulled the bolt back, and Harry was standing before them. Harry felt as if he were George Patton fresh from some resounding victory. He did not think what it was, did not picture the darkness and death, only felt a lingering glow, a brightness.

"Is that any way to talk to the last Ripley?" asked Harry.

"What is that all over your face?" asked Snake.

"Number one," cackled Harry.

"One," said Leslie.

"It's number one," laughed Harry. He walked to the cooler and took out a six-pack of Budweisers and opened one.

"I want to know what in the hell you're doing," said Snake. "What are you doing with that stuff all over your face and out driving around?"

"Number one!" shouted Harry. Leslie clapped briefly, until Snake shot him an exasperated look.

"What are you talking about?" Snake asked. He felt dizzy, and so he sat down. Harry could see that Snake was bleeding, that blood had soaked through a wad of gauze on his shoulder.

"Cut yourself shaving, son?" asked Harry.

"Screw you," said Snake.

"He fell down," said Leslie. "We're going to fly away."

"Fly away?" said Harry. He dropped the empty can and opened another. "What's the dummy talking about, John Henry, 'fly away'? What's that on his face?"

"This," said Snake, looking around. He felt like crying. "I cain't stand this anymore. It's nothing but hell. It's hell."

"You're not nowhere near hell yet," said Harry.

"Heaven," said Leslie. "This is not hell. It's heaven. I am with you."

"What's the dummy saying?" asked Harry. He felt wonderful. Harry cupped his hand to his ear as if to hear Leslie, joking.

"I am with you always," said Leslie.

8

MONK REUBENS GOT the call just after dark that Sunday night. He was sitting at the table, eating the chicken his wife, Mona, had fried late that afternoon as he had dozed and watched the Braves, worn out from working on the Longley murder. He was falling in and out of sleep when the phone rang, and he got up automatically and headed down the dark hall to answer it.

"Hello," said Monk in his deep, tired voice.

"Monk, you better get over here," a voice said. "All hell's broke loose." He recognized the voice instantly, his chief deputy, Greg Crowell.

"What?" It was all Monk could think to say.

"I'm over at Dr. Smith's house," said Greg breathlessly, "and somebody's done killed him and his wife and his brother visiting from New Orleans."

"My God, you're kidding," said Monk. "You're at the house?"

"There's blood and stuff all over the dining room," said Greg. "Miss Oxford, you know next door there, she come over to borry something, found 'em all in the dining room. It's enough to make you puke."

"I'll be over in a minute," said Monk. "You call Osborne at the state patrol barracks." Monk hung up and looked and saw Mona staring at him, holding her blue-checked apron at waist level.

"What is it?" she asked. "Did they find who killed her?" She wanted to believe they had found the killer; everyone did, because they were afraid. Now, Monk knew, they would be terrified.

"It's something horrible," said Monk. "That was Greg. He's over at Doc Smith's. Somebody's killed him and his wife and his brother visiting from New Orleans." Mona's hand came up to her mouth, and she groaned audibly.

"There's a maniac loose," she said. "God help us all."

By Monday morning, the people of Rockton had sunk into an agonized terror. The Rockton Pawnshop and Jimbo Paul's Ammo and Archery sold out of their guns—rifles, pistols, and shotguns—an hour after opening. The mayor made a proclamation. Television stations from New Orleans had reporters camping all over the town, and a writer from Los Angeles was bothering everyone, trying to obtain exclusive rights for the story. The first special edition of *The Rockton Sun* in thirty years was on the streets by midafternoon with two-inch-high letters: KILLER STALKS ROCKTON. The headline brought outrage from the city council, which was trying to keep everyone calm, but the edition sold out in an hour. Law enforcement officials were crawling all over Dr. Owen Smith's house, and the killing of Agnes Longley seemed almost secondary now.

Monk Reubens did not sleep at all Sunday night.

+ + +

Truly was holding a doll and thinking of children when she saw Nova standing in the doorway. She was dressed in a pretty yellow sundress and almost smiling. Her skin was black as the sharps on a piano. She stopped smiling when she saw Truly's face. Nova knew what it was: Junior Crawford was killing his daughter slowly. Hadn't her own father done it until Mr. Joe Westerman had shot him? Nova could not bear that Junior was hurting Truly.

"Is anybody up?" asked Truly. Her voice was full of dust, weak and harsh.

"It ten o'clock," said Nova. "Mist' Junior done gone to meet with the Citizen Committee or something. Miss Ada in the studio painting Miss Longley death with that poor cripple old dog." Nova tried to smile and then she shyly came over and sat next to Truly.

"Dr. Smith and Miss Smith and his brother were murdered yesterday," said Truly. She felt numb all over. "I heard it on the radio."

"Everybody done know about it," said Nova. "Lena done got out our pistol, and Ailene spend last night wailing."

"I went to bed early," said Truly. "Nobody told me about it. Do they know?"

"Yo mama and Mist' Junior?"

"Yeah."

"Everybody know. You looking mighty pretty this morning, Truly." Nova touched Truly's hair and Truly felt sick.

"Jesus," said Truly.

"You pretty," said Nova, stroking her hair. "It's all they is now." Truly looked at Nova and then turned away, staring out the window, feeling somehow more excited than ever in her life, yet hating Nova with all her strength.

Nova had been gone for nearly five minutes before Truly moved. She wanted to see Snake to ask him how he felt when he was killing all the others, how it felt to see hot blood all over the walls, dripping, burning into the floor.

Harry Ripley did not wait for the boys to get up Monday. He arose before even Leslie, dressed, picked out a nice army-issue .45 from Snake's gun room, and drove off toward Billy Homer's house. He could barely breathe, and he was sweating all the time, but he felt good. Billy lived outside Rockton in a run-down white house that had once been very nice. Billy had once cheated Harry out of seven hundred dollars in a poker game.

The sky was full of blossoming red clouds that morning just as Billy Homer was shaving and hearing about the killing of Dr. Smith. Billy farmed, grew soybeans, but he worked at it desultorily, not really caring if he made much money. He mostly lived and died by gambling. He loved to gamble, had never loved anything quite as much.

He finished shaving and went into the kitchen. He lived by himself. He put the blue kettle on the stove to boil for coffee and did not see the man with the Magic Marker goatee standing in the bushes at the edge of his yard, but he heard Lobo barking. Lobo barked at everything, strained at the chain. Billy thrust his clean chin out the back door and screamed at the dog to shut up, but it kept barking. It barked louder.

The gun was ready. Harry Ripley came around the corner and saw Billy standing there in his underwear, looking old and foolish. As soon as Billy saw the man, he knew it was the killer, but he could not move.

"Number two," said Harry, barely able to keep from laughing out loud.

"Who in the hell—?" began Billy, but he did not have the chance to finish. Harry shot him three times in the chest, and Billy fell backward through the doorway. Harry walked slowly up the steps and inside, stepping over Billy, who was lying there with his eyes open, blood pouring all over the broad pine floorboards. A kettle was starting to whistle on the stove and Harry took it off and poured himself a cup of Sanka and sat at the kitchen table and drank it. Harry felt the pain coming in his chest again, but he closed his eyes and the pain went away.

Now there was only one more on his list, and he could go ahead and kill himself. Harry had fallen in love with his own murder. It would not be suicide; he would murder himself. It would be blood for blood, violence that tears all things down. The only thing that bound us all to this earth, Harry thought, was violence. He stood over Billy's body for a long time and watched the sunburned field of soybeans wave in the dry wind.

+ + +

Ada stood before the easel and sketched, with charcoal, the inside of Agnes Longley's house. She drew the formal dining room, and there on the floor the slumped form of Agnes, dead. Ada felt dead, and she was determined to rise from her death.

Her life was like a child's machine that has broken but keeps running, chiming for years, hobbling around the shadows of some forgotten room. The only thing that Ada loved about her house anymore was the studio, the smell of fresh paint and gesso, the sharp light, the feel of the fan blowing warm air over her skin. She finished the sketch and thought of Georges Seurat, how he had been ignored, even derided, by his contemporaries. Like Georges, all she wanted was love. Is it so much for one person to want love? she wondered. In love, you forgive for that deep bond. But the bond with Junior had been flimsy for years, and now it had snapped like a balloon from its string.

She set the brush down. Butch was sleeping in the window seat, and Ada was now afraid of him, terrified, and her breath went out and she could not seem to get it back, no matter how hard she gasped. Her choking awoke the dog. He sat straight up and stared at her, head turning back and forth, trying to understand what it meant. Ada backed up toward the door. Her hands were shaking so badly she could barely open it, and when she did, Butch ran past her and down the stairs, straight out the front door, which was standing open. Ada sat on the floor and cried.

She was still crying when she heard Junior's heavy footsteps as he came slowly up the stairs toward her.

"What's wrong, precious?" he said.

"Get away from me," Ada shouted.

"Your dog done run off," Junior said, "run right by me."

"Don't you touch me," she said.

"You look sick, precious," said Junior. "I was just downtown. The Citizens' Committee is starting a group to go look for this bastard's killing folks in Rockton. I just come home to get my pistol."

"Get it and get out," Ada said. Junior got to the top of the stairs, and he squatted beside Ada and looked at her. Maybe she was sick, he thought. Ada saw him leaning down toward her, red-faced and lathered with sweat. She slid past him and ran down the stairs, barely recognizing the word he kept calling as her own name.

+ + +

Snake bandaged his shoulder that Monday morning and opened Ripley Garage at the normal time, Leslie trailing distractedly, bubbling about the resurrection and the life. Snake's shoulder throbbed, and he did not want to open the garage, but he could not close the damned place without attracting attention.

Already, Snake knew the heat would be terrible that day. The cattle in nearby fields hung their heads in disbelief. The plants looked dazed, stunned, and the edges of the tar-and-gravel road had begun to ooze like maple syrup before eight-thirty. A wind blew for a few minutes, but it only whirled the dust out front of the garage and sprayed a fine grit against the broad front window. Harry had hired a traveling painter to put RIPLEY GARAGE on the window, but the man had been a fool and had painted it on the outside. Now the words were nearly gone except for a faint outline. Snake had turned on the clattering air conditioner first thing, but it could huff only barely cool air across the store. Snake ate a Dolly Madison apple pie and drank a Pepsi while Leslie went in the back to look at his comic books and read the Bible.

Snake had not turned on the radio or television that morning because he did not want to hear about Agnes Longley. Living with Leslie and Harry, running this dying garage—both were terrible, but what had happened in Rockton touched the holy center of terror. For Snake Ripley, fear had replaced anger for the first time in years. He sat and stared into the store. He could hear Leslie flipping pages and humming. When Leslie began to sing "How Great Thou Art" in his high tenor, that squeaky choirboy voice, Snake slammed his hand down on the counter, grabbed another Dolly Madison apple pie, and squeezed it until the filling oozed between his fingers.

Hal Owens was getting out of his Snap-On Tools truck before Snake knew that he had even come. When he came in, Snake could see that his shirt was soaked with sweat and the blue fabric was dark under his arms and from his neck to his trousers.

"You got you gun here?" asked Hal. Snake stared at Hal, thinking how stupid he looked. Leslie was still singing. "What's that, the Moron Tabernacle Choir?" Surprised by his own joke, Hal started laughing soundlessly, his stomach shaking. Sweat poured down his face.

"Gun?" asked Snake.

"Don't tell me you ain't heard about the maniac's running around," Hal said. "Well, the entire damn world's right here. They's crews from CBS, NBC, ABC, and everything you ever heard of. Wilson Holt said he seen a guy in a beanie says he from *Jewish World News* up at Sara Nelson's restaurant. People gone start shooting each before long."

"A maniac's running around?" said Snake. I'm starting to sound like Leslie, Snake thought, and as he often did when Snake thought of him, Leslie came wandering out, no longer singing.

"Damn, you people down here really are in the boonies," said Hal. "What we got's murders coming out our ass in the fair city of Rockton. First there's poor old Agnes Longley, then Dr. Smith and his wife and his brother, who was up visiting from New Orleans. Then up at Horton's I heard the cops were all over Billy Homer's house, said he'd got shot, too. Ain't a kid on the streets in Rockton. They closed the pool and all. Heard on WYYY a list of closings long as your ass. They're having prayer services all over town tonight. Must be fifty million cops in town. Great for business. You want some socket wrenches or something?"

"God-almighty-damn," croaked Snake. What could have happened? Did he leave a fingerprint in Agnes Longley's house? What was Truly Crawford doing now? Everything seemed harsh and distant to Snake. "They got any idea who did it?"

"Like I said, it's a maniac," said Hal. "I'm ready for the sumbitch, though." He reached behind his back and pulled from his belt a .38 Police Special and held it up and looked at it admiringly. "If I see him I'll tell him to lean over, put his head between his legs, and kiss his ass good-bye. If I was you, I'd have machine guns guarding this place, it's so far out in the sticks. Sure you don't want some more stuff? Jesus, what's that on your hand?"

Snake looked down and saw that his palm was still smeared with the filling from the fried pie, and he took an old rag from beneath the counter and wiped it off.

"Nothing," said Snake. "So they don't know who did it?"

"Not yet," shrugged Hal. "We know it wasn't Bubba O'Dair. They've eliminated him since he's been in jail after killing Missy with that statue. Might be anybody else. They're trying to find out what all the victims had in common. They come after my Vicky, they'll be sorry. She's sitting in the parlor holding a .357 Magnum. Snake, your air conditioner doesn't work worth a shit."

"Explode it," cried Leslie. Hal stared at him.

"Hush up, Leslie," said Snake. He tried to think of how to act, how to act as normally as possible, but nothing seemed normal anymore. Snake Ripley smiled and forced out a dry laugh. "Jesus, sounds like the whole damn town's nuts. Yeah, I got to get me a new air conditioner. I'll keep my eyes open."

"Explode it," said Leslie. "I love the smell."

"I see the fool's killing people. I'll explode it, Leslie," Hal said. "Y'all take care. I gotta go."

"Hot as a bastard out there," Snake said.

"They said it's going up to a hundred and five today," said Hal as he swung back out the door. "That'll be a record."

Hal's truck scratched off, leaving small tornadoes of dust that drifted around the gas pumps and then disappeared. Snake was touching his shoulder and feeling his mouth as dry as the world around him when he remembered what Dr. Owen Smith had done many years before.

Junior Crawford and the Rockton Citizens' Committee met during lunch at the Little League field to discuss the terror that had spread through the town. Many wore sidearms, including Junior, who looked pink, huge and sweating. As he often did, Junior assumed that he was a leader.

Most of the other men were poor farmers or were employed at the lumber mill or the furniture factory. Nearly one third worked at Rockton Mills, a textile company that still pretended cotton was Rockton's number-one industry. More looked tubercular than prosperous, and few had education past the ninth grade.

Junior stood in front of the concession stand under a sign that said THE YOUTH OF TODAY ARE THE MEN OF TOMORROW. He wore gray slacks and a sweat-soaked blue shirt. Folds of flesh hung over the collar. The men sat in the stands, looking haggard, most of them on their lunch break. They looked suspiciously at Junior because almost nobody in Rockton liked him, and he was new to the Citizens' Committee. But they recognized what he could mean, his wealth and influence.

"Now men, we are facing one hell of a menace here," said Junior. He began to stride back and forth, arms tucked behind his back. Several of the men grinned the way you grin at the silliest boy in class at school. "I've talked to Monk Reubens this morning myself, though. I guess by now you all done heard about Billy Homer. There's five people shot dead in this town, five murders in the past few days."

"You ain't counting Missy O'Dair," said Ike Whisnant, a tall, thin man who hated blacks worse than death.

"Yeah, but we know Bubba beat her to death with that statue," said Junior. A few nodded and mumbled, yeah, that was just old Bubba beat her to death. "This is a maniac on the loose. This is like the beginning of the end of the world. You boys ever read Revelation?" Junior was beginning to get wound up, and they sat forward on their seats, suddenly interested. "When you start having people getting killed for no reason, when you start having niggers thinking they can have everything we have without earning it, when the world quits making sense and everything comes unmoored, flying ever' whichaway, then it's a sign that we may be facing the end of the world."

"God done said he'd never end the world with a flood no more," said Reverend Harris Calhoun.

"Don't be an asshole!" Junior thundered. "The world we built with our hands is starting to crumble around us."

"You think niggers done this?" asked Ike.

"I don't know why not," said Junior. "Anyway, Monk said we could help look for this maniac nights if we want to be under his supervision and there's no guns. I said I'd bring it up."

"What we supposed to do if we find him without no guns?" asked another man. "Ask him polite to cut out shooting folks?" Bitter laughter swept through the crowd. Junior grinned. Sweat poured off his fat face, and he held up his thick arms to quiet the men.

"Well, I'm taking a gun," said Junior, "but I'm just gone hide it good, that's all. You all do what you want to. Y'all mostly day shift, let's meet at the jail at six-thirty this evening."

The meeting broke up as the men headed for something cold to drink, to get out of the brutal sun. Junior lazily walked to his Cadillac, climbed inside, and started it, turning on the air conditioner and lighting a cigar. This was what he was meant to do, to be a leader, and even if his stupid wife could not see it, he was going to follow this course now. Maybe I'll run for Senate, Junior thought. Hell, I could do twice the job those other jerks do, and I'd devote full time to the job. But hell, they'd probably hold the dishonorable discharge against me. Pricks.

He drove home. Truly's car was still parked behind the house, and Junior felt something like pleasure that his daughter was home for lunch. He came into the kitchen, where

Nova Jernigan was standing over the stove stirring a lazily steaming pot of field peas. A white handkerchief was tied around her head and sweat streamed down her cheeks. When she saw Junior she stared down into the peas as if seeking some answer.

"Well, you can rest easy, Nova," Junior thundered. "The Citizens' Committee is going to catch this madman's terrorizing the town. I just came from a meeting."

"I thought y'all just cotched black folk," Nova said. She did not look at Junior. She took a sizzling ham from the oven and set it on a counter to cool.

"Are you being smart with me, Nova?" Junior asked.

"Nossir, I ain't," said Nova. "I didn't know y'all was in the crazy-people business. I see now you is."

"That mouth's gonna get you in trouble," said Junior darkly. "I'd think you'd be grateful for us saving you from this madman's running loose in town." Nova turned and looked at Junior, and he felt a chill of terror fill every pore.

"Miss Ada dog bit the mailman," said Nova with a cool gaze. "He say he gone sue you. That dog, he still be running all over the place."

"Dammit," said Junior. "This is the time she's got to have a fucking dog. That's her business. I'm tired of covering up for her. She'll just have to get her rear out of this one by herself. Maybe she knows a good lawyer."

"Maybe she do," said Nova. "Anyway, he back in the house now."

"She's got a lawyer in the house?" Junior shouted.

"Miss Ada dog back in the house," Nova said. "He come in and rip that red sofa you granddaddy brought back from Europe to pieces."

"Son of a bitch!" Junior exploded. His grandfather had seen the sofa at a store in Vienna, a thick, heavy piece on which Junior would often lie and sleep after supper. It was worth several thousand dollars. Junior ran through the dining room and into the parlor, where Butch was sitting on what was left of the sofa, looking delighted and relaxed. Bits of stuffing and red fabric were scattered all over the room. Butch jumped off the sofa when he saw Junior and came limping over to him, tail wagging. "You stupid jerk!" Junior kicked the dog hard, but it dodged most of the blow and backed up, briefly showing its teeth before loping into the kitchen. Junior surveyed the mess, feeling an explosive rage beginning to choke him. What had he done to deserve a household like this? His own mother had known her place, by God, had kept the house perfectly spotless and had obeyed his father, just like the wedding vows said. Junior walked with icy anger back into the kitchen to tell Nova to clean up the damn mess in the parlor.

When he came into the room, he saw her squatting by the stove talking quietly to Butch, muttering something that sounded like an incantation. Voodoo, thought Junior. That's what these people can do: talk to animals and make them do things, take dolls and thrust pins through their bodies to kill their enemies. Junior no longer believed in God, but he believed in the power of terror. In that nighttime kingdom, any wild horror of dreams could happen. Junior nearly jumped onto the counter when Truly appeared behind him.

"Sweetness, you scared the life out of me," Junior said. Truly had been sitting in her room most of the morning.

"I'm starving," she said. "Anybody else get blown away yet?"

"That's not very nice, sweetness," Junior said, grinning.

"Anyway, the Rockton Citizens' Committee is going out to-night, and we're going to find this maniac and make this town safe again."

"Oh wow, I'll never feel afraid again," giggled Truly. "Nova, that dog just ripped Great-Granddaddy's sofa to smith-ereens. You two make a cute couple."

"That not very nice," said Nova, standing and letting Butch outside. "But you don't hardly never say nothing very nice."

"You apologize this minute," said Junior angrily.

"I sorry," said Nova. "Lunch ready. Truly, you go tell you mama lunch ready. I clean up that mess when I through with lunch and all."

"Don't you ever talk to my daughter like that again, or you'll be making money lying on your back," warned Junior.

"How can you make money lying on your back?" asked Truly.

"Now, sweetness," said Junior Crawford.

Ada Crawford came downstairs for lunch dressed in her artist's smock, and when she saw the sofa she smiled briefly and then went into the dining room, where Nova had set the places. The richly decorated blue plates were loaded with fresh peas, buttered corn on the cob, and sliced ham. Beside each plate was a small bowl of chopped onions. Nova brought in tall glasses of sweet tea as they sat. Junior liked the tea so sweet that it curled your lips. That was the way his mother had made tea, the only way it should be drunk, Junior thought.

"Let's have grace," said Junior. Ada stared at him with disbelief, at his huge sagging pink jowls, at his sweat-stained shirt, at his hands. His fingers were so fat they were splayed, like the toes of a large dog. Nova leaned against the door frame and bowed, and Truly folded her hands like a little girl and put them under her chin. "Dear Lord, we thank you for the Rockton Citizens' Committee, which is going to catch this crazy man, and we thank you for letting us take time from our main goal, which is dealing with niggers. We thank you for this home, and for everything we have except that damn dog, which I'm going to shoot if I see him again."

"And we thank you for our health," said Truly earnestly. "As long as we have our health, nothing else really matters."

"Amen," said Junior Crawford.

Monk Reubens walked around the overgrown backyard of Agnes Longley's house, hoping that something would seem out of place. That's how you looked for clues, Monk had learned years before: find something that does not fit and worry it to death. He was a quiet man who was only forty-two but had been police chief in Rockton for years, and now, dripping sweat, he stood and looked around the yard that had already been combed by all kinds of lawmen.

A cast had been made of a sneaker footprint. It had been sent to the state crime lab, but so far, no fingerprints had been discovered at any of the three murder sites. Monk was afraid somebody would accidentally kill the delivery boy from the drugstore next, or something worse. Everybody in town was waving a gun and posturing with bravado.

Monk wondered if it would ever rain again. The heat was making people crazy, making everything seem as if it shimmered, dreamlike. The crops were drying up and soon would be dead. Monk knew that all this was borne down upon his shoulders. He cleared his head and tried to imagine how it had been for Agnes, the killer coming in, her surprising him, and then shot, having perhaps a second or two of the awful knowledge of death. Monk had been in Vietnam and knew death, but this was different, somehow more obscene. In war, dying is part of your profession, but here it was obscene and awkward, even natural deaths, because the country means *life endures.* You never said someone dead had a long, full life unless he was over ninety. And now Rockton was almost boiling in the blood of obscenity.

The one footprint had been found in soft soil just off the back porch. Monk sat on the steps and looked at it, where it pointed. Agnes Longley's backyard was lushly overgrown, a mutant. The forsythia bushes, long out of bloom, fell over from their crowns into leafy piles. A trellis that had once gloried in roses had rotted, and the faint red blossoms were now hiding among sharp shoots of Johnson grass. A mimosa tree clung to its sticky pink blossoms. The air was filled with heat and the hothouse aroma of plants overripe, overgrown. Monk looked again at what was left of the footprint. It pointed behind the houses next door. Pretend it is a straight line and follow it. Who had told him that?

Monk stood, dripping, and started walking as if the footprint were a guide. The sun was fire. Monk wore large black service boots, and they squeaked with perspiration. He walked behind two houses, eyes up and then down, up, then down, looking for anything. The state patrol investigators had looked over the area, but often, Monk had found, the best stories start with the smallest fact. Everyone knew Monk's father, Red Erwin, an uneducated man, who was the best storyteller Rockton ever had. Often he would sit with Monk and tell stories that started with some minor incident that would keep enlarging until the whole world seemed to be involved. When he was dying, Red had told Monk that life was like the ripples when a stone is thrown into a lake, always going out, always coming back.

Monk thought of his father. His death had seemed obscene, too. The cancer had been found too late. Monk could imagine it blossoming and growing. His father had died near Christmas, but cancer always made Monk think of summer, the growing season. His mind drifted, and when he hit the paved road that led into the Rockton City Cemetery, Monk was surprised. His mother and father lay here, just up where the road curved. On the right side of the road was the old cemetery, where scions of the town were buried. On the left, in a field that looked like a pasture until you got closer and saw the graves, only flat bronze markers were allowed. Monk hated the small rectangles of names and dates.

Monk walked onto the liquefying tar-and-gravel road and let his eyes wander lovingly over the granite and marble shafts. A mound of flowers was thrust up near the center of the old cemetery. Agnes Longley had just been buried there. At the far end of the new part, a backhoe glistened in the sun as it idly dug several more new graves. It made sense to Monk that this was where death had begun its crawl toward Agnes Longley. He was standing quietly looking toward the north.

"I sure hope you catch them," a voice said, startling Monk. He turned and saw Cromer Carson, an elderly man who had retired from the sawmill business a few years before. Cromer walked all over town.

"Lord, Cromer," said Monk, "you scared the life out of me."

"Thought you heard me coming," he said. They were both silent for a time. "I got me some property here." He nodded toward the new part of the cemetery. "I reckon I know more about this cemetery than any man alive. Walk out here at least once a day and memorize the stones. Getting too many to keep up with. One day you can walk out here and memorize me."

"You'll probably be walking around here long after I'm gone," Monk said.

"Not likely," Cromer laughed. "But dying's lost its natural order here. Nothing worse than people going before their time. Course, I don't really know what someone's time is. I guess when God's angels stretch out their wings and ask you to fly away, it's time."

"I guess, Cromer," said Monk.

"You find that man," said Cromer, who turned and was suddenly gone, humming a hymn whose name Monk could not remember. Monk walked up the road into the old part of the cemetery. The caretaker was cutting grass a hundred yards away, and the drone sounded like some huge, lazy insect. Monk knelt and looked into the grass. The harsh light reflected off something.

He reached down and picked up an inch-square piece of porcelain with a dull pink surface. When he turned it over, he saw, like a growing rose, a single, perfect bloody fingerprint.

9

SNAKE RIPLEY STOOD before the mirror and slid into his boxing shorts, watching the muscles in his shoulders flex around the clean white bandage. The light in his room oozed from a single suspended sixty-watt bulb, and even though it was nearly eight-thirty, the heat clung to Snake as if he were in a huge oven he could not escape. He turned to his bureau and took the bag gloves under his arm. The gloves were cherry red.

Harry sat in his recliner watching *Wheel of Fortune* and drinking bourbon. He sat in his boxer shorts. He had slept much of the day on the couch after washing the Magic Marker beard from his face, scrubbing, scrubbing until his stubbled face was dark and raw. Harry sipped the bourbon and felt the fire in his throat and stomach. He liked the way it made him sick for a moment and then turned to something else, a sunset or an embrace.

"How in the hell can you be hitting the bag in this weather?" grinned Harry.

"Shut up," said Snake. "You're dead."

"No I ain't," said Harry. "You are."

"Shit," said Snake. He walked past his father and into the kitchen. Dirty dishes were stacked everywhere, and a frying pan on the stove was filled with a crust of rancid oil. Snake stood in the silent kitchen and looked around. He could hear Pat Sajak from the other room telling a contestant he could make another spin. Snake could tear this room into the shreds of what was left of the Ripley name, throw dishes against the walls and windows and watch things break. In five minutes of uncontrolled mayhem he could destroy a room. Once, when he was a senior in high school, he had come home to find Harry beating Leslie almost senseless. Snake had taken a gun and chased Harry away, tended to Leslie, and then ripped the living room to pieces with his hunting knife.

Save it, Snake thought. That was Harry's advice when Snake had been in Golden Gloves: save it, keep the anger inside of you, and try to hurt the guy you are fighting. Harry had learned it on troop ships when often he did not think he could stand the sea anymore. Harry Ripley was terrified of drowning because he could barely swim, something he hid from his fellow soldiers, and being on the ocean was like being in the gaping maw of a beast of prey. Snake saved it and came out into the backyard.

Though darkness was trying to settle along the pastures, a thin line of light and heat clung to the horizon, and the air was full of gnats and lightning bugs. Snake had read that some cattle in the tropical latitudes were driven mad by gnats and would race bucking across the plains until they fell dead. Snake felt like running until his heart exploded. He did not know what to do anymore, and so he would come work out.

Leslie was standing on top of the rusting hulk of Snake's old '62 Bel Air. It had been Snake's first car, and when he burned the engine up, he'd had it hauled to the backyard and parked beneath the arching arms of an old chinaberry tree. The tree had been there forever. When he and Leslie had been boys and the world still seemed clean, they had chased each other with handfuls of chinaberries, throwing them and laughing. Now the tree seemed like an arthritic old tyrant, crooked fingers reaching out. Leslie's head was lost in the lower limbs, and his arms were stretched out straight to his sides. A claw hammer dangled from his belt.

"Leslie, get off my car," said Snake softly. Leslie looked down at Snake and smiled. He squatted and jumped down beside his brother.

"Hi, Snake," said Leslie. "You going boxing tonight?"

"Don't climb on my car anymore," said Snake. He turned and walked toward the barn, and Leslie trailed happily after him. They came into the barn, and Snake pulled the chain on the bulb. The familiar smells of hay and dirt did not cheer Snake. What was death? What was it like? He could not shake the sight of that old woman lying on the floor, pouring out her blood along the planks of her kitchen. And what of those other deaths? Dr. Owen Smith? Snake knew, and found it too horrible to believe or even contemplate. Did Harry kill the others? If he had, it made the Ripley family the most hated men in the history of Rockton County.

Snake began to bounce on his feet, but the lightness was all gone. He felt heavy and weak, but he began to flick lefts, rights, and combinations as he leaned into the heavy bag. Leslie sat in the dust and watched Snake. Leslie loved his brother and exulted in the snap of his fists and the way his hard muscles worked as he boxed.

"Hit it, Brother!" said Leslie.

"You want me to hit it?" Snake panted. "You want me to hit it, Leslie?" Snake bore into the heavy bag and started thrashing it with a lifetime of frustration and anger, dust flying each time his shrouded fists slammed into the cotton case. Snake could usually work on the heavy bag for three or four minutes before sinking, exhausted, into the dust of the barn, but this time he would not stop. He cursed and groaned and grunted. He began to cry. He began to see a fine red mist hit the white bag each time he punched with his right hand. Leslie marveled at the blood that was streaming down Snake's shoulder, over his chest and then into his trunks and finally down his leg. Leslie thought of girls and Jesus Christ and felt wet and excited. Snake at first stroked the bag wildly, but then he settled into a rapid tattoo, even as a heartbeat, and went for nearly ten minutes before he sank to his knees, then fell down on his elbows, crying.

"Good hitting, Brother!" said Leslie, clapping his smooth hands. "This is your blood that you shed for me." Snake rocked back on his hips. His face was white, deathly, and his right side was coated with blood. His mouth hung open and he wheezed in as much oxygen as he could, but it was barely enough.

"Leslie . . . please stop this . . . religion . . . stuff . . . it's just not true," Snake panted. Leslie stopped smiling and stared at Snake, not understanding what he was saying but loving him anyway. They were still staring at each other when suddenly Truly Crawford's car was purring in front of the barn door. Snake jumped back, having just heard the engine, and he tried to get up, but his legs were like the statues of the apostles he and Leslie had made one summer in Bible School. They brought them home and Harry had put the clay in the oven and made the boys watch through the window as they began to melt, legs going soft. They had both cried and cried while Harry laughed himself sick.

Truly came flouncing into the barn, wearing a matching shorts outfit of lime green: tight shorts that clung to each curve and crevice and a shell top under which she obviously wore no bra. When she saw Snake, saw the sweat and blood and dirt that coated him, saw his mouth open, his shoulders and chest heaving, she felt weak with excitement and desire.

"Jesus wept," said Truly. "You're bleeding like a stuck pig."

"Jesus wept," said Leslie. He stood and walked to Truly and hugged her, and she let her arms come up to him, but hugging Leslie was like hugging an idea, and Truly did not take her eyes off Snake. "Jesus wept." Leslie kept repeating the phrase like a talisman to ward off the darkness as he wandered out of the barn and toward the field.

"He's clear off the diving board," Truly said.

"Leave my brother alone," said Snake. "Just leave him alone."

"Just conversation," said Truly sweetly. She squatted in front of Snake, knees wide apart. "Tell me something. What was it like to kill Dr. Smith and the others? Did they squeal?" Snake scrambled toward Truly and struggled to his feet, pulling her up by the front of her lime-green shell blouse.

"You stupid bitch," he hissed. "I didn't kill anybody but Longley, and that was self-defense. But I think I know who did this other stuff."

"You really did it, didn't you?" Truly asked. Snake held her close and the blood darkened her top. "Come on. Who would I tell? I hardly know a soul in Rockton anymore. Except our maid, Nova. Could I tell her? She probably wouldn't tell anybody."

"You are the most screwed-up person I ever met," Snake said.

"You never met my sweet daddy," said Truly. "You ought to come to my house. There's a crazed Doberman running amok. Who did it if you didn't?"

"I think it was my father," said Snake. Truly looked disappointed.

"How do you know?"

"He's been gone a couple of times, and Dr. Smith's the man who killed my mother," Snake said.

"Wow," said Truly, "this is kind of like the Manson family or something."

"You bitch," said Snake. He pushed her hard into the wall of the barn, and she fell among the drippings of blood and dust. "They're going to send me to the electric chair."

"They'll never find out it was you," said Truly, regaining her feet. "Why should they? Just forget about it. Come on."

"What?"

"Let's go for a ride," she said. "It's so hot I'm about to puke."

"I don't give a damn," said Snake.

"Come on," she said. She walked to the car and leaned on the front fender, legs apart. Snake hated her, loved what she possessed, knew that like everything else in her life, she possessed him just like Jesus possessed Leslie. "Let's go for a ride."

"I'll get blood on the upholstery," Snake said weakly.

"Great," said Truly. "I've already got it all over me. Don't you just love the sight of blood where it's not natural, honey? Let's go for a ride."

"What's happening to me?" Snake whispered as he walked around and got in. Truly never felt better than when she was driving her car fast. She lit a cigarette and popped the first of a six-pack of Miller Lite, handing another to Snake. She put the car in first and drove clean around the Ripley house, knocking down the rotted remains of a clothesline pole that had clung for twenty years to the side yard. For a moment, the crossbar hung on the windshield in their faces, but as Truly cut left and headed screeching up the road, it fell off onto the hot, wasted earth.

+ + +

Junior Crawford stood in the shadows of the argon streetlamps that surrounded the Rockton Jail. The building loomed over Junior and nearly fifty men of the Rockton Citizens' Committee who had come to hear Sheriff Monk Reubens tell where he wanted them to search. Junior had not told the complete truth about Monk wanting help from the committee. What Monk had actually said was "We'll see," but Junior figured that was good enough.

Junior stared up at the tower. The jail had been built in 1840, and for more than a century men and even a few women had been hanged in the tower. Half the schoolchildren in Rockton had written papers about Selby Catlett, a feed salesman who in 1856 had killed his wife, suspecting her of being unfaithful. Selby was an enormous man, and they had hanged him three times, the rope breaking under him at each drop of the trap. At each hanging, he became more enraged, and in despair the sheriff took him out back and shot him twice in the chest, but even that did not kill Selby, and the sheriff was so unnerved he could not shoot him again, so he got an inmate to beat Selby to death with a shovel. The screams of the man so horrified the town that no one else was executed in the tower or even in town until after the war, when killing no longer seemed so unusual. The story that Selby Catlett's screams could still be heard was one of Rockton's enduring myths. In 1957, a country singer from Slidell, Louisiana, wrote and recorded "The Ballad of Selby Catlett," but it didn't do anything.

Junior's stomach extended far out over the twisted waistband of his khakis, and in the strange orange light he looked huge and pink, his teeth too small, too close together. He still felt so full he was almost sick. Nova had cooked fried chicken for supper, and he and Ada had dined alone under the chandelier in the dining room while Nova lurked nearby in the kitchen.

"What did you do today?" Junior had asked, trying for no reason to make conversation. Appearances were important to Junior Crawford, and staying properly married was vital to a man of his stature. Love had nothing to do with marriage, Junior thought. Marriage is a business arrangement, Junior's father had told him, and nothing else.

"Nothing," Ada said, pushing her corn from one side of the plate to another.

"You still painting Miss Longley's death?" Junior asked. "I can't understand why you're wanting to paint something so sick. I can't understand imagining something and then painting it. Why in the hell would anybody want to do that? But I guess it's good for women to have their little hobbies. Keeps you out of trouble."

Ada had stared at him with supreme hostility. "Just shut your damn mouth," she said.

"What?" said Junior. A kernel of corn clung to the greasy circle of his mouth. "You can't talk like that to me in my own house."

"This is no house or a home," said Ada, rising, thinking of Van Gogh and how much he loved even the crudest woman he ever met. "It's an asylum and a pigsty, but it's no place for anybody to live."

"You're talking like a little fool," said Junior as Ada had headed upstairs to her studio. He shouted after her, "Even our damn little house nigger knows better than that." Nova had sat at the kitchen table, toying with the point of a broad butcher knife, dragging it along the wood, leaving a white scar. Hell, Junior thought, what he needed was some kind of heroic action, catching this creep who was killing people in Rockton. Then his marriage would be stable. "Nova, get in here."

Nova had walked slowly into the dining room after setting the butcher knife down where the scar stopped on the table.

"I gots to clean this off to give the scrap to Miss Ada dog," whispered Nova.

"Is that mutt around here?" Junior asked. "I'll get my gun."

"You hurt Miss Ada dog, I tell you tried to rape me," said Nova.

"You think anyone's going to believe a little nigger gal like you?" asked Junior.

"Don't matter," Nova said, getting Ada's plate. "Just say it will ruin you."

"You stupid little whore," said Junior, but he did not know what else he could do. He sat for a moment, steaming, and then got up and followed Nova into the kitchen, where he saw her squatting on the floor behind the table. Junior came around the table and saw Butch sitting by the stove, tail thumping the floor. The dog's tail hit the floor and stayed there. The animal's eyes seemed to glaze.

Junior was still thinking of the damn beast as he stood in the parking lot and waited for Monk Reubens to come out and talk to them. While he waited, Junior was irritated by the sounds around him: car keys tapping fenders as the men leaned back, stood, and leaned back; cars that rushed by with no rhythm; the screeching of crickets in the trees that came to the edge of the parking lot. A nearly full moon, a red moon the color of blood and water, was rising behind the jail tower. Junior was wondering just where Selby Catlett had been beaten to death, when he saw Ezra Carter walking toward him.

Ezra had been a high school classmate of Junior's, and he always walked like he was on stilts that were about to break and fall. He was about six-four, and when he wasn't smoking an unfiltered Camel, he was usually lighting one. Even in school, Ezra had stunk of cigarette smoke. His hair had now gone gray, but his face was the same. His temples were too close together, as if his head had been clapped between two heavy cymbals, and his face was too long.

"The hell's he gone come out and get us going?" asked Ezra. "I got the best damn high-beam light Black & Decker makes, and he's in there farting around while this guy's probably out shooting more people."

"He'll be out in a minute," Junior said without much confidence. Ezra shook a Camel from his crumpled pack and lit it, hands cupped over the flame just as he had done it in the navy many years before.

"Tell me the truth, you think a nigger done this?" asked Ezra.

"How would I know?" asked Junior, a little irritated. He turned away from Ezra and saw Monk Reubens standing up by the door of the jail as if he had appeared there as a spirit. Junior hitched his pants and set off walking toward him.

"I never told you to bring these men," Monk said. He was very tired, had not slept much for three days, and he wanted to get home to Mona and his supper.

"Not technically," said Junior, "but you didn't tell me not to."

"Come in here for a minute," said Monk. Junior followed him into the ground-floor office of the jail tower. Prisoners were kept in cells on the second and third floors, and often they would lean out the bars and talk to relatives standing in the parking lot. A couple of state patrolmen were huddled in a corner looking at a map. "Sit down." Junior sat in a chair next to Monk's cluttered desk.

"We're ready to kick ass," said Junior. Monk smiled, thinking, Jesus, what stupid fools these are.

"I want you all to go home," said Monk softly.

"But hell, we—"

"Just listen to me, Junior," Monk said. "Right now we'd be shooting in the dark. But we've found something. We may have a suspect within thirty-six hours. When we do, we might need some help. The best thing you men can do is look after your wives and children. Go on home and keep an eye on Ada and Truly, Junior."

"You might have a suspect?" said Junior. He did not like

this turn. The man might be arrested and charged before Junior could even get on the scene, a disaster for him.

"Might," said Monk. "Now please just go on home."

Junior told the men outside that Monk had important plans for them, that they should be prepared to move in the next thirty-six hours, but not tonight. Again Junior had lied, but that didn't matter to him. Hadn't his father always told him this: "Get what you need. It doesn't matter how, but that you do it"?

The night was still young, but Junior was heading back toward home, thinking of how he might trap and kill Butch and make it look like an accident.

Leslie Ripley ran in the dark fields, light as a blowing cloud, arms up. In the summer you could see only the brightest stars. He had completely forgotten about Jesus, was now thinking about Truly Crawford, how she had hugged him, and he had felt her breasts flatten along his chest. She was in love with him; he knew it and so he ran along the fields, laughing. Love!

The world was a strange, lovely place to Leslie. He did not mind the mysteries that angered his brother so much. Each part of it was wonderful: love, death, rain, smoke, mustard, even grief. Leslie was an emotional sponge, touching his feelings, never resenting any of them. He knew, now, that he was changing, that he was slowly losing his grip on the rapid conversations of men; he was perceptibly slowing down, and he felt as if any moment he would fly into the darkened sky. That was his destiny, to change from boy to bird, from human to God. And now, with Truly's love, he would take her also, and they would fly along the dark crest of the red moon.

"There is no death!" shouted Leslie happily. He ran through the waist-high grass, bubbling with laughter. "There is no death!" The idea had come to Leslie earlier that day, that Jesus had promised that no man who believed would die. He knew that Snake did not believe nor did their father. Leslie would believe for them so they would not have to die. He would believe for Truly. Then he realized he could believe for everyone on their road, everyone in Rockton County, then everyone in Mississippi. Even the world! he had thought. And when he had realized that he could save them all, Leslie felt like a bronze bell that rang across the countryside, clear and sharp. "There is no death!"

Leslie ran out of the field and into the edge of pine woods. No one knew the woods here better than Snake and Leslie. Since they had been boys, they had explored them, made paths and a series of lean-tos. At first, the woods were thin pines, then thicker, then the land, miles from their house, sloped into one of the most inaccessible swamps in north central Mississippi, nearly three hundred acres along a marshy creek. In the winter, Snake and Leslie had explored it all, left markings on trees, but this time of year, no one could penetrate more than a few hundred feet before becoming lost in an unbelievable tangle of vines and brambles. Leslie sat on the ground at the base of a large Virginia pine, breathing hard. He thought of the swamp. Only once had he and Snake gone there in summer. Harry had beaten them both, and they were going to run away and live in the swamp. Snake had just seen a movie at the Rockton Theater about a man living in a Louisiana swamp. They had gotten half a mile into it when they had seen, coming toward them in the water in an unending sinuous line, a water moccasin, and the horror of that image, of approaching death, drove them home. Harry had laughed at their story. He didn't care if they ran away; hell, they did it all the time. Besides, the only man who really knew all that land was Harry Ripley.

Leslie forgot about the swamp. He thought again about Truly Crawford. She had hugged him. If she loved him, what did love mean? He had loved a girl once, in the ninth grade, about the time he realized that he was being irrevocably left behind, that his mind was becoming worn out, that he could not think anymore. Her name was Angela, and she had been in school for only two weeks while her father worked at the Rockton Fair. She had liked Leslie, the soft eyes and distant look. Most boys were so aggressive. The others made fun of Leslie, but he did not mind, and in that Angela found something to care for. She had learned never to love anything, because you leave it so soon, but she could not help loving Leslie, and when they had parted both of them had cried. But this was more than Angela, Leslie thought. He tried to think. Nothing connected for Leslie.

Yes, he suddenly thought. Truly loves Snake because she knows that he, Leslie, will save the world. That's it! Leslie ran back out of the thin pines and into the moonlit field. His feet were barely touching the earth.

"There is no death!" he shouted. Anytime now, he thought, over this next rise, his arms would burst into wings.

10

ADA CRAWFORD'S KEY ring had a picture of Snoopy and Woodstock and was round and soft. She held it lightly as she ran down the back steps of her house toward the El Dorado Junior had bought her the year before. Butch was at her heels, limping along merrily.

"Good dog, good dog," she panted. She imagined the beast about to leap, about to come for her throat and rip it out, but Butch just ambled behind her until she got to the car, slid along the fabric seat, and shut the door. Butch jumped up and put his face to the window. "Jesus Christ." Ada started the car and turned the air conditioner on full as Butch fell back and swayed toward the steps. When night came in the summer, Ada would drive all over the county, sometimes out of it. She would look at the silent streets and roads as an artist, seeing the power of the country, the stark lines of barbed-wire fences. Now, she stared blankly at Snoopy and Woodstock, wondering if she would go to Rich Barksdale's house. She thought she heard the growl of an engine. Junior. She drove around the house and to the street, but it was only Mr. Ed Oswald, an arthritic old man who lived at the end of Wentworth.

Ada thought of Rich. She had met him the fall before when he taught a watercolor class at the Rockton Public Library. He was nearly fifty, tall and lean, with gray hair and a goatee that was too neat, tapered fingers, and square nails. He had moved to Rockton to paint a year before that, and few people knew much about him. He and Ada had become friends, much to Junior's disgust. Once Ada had Rich to supper, and Junior insulted him continually until Ada had screamed "Jesus Christ!" at the top of her lungs, and Junior had gone upstairs. Once, following a lesson, she had gone with Rich to his house. He lived on North Main Street in Victorian splendor, and his home was filled with precious ceramic dolls and elegant furniture, along with framed watercolors. She had never seen a house decorated with such taste, reflecting such good breeding. Rich moved through his icons like a king among his loving subjects, she thought. The coffee table held copies of *Architecture* magazine, and a silver bowl was filled with expensive Swiss chocolates. The day she visited, they had sat side by side on the couch, and she had been swept away with admiration for his work, which was largely of magnolia flowers. While they sat, he had laughed easily for a long time, and she had felt hot and weak. He had kissed her on the cheek when she left, and she could not forget, as she had driven home, how loveless her own marriage was.

Now, exulting in the gentle wash of cold air from the El Dorado's vents, she thought about Rich, about his long fingers, the way he held the brush and waved it on the thick artist's paper. She could drive over there. Would he be glad to see her? They had not been together for several months now.

"Maybe he'll need me," said Ada out loud. When Ada drove in her car at night, she often talked out loud, sometimes carrying on both sides of a conversation. She felt her face grow hot. "Excuse me, Rich, but I was just in the neighborhood. Would you like to fornicate?" She tried to laugh but the sound was harsh and full of anger. Rockton was a small, ordered town of 2,500, and the courthouse had been on the square for more than a century. She drove slowly past it on Main Street, thinking of how it had looked when she and Junior had first been dating. She had come down from Memphis and met his parents, had spent the night in the house where she now lived. Lord, Junior was something in those days, trim and smart. But as each day passed, he lost himself in the indolence of those who do not work. Now, he had become some monster, a mass of ghastly flesh and arrogance.

"What makes monsters of men?" asked Ada. "What makes a decent man become gutless trash? Junior, you are gutless trash." The car was getting frigid, so she turned the air conditioner down. "I could freeze my ass off in here." She looked at herself in the mirror and was not ashamed. Ada drove up North Main Street and slowed at Rich Barksdale's house. His lights were on, which did not surprise her because it was only nine-thirty, and Rich had told her how he stayed up late, painting. A night person. That's what Rich was. Hadn't he used those words himself the day he had kissed her on the cheek? Ada wanted to stop but she could not do it yet, so she drove past his house two blocks and turned right, heading out toward Rockton High School, which was at the edge of town.

The school had high chain-link fences and a massive front gate from which a padlock dangled. "Looks like a damn prison," Ada said. Two or three streetlights lit the expansive campus, but once she had passed it, she was in the darkened countryside. That school. Four years before, she and Junior had seen Truly's graduation exercises in the gym, had been so pleased when she got her diploma. But she hadn't been magna cum laude. She hadn't even been cum laude. "I tried to give her the soul of an artist, and her father gave her the soul of something dark and wicked. She's wicked. She's the love and curse of my life. Van Gogh would not even have loved her. In his day she would have been a woman of the streets." She thought bitterly of Junior. "He's making her a whore."

Damn this, Ada thought. Damn it all to hell. She turned around and headed back toward North Main Street.

"If he asks, I'll say yes," Ada said. "Damn his soul, I'll say yes."

+   +   +

Harry Ripley slid into his rumpled trousers and came out the back door. The light was on in the barn where Snake worked out, but no one was around. Where in the hell had they gone? Was that a car he had heard while he was watching Andre the Giant beat the shit out of Big John Studd?

Harry walked down the rotting steps in his carpet slippers and into the yard. The grass was still hot from the day. The whole world seemed ready to explode in flame. Harry looked up at the faint stars and thought of his wife, of what he had done in the past two days. He tried to think if it had been wrong. It had not. Dr. Smith had to die, he always had to die for what he did, and Billy Homer, well, that was icing of some sort. Easy. Both of them were easy. Now he was thinking of number three and how he would do it. Not tonight, maybe tomorrow night. Let him come home worn out from the garage, worn out like me, and we'll both go to glory together. *I hate him,* thought Harry, *for being so much like me.*

Harry was halfway back to the house when he thought he heard something in the old pasture. The only thing Harry feared now was capture, that they would get him before he got Henry. He could not let that happen. Sagging, sweaty, and gray, Harry tiptoed to the end of the barn, and in the moonlight saw Leslie running across the pasture, shouting and laughing. Harry was filled with revulsion, almost pity. Why had God let that boy come into the world, anyway? Leslie had been damaged, and nothing could be done. After he and Henry were gone, Harry thought, Leslie would own the garage and the house. He looked up again. Leslie had stopped at the crest of a hill and was shouting at the sky, waving what appeared to be a hammer at the stars. A fast-moving pain hit Harry in the breastbone and then was gone, and Harry rubbed his chest, not really caring if the breath went out of him like air from a balloon.

Leslie looked down toward the house and saw his father standing behind the barbed-wire fence, wearing pants but no shirt.

"There is no death!" shouted Leslie, face suffused with sweat and joy. He came running down the hill, letting his weight carry him up to the fence. "There is no death!"

"What you yelling about, Leslie?" asked Harry, suspicious. Leslie stopped, breathing heavily, thinking about how much his father's chest looked like an old woman's. "Death?"

"There is no death in me," said Leslie. He realized that he could save Harry. Now he and Harry and Snake would live forever.

"Christ," said Harry, backing up a couple of steps.

"Yes," said Leslie.

"Where you got all this religion shit is beyond me," Harry said.

"You are the father, and I am the son, and that is the way to Truth," said Leslie. Harry began to laugh, a choking, raspy laugh that sounded in the still, hot night like someone filing rusted metal. "I am the way to your salvation."

"You are the dummy, and I am the keeper of hell," said Harry. "This here ain't heaven, dummy. It's the only thing they is of hell on this earth. You put your ear down on that pasture and listen close, and you'll hear the fire. The Devil's right under us, burning up the world. Why you think it's gotten so damn hot, Leslie? You want religion? Well, damn, you put your ear down and see if you can hear Satan. He's calling for us Ripleys, Leslie. We all going to burn forever in hell."

"No," said Leslie, confused. "I am with you always." Harry came to the fence and held it and stared at the only son he would allow to live. Leslie would be the perfect witness of what had become of the Ripleys.

"Lie down and listen to hell," cackled Harry. Leslie tentatively kneeled and then lay flat on his stomach in the grass. The ground was hot to the touch. The grass was dry and broke under his face. Leslie put his ear to the ground, closed his eyes, and listened. He was covered with sweat, foaming just like his only brother when he worked out in the barn. Leslie Ripley listened.

At first, he saw a hawk, and he laughed for all the joy in his heart. Harry spat on the rusted barbed wire and the spittle hung, stretched obscenely, and broke. Leslie watched the hawk in his heart and felt himself rise, but then it changed: he heard something like a dynamo churning, like the engine of Snake's old truck or the sound of a soft machine gun, like the purring of a metallic cat. Then the world was consumed in flames around Leslie. He could see, waving in stalagmites and stalactites, the flames of hell, the vast minions of darkness tortured by their eternal pain. They all shouted, "Save Me! Save Me!" as they burned, and their arms waved wildly, and their fingers were flame, shooting flame, and the screams were pitiable, and a burning wind scourged them as they ran. Leslie began to shake and to cry: this is what God had meant for him, to be his burden for this earth, to die that these people might not burn under the earth of the Ripley farm. Leslie sat up, breathing hard, terrified that the casual geography of hell had placed it directly under their farm. This was a sign.

"This do in remembrance of me," said Leslie. Harry fell to his knees, laughing and shaking his head.

"You hear hell, Leslie?" asked Harry. "I always thought hell was in the water, in the ocean. But I guess each man gets to pick his own hell and his own God. Unless he's a dummy and don't know the difference."

Leslie picked up his hammer and slid it back into his pants. All was clear to him now, and once again he felt light and happy, forgetting who the man at the fence was, standing there like some vagrant, like some whisper of death, the everlasting sentinel of hell.

+ + +

It was 10 P.M. and Truly Crawford was pushing ninety on the straightaway four miles south of Rockton on Deerskin Road. The road was heaven for sticky black tire skids, for drag races and cutting doughnuts. Black tread streaks wove back and forth across the nearly liquid tar and gravel, as if someone were weaving a basket.

"I feel like a complete fool in these shorts," said Snake. "And I've got blood all over your seat. You're never going to get this off here."

"What makes you think I'll even try?" asked Truly. "Why did you say your father wanted to kill Dr. Smith?" Snake sighed. The blood had stopped flowing, but his shoulder throbbed pitifully, and his chest was masked with a dark stain of dried blood.

"He killed my mother," said Snake. "He was late when he delivered Leslie. He let my brother choke on the cord, and he didn't get enough oxygen, and that's what happened to him. He let my mother bleed to death in that damn piece of a hospital he had."

"Jesus," said Truly. "I always just thought Leslie had a learning disorder or something."

"Shit, we didn't take out an ad in the paper to announce it," Snake said. "He seemed okay for a long time, and then it went downhill. A lady from New Orleans told us it was like having a head full of gears that started meshing less and less each year. He's gone to pieces. Everything's gone to pieces."

"I still love you," said Truly. Snake laughed bitterly.

"All you love is what I got in my pants," he said.

"That's not all I love," Truly said. "But it is one of your best features."

"You're just like the Ripleys," said Snake. "That's why you like me, Truly. Who are you trying to punish?"

"Punish?" asked Truly. "I never thought of it that way. Everybody, I guess. Everybody deserves to be treated like filth. The entire world is filth."

"I'm sick of being filth," said Snake. He felt lonely. "I'm sick of being poor and trash, and I don't know what is happening to me or to Leslie. I don't know why God give me that old man for a father. Leslie's the only thing I ever loved that loved me back."

"Too bad you didn't have *my* daddy," laughed Truly. "Then you'd be an upright citizen."

"Turn around somewhere and go by the garage," said Snake. "I'm hurting like hell. I got some pills there." Truly knew the way. In rural counties, everyone knows the way, knows every dirt lane and where it ends. In fifteen minutes, she was pulling in front of the Ripley Garage. "Out back." She stepped on the accelerator and slid in the dust past the gas pumps and around back near the railroad tracks in the thin glow of the light on the telephone pole. Snake unfolded out of Truly's Jaguar, feeling sick and afraid.

Snake looked up to see the wind blowing grit in small puffs down the railroad tracks. He walked to the back door and opened it, and Truly went inside with him. He often came here at night and sat in the dark. The stockroom was nearly black, but when they came out of it into the office, the single fluorescent light that always stayed on lit their faces with a ghastly, lingering flare.

"Go get us a six-pack out of my cooler in there," said Snake.

She stared at him in the shadow, body all muscles, hard

planes of flesh, right side dark with dried blood. She stared at his gym shorts. Truly did not know why she always wanted sex; while she was doing it, she felt light, soaring, in control, but when it was finished, she felt revulsion, the desire to scream. Truly got the cooler. Snake went behind the counter and took his rag in his left hand and began to wipe off the blood and sweat. But the more he wiped it, the more it became smeared. "Dammit!" He threw the rag on the floor and tottered around the counter and sat on the floor. Truly came back with a six-pack of Coors and sat beside Snake. They opened their beers and drank in silence for a long while.

"My daddy used to bring me here when I was a boy," said Snake. "We'd come up here at night and sit and listen to the fights on the radio."

"What did your daddy do?" said Truly in her best Southern-belle drawl.

"Nothing much," said Snake. "He just come around the counter here and beat the holy shit out of me for pulling for the wrong guy. He always thought I was pulling for the wrong thing. Didn't matter what the hell it was. If I was for it, he was against it."

"My daddy never disagreed with a thing I ever said," Truly said. She gulped her beer and then belched raucously. "Didn't matter what I said, it was okay with old Junior Crawford."

"And look at us," Snake laughed. "Sitting in this run-down garage nobody wants, living like animals. I don't think I can stand it another minute. I could cut my throat from ear to ear."

"Huh," said Truly.

"What?"

"That reminds me of the first dead deer I ever saw," she said. "My father had killed it and brought it home. It was on the hood of his car and blood was pouring down the fenders. I cried and cried when I saw it. It had pretty eyes. I couldn't believe my father would kill anything that pretty."

"Some people think deer were put here just to kill," said Snake.

"What isn't?" asked Truly. Snake finished his beer, opened another, and drank half of it with his eyes shut tightly. He stood and took the beer can and threw it the length of the office, where it hit the wall and glanced off without much effect. Truly stood and threw hers, too, and her arms came around him. He kissed her with such force, even violence, that Truly was astonished, and in less than ten seconds they were both naked. Truly hopped onto the counter.

There seemed to be blood everywhere.

It lasted less than five minutes for Truly and Snake. Snake backed away and put his hand over his face and walked around the office naked for a moment. Then he began to cry. Truly yawned and moved into the back room and did not come back out. Snake finished sobbing and looked around for her.

"Truly?" he said. "Truly, dammit, what are you doing?" She did not answer, so Snake slipped back into his soiled gym shorts and walked into the back room. The door to the outside was open. Inside, it was so hot Snake could barely breathe, and out here it was hardly better. "Truly?"

"Here!" she shouted. Snake looked up the railroad embankment and saw Truly, still naked, walking unsteadily down a rail, her breasts jiggling and waving as she tried to balance herself.

"Jesus Christ, get down here and get your clothes," Snake said. "There's a damn train due at ten-fifteen."

"Really?" said Truly. "Awright!" Snake's shoulder had begun to bleed again. He couldn't believe he had not even gone to a doctor, but he simply couldn't. He knew it.

"Please get down here," Snake pleaded.

"Why'd you put your pants on?" asked Truly. "Get naked and come on up here. Let's do it on the railroad tracks."

"There's glass all over the place there," Snake said. "That's where we bust bottles. Would you please come down here?" Truly yelled with joy, and Snake looked back toward the road, but no one was there. He was thinking about what to do next when he heard the whistle of the train down at the Ruark Road crossing not half a mile away. "I hear the train."

"Come on up!" screamed Truly. "Let's give them a show." The hell with her, Snake thought, the hell with her. He got in Truly's car and sat for a moment, but then he knew he would have to get her. Just like he would have to take care of Harry and Leslie and this damn garage. He got out and ran up the bank just as the train came around the curve. Truly had her arms up and was waving at the train. She screamed and sang "Bad Moon Rising" and cupped her breasts and waved them at the engineer. Snake grabbed her and dragged her screaming down the bank just as the train came by. The engineer, who had seen it all, stared and hooted at Truly. The train was long, clattering cattle cars, boxcars carrying fertilizer.

Truly was laughing as Snake held her wet body, and they came to the car. She felt as if her life were just beginning.

+ + +

Ada had driven by Rich Barksdale's house three times before she gritted her teeth and pulled into the semicircular driveway, right up to the huge fluted Doric columns. Lights were on in the parlor to the left. She could see the dark oil portrait of Rich's great-grandfather hanging over the mantel. She had been fascinated by his story, by the cracked canvas that had been varnished so many times the man's skin was a dark yellow.

"What in the hell am I doing?" Ada said as she looked at herself in the rearview mirror and put on fresh lipstick. "What in the hell am I doing?" She opened the door and stepped into a world that felt like fire. The heat swept into her mouth, her throat, her heart. Her skin immediately began to ooze sweat. She slammed the door and walked up the broad stone steps that had been worn down by generations of Rocktonians, back to the time of elegant and loving men who went off to fight for a lost cause. Ada loved to read about the Civil War, of the men like Robert E. Lee and Jeb Stuart, gentlemen who treated women with kindness and love. Rich is like those men, she thought.

She walked right up to the door. Her heart was clattering so fast her breath felt ragged, a foaming, out-of-control engine. She felt ridiculous and wondered if her breath was all right, if she was beginning to smell sweaty. She rang the bell. It sounded far away. Through the cut glass on the right side of the door she saw Rich coming down the parqueted hall, wearing a velvet smoking jacket and a paisley ascot, smoke escaping from a briar pipe he clenched in his even teeth. *Sweet Jesus*, Ada thought. The door, heavy and smooth, swung back.

"My God, Ada Crawford," said Rich in his deep, elegant voice. "What in the world are you doing out this time of night?" He smiled beautifully, and Ada felt the rush of very cool air coming around him.

"It's late," she said, almost giggling. "I was just out driving, saw your light on, and thought I'd say hello." She felt her face fill with blood, and she felt worse than foolish.

"Come on in and let's have a glass of wine," said Rich. Oh God, thought Ada.

"An offer I can't refuse," Ada said. Rich held his arm behind her a few inches and escorted her into the house. A crystal chandelier sparkled in the hall. Everything smelled of furniture polish. She heard voices. *Damn, voices.*

"I've got some friends here you'll want to meet, Ada," Rich said. "How's your painting going? Still working on those watercolors?"

"I'm trying," she said. "And I've been reading about artists. It's such an exciting thing, to read about their lives. It's all so romantic." *Damn,* she thought. *I'm such a fool.*

"One of the reasons we all love it," said Rich. Ada could not believe how smooth and perfect Rich's skin was. Like his beard was just beneath the translucent skin, though he seemed freshly shaven. He was tall and slim, and his nose was perfectly aquiline, the kind Junior always made fun of. "I've got some artist friends from Memphis down. Come on in." He took her hand. His flesh was warm and soft. They walked into the parlor, where two men were admiring a china vase.

"Rusty Grady and Tristan Mitchell, this is Ada Crawford, one of my former students here in town," said Rich. Ada clutched her purse and stared at them. Something about them was exactly like Rich, very slender, almost too perfect. Rusty had a neat mustache, and Tristan wore round tortoiseshell glasses. Both men had razor-cut hair and neatly creased trousers. Rusty wore tassel loafers, and Tristan had on Italian shoes that were snugged with eight eyes. Chamber music filtered into the room.

"Pleased to meet you," Ada said.

"An artist," said Rusty. "What's your medium, dear? Do you do watercolors like Richard? Tristan and I both collect his work. Y'all are lucky to have him here in Rockton."

"Well, I'm using oils now," said Ada. "Yes, we are lucky to have Rich here."

"Oh God, this is embarrassing," said Rich. "Wine?"

"Burgundy," said Ada. Rich disappeared. Rusty set the vase back on a glossy étagère.

"Just terrible what's happened here," said Tristan. He had a vague accent that Ada could not place. Neither man seemed more than thirty, much younger than Rich.

"What?" asked Ada. Tristan looked at her suspiciously.

"The murders, honey," he said. "My God, the entire civilized world's here. I heard Dan Rather talking about Rockton on the news last night."

"We weren't even sure we wanted to come down here," said Rusty. "God, it just makes me sick to my stomach."

"Oh God, yes," said Ada, shaking her head. "I thought you meant here, in Rich's house. Of course it's terrible. I knew them all. It's this heat. We haven't had rain here for weeks. Sure feels glorious in here, though, doesn't it?"

"Just fabulous," said Rusty.

"What kind of work do you both do?" asked Ada. Rich came into the room and handed her a goblet of crystal, old family crystal, in which he had served her wine before.

"I run my own gallery," said Tristan. "It's small now, but growing. Rusty's a stylist at Chiffon's."

"What's that?" Ada asked.

"A hair-design parlor," said Rusty. "It's at Lenoir Square." Ada felt strange. She sipped her wine and nodded.

"You work, honey?" asked Tristan.

"No," said Ada, "I, uh . . . just paint. I'm just an artist."

"Where have you shown?" asked Tristan. "Do you have an agent?"

"God, nowhere," said Ada. She laughed nervously. "I'm just an amateur." An awkward silence filled the room with the music. Tristan came to Rich and reached out with a perfectly manicured fingernail and scratched at his lapel.

"I think you've got that cheesecake on your jacket," said Tristan. He scratched at it eagerly. "Richard, you're such an insufferable slob sometimes." Tristan thrust his finger in his mouth and then pressed it to the spot and scratched. "Honey, you'll never get this off, never."

"God, Tristan, get your hands off Rich," said Rusty. "We have company." Ada felt suddenly as if she were being consumed in flames. How could she have been so utterly stupid? How? She tossed off the glass of wine and started walking toward the door.

"Where are you going, Ada?" asked Rich. "We're going to look at some new prints I'm buying from Tristan."

"Got to go, got to go," choked Ada. She handed Rich the glass and mumbled a few vague good-byes, and before she could remember what was happening, she was back in her Cadillac, driving through Rockton. If she had looked in the mirror, she could have seen the mascara streaking her cheeks, making them dark and wet.

+ + +

Mona Reubens curled up next to her husband and put her hand gently on his chest.

"They'll have the results back by late tomorrow afternoon?" she whispered. He sighed, a great long exhalation of sadness and defeat. The window air conditioner clattered as if it had a death rattle.

"If it's on file," said Monk. "Could be somebody not ever fingerprinted."

"Maybe we'll get lucky," she said.

"Somebody who's never been in the service, been arrested, gotten a liquor or beer license," mumbled Monk, heavy with approaching sleep. "Chances are it won't be anything."

"You're doing the best you can," Mona said. "Everybody knows you're just doing the best you can."

"That's not really enough sometimes," said Monk. Mona listened to his breathing change. He was edging into sleep. She had never been able to give him the son he so badly wanted. She felt so sorry for him that she could cry.

11

LENA JERNIGAN AWOKE long before dawn and walked onto the back porch in her thin cotton dressing gown. A hot wind lifted the gown, billowing it around her ropy legs. She was three years older than Nova. Ailene was leaning over the sink washing her face, wearing only worn white panties. The sink was on the back porch and always froze in winter. Ailene was a year older than Lena but was even thinner. Ailene had no breasts at all; she looked like a teenage boy, a slight swelling at the nipples but that was all.

The Jernigan sisters lived three miles from Junior Ripley's house, on a slope that overlooked the Rockton City Cemetery.

"Look at that," said Lena. "She be the most pitiful thing I ever seen." Ailene looked up and saw Nova sitting in the backyard, staring down toward the cemetery. Between their house and the cemetery was a forbidding jungle of kudzu. "She just come home and sit and stare. She say anything to you about what wrong?"

Ailene said, "Not directly. I think she just sick of crazy folk and this heat. I told her she work for Junior Crawford, she get crazy, too. She tell you about that dog?"

"Say it running loose," said Lena, "Say it gone bite somebody ass off. How come don't no crazy man never shoot somebody like Mr. Junior Crawford?"

"Don't seem right, do it?" said Ailene. "I need you Mitchum. Yesterday I sweat through my clothes before my shift half over."

It was almost time for Nova to come in and get ready for the walk over to the Crawford house. She felt the sun's power as it swelled in her face, in her eyes and mouth, and she believed that something was about to happen, that the entire earth was about to break apart, that the world was about to totter and roll away like the stone from Jesus' tomb. All the passion for which she had waited had now been ruined. The Devil had begun to choke her, forcing her to feel for Truly Crawford what she wanted to feel for one special man in her life. But why had Lena and Ailene never married yet, them already heading for thirty? Were they, too, confused by what love meant? Why was love such a terrible dilemma? Truly's face was light and terror. But Junior. Junior Crawford was the Devil himself, and Nova could not forget how he had looked in the kitchen. She could not tell Lena or Ailene about what had happened. Across the jungle of kudzu, three tents flapped in the hot breeze that raked across the Rockton City Cemetery. Maybe she could kill Junior and everyone would think it was just the maniac.

"I couldn't kill nobody," cried Nova out loud. On the back porch, Lena and Ailene heard her.

"What she say?" asked Ailene.

"Just groaning, appears to me," sighed Lena. "I feel so bad for her, Sister. She just finding out what it like to be black and a woman in this world, and it killing her inside."

"Got to live," said Ailene. "Onliest thing we got to do. Live."

Nova stood, shaking her head, and walked back across the yard toward the house. She saw, through the tattered backdoor screen, the faces of her sisters, staring at her. Their eyes were wet with pity, and Nova Jernigan knew who it was for.

+ + +

Harry Ripley, Snake, and Leslie sat at the kitchen table eating breakfast. Snake had rebandaged his shoulder, but it was hurting more and more. Harry cut into his greasy fried egg and thrust the dripping yellow between his bloodless lips. Snake had cooked breakfast, but he felt sickness and anger as he watched Harry eat. Leslie ate and moved as if he were listening to some private music.

"You did it," said Snake, his voice flat. Sun boiled up over the window ledge and spread along the table. "You killed all those people. You're who they're looking for." Harry grinned.

"Number three," said Harry. "Number three."

"The Trinity," smiled Leslie.

"What's that, dummy?" asked Harry.

"Three is the Trinity," said Leslie. He cut his egg and held the dripping yolk up to his lips. "This do in remembrance of me." Harry cackled with laughter.

"Son, your shaving cut looks a little worse today," said Harry.

"Shut up," said Snake. "Just shut up." He was thinking of the night before, when he had dragged a giggling Truly Crawford back down the railroad embankment, made her dress. She had taken another six-pack and scratched off in her car while Snake had brooded in the dusty silence of the Ripley Garage, trying to decide what to do. Nothing made sense anymore. "I know it was you."

"Well, there's number one," said Harry, "number two, and then there's number three. Number three is the greatest of all."

"I will be with you always," said Leslie.

Harry laughed and sipped the coffee that lazily steamed in his mug. Snake had already decided that he could not go to the garage today; he had to think. When he was troubled, Snake would sit for hours trying to clear the debris from his mind. The hell with all this, Snake thought. I'll just leave and see if anybody follows me. No way I can go to work today.

"I was up early this morning," Leslie said, standing and walking to the window over the sink. It had not been washed in years, and a greasy haze made everything outside seem bound in a gritty fog. "I walked up into the pasture, and the hawk came low over me, and I held up my arms and asked it if this was the end of the earth. And you know what it said to me?" Leslie turned and looked at his father and brother, smiling beatifically. "It said, 'I wish I was an Oscar Mayer wiener.' If that was not God or our mother I would be surprised." Harry began to laugh, a choking, wheezing laugh. Snake thought he might kill Harry, might just storm into the front room, get the big .357 Colt Python, come back, and blow Harry all over his coffee cup. "I think it was God, because our mother died so very long ago, and God lives in all of us. God could live in a hawk if he could live in Jesus. God could live in anything. Hawks who can talk live with God on his throne in heaven." Leslie paused and smiled at them. "I am going to do something wonderful for both of you."

"DUMMY DOES SOMETHING WONDERFUL," said Harry. "That'd make a good headline."

"Better than being a damn mad-dog killer," said Snake. Harry's eyes, which were drooping in their red rings, went dull and flat as he turned on Snake.

"You think being dead's worse than this?" asked Harry. He took the remnants of his eggs and grits and stood on his stork legs and threw the plate against the wall above the stove. The residue slid down the cracked plaster. "You think life is worth living? You been listening to damn Billy Graham or something on TV, boy? Look up there." Snake stared into his plate. "I said, dammit, look at that wall!" Snake looked up from habit and saw the mess. "That's all life is. Scum on plaster wall. Bet you thought life was gone be something beautiful, didn't you, boy?"

Snake jumped up and walked swiftly into the front room and got the Python. He came striding back into the kitchen and went around behind Harry, who was still grinning. Snake wrapped his strong left around Harry's neck and put the barrel of the .357 to his head and thumbed the hammer back.

"No!" screamed Leslie. "This is not the way to eternal life." Harry smiled, revealing his bad teeth.

"I'm going to blow your brains out," said Snake. "I've

been taking it from you for my whole life, and I think I should dish it out a little now."

"Go ahead," said Harry. No one moved for more than thirty seconds. "I knew you didn't have the balls, boy. You still believe life's worth living, don't you? Go ahead." Leslie fell to his knees in a patch of brutally hot sunlight that streamed through the window.

"Father, forgive us for we know not what we do," Leslie said. "Forgive us our transgressions and for Harry being such an ass and Henry being the brother of hawks. Please forgive my brother, Henry, for being the brother of hawks." Snake saw Leslie and fell back a step. The blood from his shoulder was pouring like water from an open tap, down his side, and then into his pants, down his leg. Snake could hear Harry chuckling. Snake turned and looked at the egg on the wall.

He whirled toward it and fired five times, the sound of the gunshots deafening in the still kitchen. Leslie jumped up and ran to Snake, holding his nose into the smoky air.

"Explode it, Brother!" shouted Leslie. "Oh, I love the smell of guns!" Snake knocked a chair over as he ran out into the backyard, sure that death could be no worse than this.

+ + +

Ada Crawford was waiting. She lay beneath the single cotton sheet and felt the breeze from the fan ripple over her. Junior was already in the shower, thank God. She reached over to her bedside table and took the *Letters of Vincent van Gogh* and tried to read it for a while. Her mouth was dry, and more than anything she felt horror and bitterness over what had happened the night before. Art was responsible for her dark feeling. If she were not sensitive, she would not feel things so keenly. Better to be a dolt like Junior, who didn't know beauty from filth, to be insensate, unaware of the great painters and how well they loved.

Were there truly men like them who loved this well—that they would immortalize love with the eternal gloss of sculpture, with the dazzling displays of paint on canvas? Surely Leonardo must have loved Mona Lisa, must have adored that shy smile. Van Gogh loved Arles and its people, loved the sun and the flowers that broke the earth and reached up for it. She set the book back on the small antique table.

Ada pushed the sheet back. She sat looking out the window at the formal boxwoods that surrounded the Crawford mansion. That sound. Something like a locomotive far away chuffing toward Rockton, but it was no closer nor no farther away. She turned to her left and saw Butch sitting on his haunches in the corner beside the rosewood chifforobe, panting heavily, his tongue lolling out of the left side of his mouth.

"You're thirsty," said Ada. Butch's tail thumped against the wall. Junior came walking out of the adjoining bathroom, naked. His white mane was askew, sticking up wildly, leaving his bald spots uncovered. Ada could never in her life remember seeing any man quite so hideous.

"How in the hell did that animal get in my bedroom?" asked Junior. Butch's tail stopped thumping, and he came upright, head down a little. "Nova! Nova!" Butch did not move or pant. He stared at Junior, eyes glassy. Ada thought Butch was going to leap at Junior. *Oh please*, she thought. They could hear Nova's sneaker-clad footsteps ascending the stairs. There was a tiny knock on the door. "Come get this damn dog out of here."

"You're naked," said Ada.

"For God's sake," said Junior. The door began to open slowly, so Junior grabbed the first thing he saw, his wife's robe on the post of their bed. The sleeves ripped as he thrust his huge forearms into it, and he had to hold up the bottom to cover himself as Nova came creeping into the room. She took one look at Junior and began to giggle.

"Is you taking up modeling?" asked Nova. Ada laughed hysterically.

"Use that smart nigger mouth to get this dog out of my bedroom," said Junior harshly.

"Come on, boy," said Nova, making a cricket sound with her tongue. Butch leapt up and circled Junior warily, head still down, eyes burning holes into Junior's chest. "Come on out the room." The dog stood in front of Junior and looked at him with the still intensity of death. Nova giggled nervously at Junior standing there in the robe. "Come on out the room." Butch never took his eyes off Junior as he limped sideways to the door, then followed Nova down the stairs.

"In my damn bedroom," said Junior, closing the door and throwing off the robe. "How in the hell did that monster get into this room?"

"I'm sure I don't know," said Ada. "You looked ridiculous in that robe. I'm glad Nova got to see that."

"Now baby," said Junior. He felt wonderful. He loved to start sweating when he got out of the shower, loved to stand naked in front of the antique bureau and dry and comb his hair. He walked up to it and hung his stomach over the edge and lifted a clean, dry hand towel from a stack that Nova kept there. He toweled his hair, and as he did, his gut shook back and forth and he sang "That's Amore," one of his favorite songs.

"Stop singing," Ada snapped. She did not know she was going to say it.

"Baby?" said Junior. He turned and stared at her, a huge black barber's comb held tightly between his fingers. The veins stood out in his nose.

"Your singing makes me nauseous," she said. She fell back against the pillow, not able to look at him. "Why in the hell can't we afford to air-condition this place? I can't stand this heat."

"I always thought you liked my voice," said Junior, obviously hurt.

"I always lied," said Ada. Junior came over and sat on the edge of the bed. His jaws worked as if he were chewing a word. Nothing, Ada thought, should have this little pride, this little sense of what was decent and good in life.

"When was the last period you had?" asked Junior. His voice was superior, slightly hard.

"What in the hell . . ." said Ada, sitting up and snapping her head toward him.

"Because I was thinking you're just going through the change, baby," said Junior.

"I'm changing," Ada said. She rolled out the other side of the bed and turned on Junior. "You're damn right I'm changing. I'm looking at something that used to be a man, and I'm starting to realize that not everyone is the slime you've turned out to be. You don't have one shred of art in your bones. You don't have the slightest understanding of love. There are men who would die for their wives. You don't have an ounce of love in your heart anymore, if you ever did."

"Baby, just be patient," said Junior, waddling around the bed. "Maybe I'm about to do something heroic for you. The Citizens' Committee is going out to find that mad-dog killer. We're going to comb through the niggers over on Henry Street today, see what they know."

"My God, you're repulsive," she said, looking at his stomach. He hunched over slightly, and his fat now completely covered his groin, as if he were some great, sexless thing. His breasts were rotund and thick as hams. "I don't know if I can bear this. I just don't know. Why do I have to bear this?" She crossed her arms over her chest like a mummy. The room was dusty and still. Outside, a car horn coughed at a dog. The silence pulsed between them. The bell on the courthouse began to chime the hour.

"Baby, you're just overwrought," said Junior. He turned and walked back to the mirror. Ada looked at his rump, which was small and folded under like some dead, hairless beast. Junior's upper body was massive, but he had no hips or thighs at all. Junior took the black comb and began to swirl his silver hair artfully over the bald spots. He began to hum "That's Amore."

Ada picked up her robe and put it on. The sleeves were split, and flapped as she walked out of the room and into the hall. Truly's door was closed. Fall might never come, Ada thought, fall with its splendor of colors, its rich palette. Rain might never come to soak the earth. Ada loved the smell of rain, and it reminded her of childhood, of sitting on the porch dreaming of how wonderful her life would be, how she would marry some wonderful man who would worship her, would do anything to make her happy. The smell of rain.

Ada crossed the hall into her studio. The smell of paint

and turpentine and linseed oil was strong, pungent. "The Death of Miss Agnes Longley" was still on the easel, twenty-four by thirty-six inches. Already, Ada had outlined Agnes lying on the floor. That was the night of the storm that never came. Ada had stood here in this room, all the windows open, watching the lightning break the sky, praying for rain. *Prayers*, Ada thought. On one wall, she had hung her most perfect still life, a vase of red and white roses. She walked slowly to it and took it down, then went to the window. She parted the white lace curtains and held the corner of the painting and leaned far out, looking at the ordered boxwoods on the east side of the house, the town side. She took the painting and with all her strength sailed it into the light.

She watched it turn, red and white, red and white, until it disappeared into green.

Rockton seemed to lurch through the motions of its business each day: Bob Hoard down at the Purina store by the tracks buying feed for his horses; Mabel Salinger in Sew What getting muslin for pillowcases she was making; Joe Danny Davis at Smith Hardware getting the blade for his old lawn mower sharpened. And yet, over each shoulder, their eyes cut toward the next man in line, wondering who had blood on his hands and who was pure.

Mona Reubens was afraid. Monk had been in the papers and on TV constantly as sheriff of Rockton, and what if the killer saw it and decided to stop him? What if the killer came to her house during the day or the night while Monk was away? Who was there then to protect her?

That morning at the breakfast table, she had presented

Monk with scrambled eggs, toast, coffee, and grits in which a liquefying pat of butter lazily swam. They sat in silence as they ate. The radio in the background droned.

"That print should be back by late this afternoon," Monk said. He moved the butter into the grits until the white and yellow became one color. "That was Calhoun with the State on the phone. He said it was clean as anything, that we really lucked out."

"But you don't know if it's somebody who's ever been fingerprinted?" asked Mona.

"If he's been in the service, been arrested, got a beer or liquor license, anything like that," Monk said. "I tell you what I think. I think it was somebody passing through looking to rob somebody, and it got out of hand. Just went berserk. Probably not even in the South anymore. Probably in Sharon, Pennsylvania, or something." Mona looked into her plate.

"That's what I was thinking," she said. Monk looked up at her. Without any makeup, her hair curled from a deep sleep against her pillow, she looked older than forty-one. Her skin was pale, almost a translucent white, and her lips visibly trembled.

"I know," he whispered.

"Maybe it's somebody who knows us," said Mona. "That's the most terrible thought of all."

"You know how to use the pistol," said Monk. He had given her a .38 Police Special two days before and showed her how to fire it. "Besides, it's all over now but finding who did it."

"Why don't I feel like it's all over?" asked Mona. "Why don't I feel like that? Why do I feel like this will never be over?"

"Before you know it, it'll be fall," said Monk, standing wearily and coming around behind her. "We'll go to the football games, get barbecue before them, and eat on the boot of the car. We'll drive up into the mountains and watch the leaves turn."

"Funeral's at two?" she asked flatly. Monk hugged her, and when he did, Mona felt his gun holster pressing into her shoulder.

+ + +

Junior and Ada were waiting at the table for their break-fast when Truly came bouncing through the dining room, heading toward the kitchen. The room was perfectly ordered, and Junior was reading the paper. He looked up just as Truly came into the room.

"Well, look here at sweetness," said Junior. Truly smiled with sickening unctuousness at her father and waved, not thinking of stopping. "Whoa there, baby. Just whoa there!" Junior grinned and pushed his chair back. "How about a hug for the old man, huh?"

"Christ Jesus," said Ada. She was still in her housecoat and was all but snarling at Junior and the idea of this house. In the past fifteen minutes she had thrown nearly all her paintings out the window, except "The Death of Miss Agnes Longley." Junior had been looking at her in disbelief, but now they both stared at Truly.

"Say it," said Junior, arms open. Truly knew. She came to him and hugged him and, leaning back, said it.

"This is my father's world."

"Blasphemy," said Ada.

"Is you ready for breakfast yet?" asked Nova. She was

standing in the doorway. "Miss Truly, I didn't know you was here. Is you eating breakfast with you folks or what?"

"No, Nova, I'm not dining *avec mère et père* this morning," said Truly.

"You not what?" asked Nova. "Is you speaking in tongues?"

"Oh my God," said Junior Crawford.

"Tongues," said Truly. "No. I'm going riding this morning, try to take advantage of this wonderful sun."

"You'll get sunstroke," said Ada. "You'll burn up your brain."

"I always wondered about sunstroke," said Truly. "Does it start coming on you all at once or is it slow?" She walked to the huge mirror on the buffet and looked at herself. She was wearing a pale-blue shorts outfit. Her makeup was perfect; she was in complete control. "When it happens, does your brain just explode or do you start to melt? I always wondered about sunstroke."

"What?" asked Ada weakly. "Why are you talking this way? Why are you doing this to me?" Truly knelt by her mother and looked up at her.

"Everything I do, Mother, isn't about you, for you, or to you," said Truly sweetly.

"That's what I keep telling her," nodded Junior happily, gesturing with the front section of the paper. "I keep telling her that same thing."

"Is you wanting orange juice or tomato juice?" said Nova.

"Why are you talking like this to me?" Ada asked, horrified. "What happened to you, Truly? What in God's name happened to you? This town's the darkest place on earth, and you seem to think it's like a picnic. What has happened to you?"

"Mother," said Truly. "Don't you worry your pretty little head." Nova watched from the doorway, feeling the power of hatred make her strong. Watch these rich white folks tear themselves to bits.

"Just what I always tell her," exulted Junior. "Nova, I want orange juice. And bring me a damn grapefruit. I want to lose some weight. If you eat a grapefruit, you can eat all you want to for breakfast and still lose weight. I read that in the *Enquirer*. Did you read that, sweetness?"

"What kind of juice would you like, Mother?" asked Truly. "Tomato juice is kind of sour and pulpy, and orange juice will burn your mouth from its acid. Which one do you like better?" Ada looked at them both, slid her chair back, and left the room.

"What'd I say?" asked Junior, his arms up in the air. "Women. What in the hell did I say?"

"Nothing," said Truly as she headed out the door. "You never say anything."

"Now, sweetness," said Junior Crawford.

Truly came into the blaze of summer. She saw the splashes of color in the hedges, out on the neatly clipped lawn. She sauntered to the color. Truly was wearing her Ralph Lauren sunglasses, and she stood holding the keys to her Jaguar and looking without expression at the scattered paintings: a still life of a vase with roses, a pointillistic puppy, a sunrise with thick, gagging brushstrokes and crows over a field, a copy from Van Gogh, a partial picture of Ada's dog, not looking at all like a Doberman but like something from the jaws of hell. Truly shook her head slowly and saw, tumbling from the upstairs window, another painting, this one small. It fell heavily, turning once. Truly walked to it. She lifted it by the corner and saw that it was of a big-eyed little girl holding a fistful of daisies, something Ada had copied from the toilet-paper package. This one was indistinct, as if painted by Monet as a child. Truly dropped it and turned around.

For a moment, she thought she heard something like the tearing of flannel sheets.

12

N O V A   S T O O D   I N   the window of the visitor's house and watched as Junior Crawford tied up Butch and began to beat the hell out of him with a stick. She had done most of her chores, and it was not yet time for supper, so she had been watching the soaps when she had heard Junior coaxing the dog forward. Junior had slipped a rope over Butch's neck and snapped it tight. Then he tied it to a huge water oak that his grandmother had planted. Butch, realizing he had been tricked, lunged along on three legs, trying to escape, growling and thrashing. Junior stood just out of his reach and hit him with a long, slender stick of bamboo. Each time Junior hit the dog, it howled pitifully.

Junior felt great. All day long he had been thinking of this. For two hours he and members of the Rockton Citizens' Committee had wandered around the black section of Rockton, storming into backyards and questioning women and children, once screaming at and abusing an old man who had been brought out into the sunshine by his daughter. After an hour of it, someone had called the sheriff, and Monk Reubens had driven over in time to find the men at a black neighborhood's public swimming pool, in a violent shouting match with five or six young men who were ready to fight.

"Dammit, Junior, back off!" Monk had shouted.

"I'm trying to help save this damn town, and you're telling me to back off?" Junior screamed. Monk hated Junior, hated all he had been, had become, would be. And yet Monk was a politician, had to be elected every four years, and you needed to stay friends when you were a politician. He had taken the forty men from the Citizens' Committee back over to the jail and told them a break might be coming in the case; maybe he'd need their help that evening. Junior was ecstatic. Monk was doubtful, but if it shut them up, why not? The men had disbanded without a reporter finding out about it all, which was something of a miracle. But many of the reporters had left town. It didn't seem like anybody else was going to get killed, so why should they stay? Go on to another town where people were killing each other. Murder gypsies, Monk had told Mona. That's what they are, murder gypsies.

Junior had gone home, triumphant, to find Nova out in the backyard picking up Ada's paintings from the lawn, retrieving them from the hedges. Junior had laughed and gone inside for a cold beer and a bloody roast beef sandwich. He sat by himself in the dining room and ate and drank, watching his face in the mirror, turning it to see how his silver mane fell neatly back over his head like waves. Then he had slept in his chair in the den, snoring peacefully. Once, Ada had come into the room and watched him for a while. His huge stomach had popped two buttons, and it was thrust out, pink and hairless, rising and falling, rising and falling.

Ada moved through the house as if ankle-deep in syrup. Her head was stuffed with fatigue and anguish. She could not face this much longer. She needed the clear, cool ache of love. She had finally gone to her room like Truly, now returned from her drive, and lay on the bed and cried herself to sleep.

When Junior had arisen from the recliner, it was three-thirty and he wanted a beer, so he got a cold Bud from the refrigerator and went outside. Butch had been loping around the yard, stopping to dig up flowers, to mark his trail. Junior watched him for nearly twenty minutes, his gorge rising. What in the hell was wrong with Ada that she wanted him to get this dog for her? Junior finished the beer and came into the house in a rage, finally finding his heavy rope in a hall closet, the hangman's knot still in it. Junior had learned to tie a hangman's knot in high school, and he loved to tie them, in window sashes, in shoe strings, spare bits of twine, in this heavy ski rope. He came back outside with the rope behind his back.

"Here, Butch, here Butch," Junior had said. "Nice dog." His voice oozed across the neat lawn. "Here Butch, nice dog." Butch had been suspicious and had come slowly toward Junior, getting five feet away when Junior whirled the rope around and by some profound accident lassoed Butch perfectly. The dog ran, Junior pulled on the rope, and Butch was trapped. It had happened in two seconds, and Junior was thrilled. He ran to the shade tree and tied the rope. Then he squatted and opened his buck knife, which glinted in the late-afternoon light. He cut a stick. Junior found just how far Butch could go. This was too good to waste, so Junior went back inside for another cold beer, then he came outside, cracking the stick as if he were an animal trainer. "Ha! Frank Buck! Bring 'em Back Alive!"

Junior had begun to beat Butch, who was straining hopelessly against the rope, snarling and whimpering with each blow. Nova heard the commotion, and when she saw what was happening, she ran from the window and out into the yard.

"You stop beating Miss Ada dog!" shouted Nova. "You stop that now!"

"Get the hell out of here, Nova," said Junior happily. He was pouring sweat, and his hair had fallen down in a dank lock over his broad forehead.

"Stop hitting Miss Ada dog!" Nova felt her soul coming up in her throat. The dog was dancing now, dancing in terror as Junior flailed away with his stick. The dog danced away and Junior chased it, always staying just out of its jaw range. "Stop it! Stop it!" Nova was screaming. Upstairs, Ada heard the sounds and pulled her pillow over her head, but Truly heard it too and came running downstairs and out into the dazzling heat of the backyard. It looked to her like a ballet. Junior was dancing with that dog, and Nova was standing nearby, holding out her hands in supplication and crying. Nova turned and saw Truly, who was walking with deliberate strides toward them. "Miss Truly, tell him stop hitting Miss Ada dog! Tell him!"

"Hi, Daddy," said Truly with a cloying smile. Junior backed up while Butch still danced.

"Well, hello to you too, sweetness," said Junior. "I'm just giving greetings to this mutt."

"Don't let me stop you," she said. Junior nodded.

"You got it," he winked. He waded back into the area where Butch could be beaten but could not fight back. Nova began to cry and ran off. Truly went and got a lawn chair and unfolded it and sat as close as she could.

The rope snapped and arched. In ten minutes, Junior was worn out and happy, and he and Truly went inside and watched a rerun of *M*A*S*H* on TV. Butch lay in the grass, licking blood from his wounds and starting to gnaw at the rope just below the noose.

Harry stood in the gun room and wheezed as he looked over the arsenal. That night, he planned to kill his older son, and he wanted to make sure he used the proper firearm. No one was at home but Harry. Snake had wandered off somewhere, and Leslie was bouncing around in the pasture. For so long he had been damaged, and now he was broken. Brains scrambled like eggs. There was the big Colt Python, and three or four .38 Police Specials. A .357 would be no good, because it just blew a man into bits. The .38 would make him suffer, but a slight error in aim and Snake might escape, even though it had good knockdown power. Ah. Harry took the Boss .12-gauge shotgun with the tight choke from the cabinet; its stock was worn and oiled to an awesome sheen. It had been a gift to him from his own father on his twelfth birthday. Harry felt like he was going to have a heart attack in the still, stuffy room: his chest was tight and heavy, and breath came in raspy gasps. Harry wore only a pair of boxer shorts. He had not shaved in two days now, and the shadow of his white beard sunk in with his pale cheeks. Harry held the shotgun up and broke it down to find it loaded; Snake often kept all his guns loaded. Harry slammed the gun shut and thought about his father. He had been a huge man with a violent temper, given to sudden towering rages, and once he had actually killed a traveling salesman who did not laugh at a joke. The old man called the sheriff, who came out and fetched the body away. They wrote the man's family in Ohio and told them he had fallen from his car while drunk and been killed. The sheriff got a note back in an old woman's hand thanking the people of Rockton County for their kindnesses. That was in . . . what, 1933? Harry couldn't remember. He aimed the gun at the front window, where the hot light was setting the panes on fire. He pulled the trigger. The blast blew the entire window out in a sparkling shower across the front porch. Harry half lowered the gun and pulled the other trigger and blew a hole in the floor. Up in the pasture, Leslie thought the sounds had been made by a hawk that was hunting for mice. This would be fine, Harry thought. Terrible wounds and a few moments to think about it. Then Harry would kill himself with the gun. Just take his time putting another shell in the gun and put the barrel to his forehead. Harry had long arms. When he was a boxing champion, his long arms were the envy of every puncher; that's what won me the title, he often told Snake, whose arms were short and so muscular they would hardly come over his head. So tonight Henry and I will be dead, Harry thought, and so what will become of Leslie?

Harry heard the back door slam and set the gun back in the rack and walked into the filthy den to see Leslie, sweat-streaked, coming in the room.

"Daddy," said Leslie. "Father."

"Leslie," laughed Harry, "Poor thing."

"Our brother is a ghost," said Leslie. "And I was not

afraid." Harry narrowed his eyes: had Leslie somehow found out that he was going to kill Henry?

"Who told you that?" rasped Harry.

"It was told to me by a hawk who could dance on clouds. He danced on a cloud, Daddy." Harry got his bottle from the table and took a swallow and surveyed the monstrous mess around them: tons of old paper, food, clothes, the final shift from man to animal. He started laughing.

"After tonight, this will all be yours," said Harry. "Stand up, boy. Attention!" They had played this game when his sons were boys, military drills that Harry remembered from the army. Leslie jumped to attention and smiled. Harry walked to the table and got his greasy old Red Man cap and brought it back over. "As commanding officer of this ship, it is my duty to give you the Navy Cross." Harry reached out and snugged the cap on Leslie's sweating head. It rested there. Leslie loved it better than a crown.

"I don't deserve this," Leslie said in confusion. He began to cry. "I never deserved an honor like this."

"Hell, boy," said Harry. "You earned it! Here, drink up." He handed Leslie the bottle and he took a gulp. The fire slid down his throat and into his belly. For a moment, Leslie thought he smelled the smoke of a gun and he knew, yes, they had fired a twenty-one-gun salute to him outside. He did not know how, but he was a hero. This was the best day of his life.

+ + +

Bubba O'Dair was in a fine mood, ripping the fried chicken skin off the meat with his perfect teeth. That was about the only thing perfect about Bubba, his teeth. Missy had loved his smile when she had first seen it in the ninth grade. Bubba was from Rockton, but Missy had moved there from Tupelo, fresh off the farm, eyes big as a dream. He had smiled at her the first day she got off the bus, and though he wasn't very handsome, that smile dazzled her, made her feel that Rockton was somehow much more than she had ever seen.

Missy had grown tired of Bubba's smile long before he had beaten her to death, and most often it had resembled a snarl, like some frustrated and starving wild beast. Bubba didn't know why he had killed her or what would happen to him now. He didn't much care. Maybe a few years on the chain gang would do him good. Wasn't that what his father had said? He thought of Missy a great deal, but he knew that her death had been in his fingers all along. He sometimes thought of their earlier days and cried, but tonight he felt good. He had done six hundred sit-ups and two hundred push-ups that afternoon.

Monk Reubens had just given Bubba the plate of food. They cooked food for the county jail out at the work camp, where state prisoners were kept. Maybe if he was lucky, Bubba would be able to come back to the Rockton County camp after a year or two at Parchment. He could work out on the roads he had raced, where he had spent half his life drunk. The prosecution was going to ask for the death penalty, but they didn't hardly execute anybody anymore, did they? Bubba wasn't worried.

Monk was alone in the jail with Bubba and Shine Caswell, an old man who habitually got plastered and pissed on a statue in front of the courthouse. None of the women in Rockton thought much of seeing Shine piss, since he was nearly seventy and had been doing it for forty years. They would grab their little girls by the arms and turn them away, but nobody knew what to do with him. Monk arrested him three or four times a month, but he didn't have any money, and it cost the county plenty to board him. So he'd be back out soon, pissing on parking meters, the statue, on the azaleas in front of the Baptist Church, on anything. The boys thought he was neat, the girls were horrified and disgusted, and the city fathers treated him like an ugly statue that kept popping up around town.

Shine was tiny and bent and loved to laugh and tell jokes. Shine also loved fried chicken, and so he slurped merrily at the thick white meat as Monk walked back to his desk. The door opened and Greg Crowell, Monk's top deputy, came in, looking worn out. He slumped down at his desk in the open room, tilted his hat back, and sighed.

"I just don't damn believe Junior Crawford," Crowell said. "He's got the blacks all upset and is turning this into a racial thing. Why in the hell would he do that?"

"He just wants somebody to hate," said Monk. "It's hard to find anybody to hate these days. You remember how it used to be. Everybody hated everybody. Now you have to really work at hate to make it any fun." Crowell laughed and shook his head. He was lighting a Salem when the phone rang, and Monk answered it. For a moment, Monk talked in monosyllables, and then Crowell saw him sit up straight in his chair, saw his mouth fall open slightly. Monk looked over at Crowell in disbelief. "Are you sure? Well, I'll just be damned. Of course I know him. We'll go down there and check it out, me and Greg and the others. Maybe he's got a good reason for it. But I doubt it. Yeah. Yeah. Okay, I'll let you know. Thanks."

Monk gently set the receiver on the cradle. Bubba O'Dair was singing "Whiskey River" while he chewed on his chicken.

"What?" asked Crowell. "What is it?"

"They got that print back," said Monk. "Traced it to a set we got on a misdemeanor case several years back. Turned out he wasn't guilty then. I don't know about now. It's Snake Ripley." Crowell's eyes seemed to fill with recognition, with fire.

"Snake Ripley," he said. "I'll be a son of a bitch. And he's got more guns than anybody this side of hell. Why would he do it? Why would he kill all those people?"

"Why does anybody do anything?" asked Monk. He stood and got a .45 from a cabinet along with a box of ammunition. "Get the shotgun and call the boys at State. Let's go see what Mr. Ripley's up to these days."

+ + +

Junior, having finished his second beer, heaved himself into the recliner and fell asleep. Truly stood and watched him, wondering when he would have his first heart attack and if it would be fatal. She knew it would not be this summer. She needed to feel alive again, and in this house she was feeling strangled and lost. She got her keys and went back outside.

Although it was nearly five, the sun was still high in the windless sky. Truly glanced at the crippled dog for only a moment before she climbed into her car. She wanted to see Snake, feel the power in his muscles, to see how he was coping with the blood on his hands. She flew down Deerskin Road, hitting 120 before easing back joyously, listening to a rock tape. She turned and drove out toward Ripley Garage, and when she got there and saw Snake's sign, she laughed, remembering how Snake never could spell, that his "illiness" was actually a hole in his shoulder that Agnes Longley put there almost as a reflex just before Snake killed her. Maybe his father had killed the others or maybe Snake had. She didn't care. Truly drove the rest of the way to the Ripley house and pulled around back. The decay hung over the house and barn like a halo.

Snake was sitting in the barn staring at his barbell, having decided that he would leave that night, just pack all he could and head out West. They could come and get him, but he didn't think he would ever be discovered. He wore his gym shorts and his boxing shoes but no shirt, letting the wound breathe. When he heard the Jaguar growling into the yard, he did not even move, knowing instantly who it was, what she had come for. How had Truly Crawford come into his life? She was just crazy as hell. I never was crazy before, thought Snake, just screwed up. And then I met Truly and everything went to hell.

Harry was asleep in the house, and Leslie was off somewhere in the pasture with his hammer. Truly got out and walked into the barn: she knew he would be there, he would always be there, where he could hit the bag and bleed and spit. She looked down at him, and he looked dazed and sullen, as if he would be sick.

"Look what the cat drug in," said Truly.

"Don't you ever feel anything?" asked Snake.

"I feel everything," said Truly.

"Couldn't prove it by me," said Snake. He sighed. "I'm getting the hell out of here tonight."

"Where?"

189

"West. I don't know."

"You going to be a cowboy? I can't picture you sitting on a horse." She sat down in front of him so close their legs entwined. Truly felt the faint pulse of electricity she always felt around Snake, and so she crossed her arms low and pulled her tube top off and sat in front of him, her bare breasts glistening with sweat.

"Jesus Christ, put that back on," said Snake. He stared at her breasts and shook his head.

"You don't really want that," said Truly. "God, it's hot. It's not fair that boys can take their shirts off and girls can't. Don't you think it would be more fun if all of us could take our shirts off?"

"I think you're crazy as hell," said Snake. He reached out and touched Truly's left breast, lifting it, dragging his rough fingers across it.

"Think you'll kill anybody out West?" asked Truly, closing her eyes in pleasure. Snake thrust her breast aside and stood and walked into the yard, heaving with fear and anger. Truly walked out into the hot light with him.

"You want Leslie and Harry to see you?" asked Snake angrily.

"I don't care," said Truly.

"I knew it wasn't me," said Snake. "It never was me, was it?" He shook his head and felt as if he would cry, though Snake never cried. "I never been loved by nobody in my life but Leslie."

"I been loved to *death*," said Truly. "It's not any better. You get loved to death, and you'll see that it's better to be just something terrible and ugly." Snake turned and looked at her and was stunned to see that Truly Crawford's eyes were well-ing with tears. "I'd rather be a corpse rotting on Main Street than loved to death. All I ever wanted was to be let alone."

"Being let alone's no better," said Snake.

"Then there's nothing," said Truly. Suddenly she felt better, and she walked inside and put her tube top back on, slipping it over her slick breasts. She came back out in time to see that Leslie had suddenly appeared and was climbing the chinaberry tree. He climbed out on a limb and swung down from it and dangled at arms' length, smiling at them.

"We should open the garage, Brother!" shouted Leslie. Inside, Harry awoke and walked into the kitchen and saw them outside. Was this a good time to kill Snake?

"What are you talking about?" asked Snake.

"People up there," said Leslie. He dropped heavily into the shade of the tree. "Come out here and see." Snake followed him around to the front of the house and so did Truly. Snake looked with his mouth open: at the garage, half a mile away, four or five police cars were parked, and he could see figures milling around.

"Son of a bitch," hissed Snake. "Let's get the hell out of here."

Truly felt her heart slamming against her rib cage, and she did not know if it was with fear or joy.

13

BEHIND THE PASTURES were the woods, and two miles past them, the terrain sloped down into a mucky bog that stayed putrid and wet even when it had not rained for months. The people of Rockton County had given it many names. On old maps it was called Hoke's Bottom, and later, Blake's Swamp. Now it was known only as the Black Swamp, and though the official county historian, Bradford Elms, had tried to prove that "Black" was merely a corruption of "Blake," nobody much cared. But they all knew it was the largest such swamp in north central Mississippi. The land was a sunken hollow that extended for miles, a geological freak crossed by several slow-moving, syrupy creeks. There was no record of anyone ever trying to cultivate the land. Even the oldest aerial photos showed it thick with huge trees. The only water moccasins in these parts had been identified there by a herpetologist from the University of Mississippi.

Hardly anyone alive knew the area better than Snake Ripley. Since he had been a boy, Snake had tramped the deepest recesses of the swamp, finding names carved on trees from fifty years before, stopping in wonder at the sight of an exotic and rare flowering plant that surprised him underneath a rotting log. If there was magic, it lay in Black Swamp, with its blooming fungi, the threat of danger, the nights full of raucous frogs and birds, even bobcats. Once Snake had tracked a bobcat for the better part of a day before finding it on a tree limb. Snake had killed it with one shot and carried it home, forty-one pounds, until his arm ached. He had tried to skin it and save the pelt, but it had gone bad, and Harry had thrown it away while Snake was at school.

One person once knew the swamp better than Snake: Harry Ripley. He had been born here, in this very house, and he had spent days hiking and camping in the swamp before going off to war in 1942.

Snake came running into the house with Leslie and Truly at his heels, and Harry, still in his boxer shorts, watched, mouth open, as they rushed into the front room.

"What are you doing?" asked Truly. She could not stop smiling. Her heart was pounding.

"Getting the hell out of here," Snake said. He knew what to do now, felt something in him breaking, as if bone and sinew had cracked and snapped loose.

"We could go in my car," said Truly.

"You're not going anywhere," Snake said. He stuffed the .357 Magnum in his pants. He filled a small musette bag with ammo and raced back into the kitchen. Leslie and Truly came with him.

"You can't stop me," said Truly. "You can't make me do a thing. I'll go if I want to."

"And get your damn head blown off, too?" asked Snake. "You want to hang on my cross, too?"

"Yes," said Leslie. His pockets bulged, and he carried the claw hammer in his thin fist like a religious relic, something rare and precious. "And I will go with you too, my brother, my ghost." Snake quickly filled a canteen with gurgling warm tap water and slung it over his shoulder. He stuffed a pack of matches in his shirt pocket and grabbed his T-shirt off the back of the chair. They would catch him in a damn minute on the road. He could spend days in the swamp and come out anywhere he wanted to, free, long after they had given up.

Harry came into the room and stared curiously at Snake.

"What in the hell are you doing?" asked Harry.

"Drop dead," said Snake. "I'm leaving."

"Wait a damn minute," said Harry. "What's happening?"

"Police all over the garage," said Truly. "We got to get out of here." Harry saw it all at once, saw his dream of the Holy Trinity of Death dying before him, saw someone else killing Henry, robbing him of this last glory.

"The hell," said Harry. He ran back toward the gun room and got the .12 gauge, jacked in two shells, and came back to the kitchen, but Snake and the others were in the backyard. Truly did not know where Snake was going, did not care, and neither did Leslie, who was dissolved in the ecstasy of transfiguration. They had almost reached the fence when Harry screamed. "Stop it, you son of a bitch!"

Snake turned and stared at the old man in his shorts on the back steps, not far from the shade of the chinaberry tree. He saw that Harry was holding a shotgun, felt his anger swell like a ripe maypop, ready to break.

Harry knew this was the end, that the jaws of the grave gaped for him in this sodden heat. He also knew that he could not yet fall into his death. This was a sacrament, a tide that would sweep him into hell.

Harry raised the shotgun to his shoulder and aimed it at Snake, who stared at the gun, not knowing what his father had in mind. Truly took Leslie's hand and ran to one side just as Harry pulled both triggers with all his might. Three pellets peppered Snake's shoulder. Snake was stunned, disbelieving that his father had fired at him, yet believing it more than anything in this world. Snake took the .357 from his belt and held it out with both hands and shot his father in the head. At first, Snake, seeing Harry fall onto the steps, thought the shot had been spectacularly lucky at this distance, but then Harry sat up, touching his bloody cheek, and Snake knew it was only a graze.

"Son of a bitch," shouted Snake. He hesitated and then turned, crossed the fence, and ran, Truly and Leslie right behind him. Truly caught up with Snake, and then Leslie, and long before Harry had run back inside and slipped into his clothes, they had made the edge of the woods.

+ + +

Monk Reubens and the others had been in front of the Ripley Garage less than five minutes, walking around it, looking for signs. Greg Crowell tugged at his crotch and spit into the blowing dust out front.

"This is weird," said Greg. "Would have thought one of
'em had of kept it open." Four or five state patrolmen were
starting to get back in their cars when they heard the gunshots. They all turned and looked down the road toward the
Ripley house. It wasn't at all clear that the sound came from
there, or what it was. "Was that thunder, boss?"

Monk looked up into the sky for only a moment. High,
thin clouds had blown in from somewhere, looking like the
dripping whiskers of an old man's beard.

"Guns," said Monk, who knew the sound. He felt paralyzed and thought of Mona and how much they still loved
each other after ten years of marriage, how little he wanted to
get killed, but how much this needed to be settled. "A shotgun. Let's get down there."

For his part, Harry had not waited. He could not wait for
police, for Snake to escape into Black Swamp without the
blessing of his father's lead. Harry could not remember having dressed this quickly, having moved like this, since the
old days in the service. He seemed to float off the filthy
floorboards as he dressed and then raced into the front room
to grab an old army-issue .45 that he had brought back from
the war. He got two clips. By God, this had some range. He
was almost out the door when he realized that his feet were
bare. Leslie's old sneakers were sitting gape-mouthed on the
back steps, so Harry sat, pulled them on, and laced them, his
gnarled fingers trembling so badly the strings would barely
cross and twine.

Harry took a deep breath and felt almost dizzy, then he
scrambled across the yard and to the fence. He leaned down
and tried to crawl through the rusted barbs, but he came up
too quickly, and his thin flesh tore for nearly five inches, and

Harry cursed and felt the blood begin to drip down his wasted back as he straightened up and started up the slope of the pasture and toward the woods. He had not gone more than a hundred yards when he stepped in a small hole and tripped, landing heavily on his left hand. Harry cursed again, and when he stood, he believed the hand might be broken. He winced.

"God will damn you, boy," he said out loud. "I brought you into the world, and I'm taking you back out." Harry held up his gun hand and screamed. "I'm taking you back! You hear that?" Harry could not see anyone in front of him, so he came on up the pasture and disappeared into the pine woods, still two miles from Black Swamp when Monk Reubens and his men got to the house.

Monk had already radioed back, telling Erma Owens, the decrepit but dependable dispatcher, to call the state and to let the mayor know about this. Monk cursed himself; he probably should have left half his men at the garage.

They drove up to the house, lights flashing, and came piling out in a blur of blue and raised guns, professionally fanning out around the cracking shack. Monk wished movies would stop portraying Mississippi sheriffs as potbellied morons; many were intelligent and articulate, and all had graduated from police academies. Few were better than Monk Reubens, and he knew that eyes all over the state would be on him. He took the position at the front door.

"Harry!" shouted Monk. "Harry Ripley! This is Monk Reubens. We got men all over the house. You and Snake and Leslie come on out of there." Monk waited, ear to the door, listening. He could hear the dry prattle of the television. "Come on out, Harry." He waited. Monk slipped the walkie-talkie off his waistband. "Y'all stay put. I'm going inside." No one said anything. The state patrol operated as backup at the pleasure of a county sheriff; it did not have jurisdiction.

Monk turned the handle, and the door fell back on its squeaky hinges, opening into the dusty hallway. Monk loved to read about the ancient Egyptians, to watch the specials on public television about archaeology. This was like opening some ancient tomb, a place of death, he thought. A hot blast of fetid air washed over him. The hallway was full of old newspapers and clothes and a hat tree that might once have been beautiful. The mirror on it had obviously been shot with a small-caliber gun, and Monk saw his own reflection split into millions of shards.

"Snake! It's Monk Reubens. Let's just do this easy," shouted Monk. There was no answer. Monk waited for a moment and then kicked open the door on his right and found himself in the arsenal. "Jesus H. Christ." Monk held his gun out at arm's length, gripping his right wrist with his left hand. The room was full of shotguns, of pistols and rifles. A shotgun was lying on the floor, trailing scattered shells that someone in a hurry seemed to have dropped. Monk moved through Harry's bedroom, still pointing the gun. The room was unbelievable. "Snake!" Monk waited. "Snake!" He came into the living room on the other side of the hall and found the TV going. The front room on the other side was the boys' bedroom, and no one was in there, either. The kitchen was in the back of the house, behind the den, and by the time Monk got there he was sure no one was in the house. It was a feeling you got. He could see his men off the screened porch, guns drawn. Monk kneeled and stared at what appeared to be drops of blood. He opened the back door slowly. "Nobody's here."

Greg Crowell was standing on the steps holding his gun, Adam's apple bobbing.

"Monk, Truly Crawford's Jaguar is out here," said Crowell. Monk stepped back into the glare and looked down at the car next to the barn. It looked bizarre, unreal, in this squalor. "This looks real bad for her."

"Did she know those boys?" asked Monk distractedly.

"This looks real bad," repeated Crowell. Monk walked under the shade of the chinaberry tree and looked around. He felt blind. He knew about Truly as everyone did, but nothing could make him believe she had anything to do with this: it was too grotesque to believe. No, she had innocently come to visit and been kidnapped.

"Fan out and look around," said Monk, and the men, guns still drawn, crept around the yard as if they were walking on glass, as if the yard were something precious and fragile. Monk walked loosely, the merciless light from the sun throbbing on his face faster than his own heart. Monk went into the barn and saw the heavy bag and the speed bag hung from the low ceiling, saw the barbell and dumbbells, the weight bench. He saw that the floor was covered with sawdust and a trail of dots whipped around it, dark blood. He was staring at the still-life abstractness of the heavy bag when there was a shout. Monk walked heavily outside and saw men standing at the fence, looking at something. When he got there, he saw that it was a piece of blue fabric, freshly torn. Just on the other side of the fence was the bright trail of blood, darkening.

"Tom says that that car is all Snake's got, Monk," said Greg Crowell. "They left here, they left in something else."

"Blood there," said Randy Carpenter, who worked with the state patrol's office on the other side of Rockton.

"In the house and the barn, too," said Monk. He suddenly knelt, feeling as if he would reach his own kindling point any moment and burst into flame. No. This town needed someone now, and if he was not the man, he would do his best to pretend that he was. He climbed over the fence and looked at the blood. It led up through the pasture toward the woods. "Billy, you better call Steve and see if we can get some more people down here."

"We got maybe four available," said Randy. "And the patrol's scattered, could be here in forty-five minutes."

"I don't know if we have that long," said Monk. "He's taken her, probably his brother and the old man too's my guess." Monk sighed heavily. "No. I'll call because I got to call Junior Crawford, too. You all go on and follow what you can up this way, but if it gets into the woods, stop and wait for more of us." Monk walked up the pasture for thirty yards and then came back slowly, more slowly than Greg had ever seen him walk. "It stays fresh going up that way."

Monk went back into the house and found the phone in the kitchen. He had never felt anything like this, not even in Nam. He felt as if he had stumbled into the jaws of hell.

+ + +

By five that afternoon, the thermometer just outside the kitchen window at the Crawford house had groaned up to one hundred and five degrees. The high ceilings helped keep the other rooms in the eighties downstairs, but the kitchen was hotter, and now Nova Jernigan sat on a high stool watching five thick, fatty pork chops fry in a bubbling pan of oil. A cake of hard cornbread was already in the oven in a black skillet.

Nova loved the smells of Southern cooking. Turnip greens boiled, filling the room with their acrid aroma. As she sat up to the counter, Nova took the large serrated knife and peeled and sliced potatoes for frying. Fresh tomatoes and cucumbers were drying on paper towels. She would slice them and break off fresh leaves of crisp lettuce to make a salad plate.

But she was almost trembling with fear. She had never seen anyone do what Junior had done to that dog. She had seen the power in the fat man's hand, the hate in his eyes. That kind of hate could do anything. Hadn't her own mother told her that hate even killed the Lord Jesus? Just before she died, she had told Nova, Lena, and Ailene that hate could eat a woman alive, that a black woman had to take more hate in this world than any other creature God ever made. Use that hate, she would say. Turn it back with your heart. If you turn hate back with your heart, the one who hates you will learn about love.

Hell, thought Nova Jernigan.

Butch had stopped licking his wounds and had temporarily even seemed calm. Nova had taken him a large pan full of water and an entire pack of bologna that Junior had bought on his way home from the Citizens' Committee's wanderings earlier that day. Nova looked out of the window and saw that Butch, refreshed, was up and pacing back and forth beneath the water oak where he was tethered. He seemed to be nothing but an unwinding ball of muscle and hair.

Nova did not see Junior come into the room, but she felt him and heard his heavy steps making the floor squeak lightly. She wanted to turn and scream. She often pictured things happening, and when people saw it in her eyes, it scared them. This was the hold she had had on Junior, the power that was now gone. She peeled the potatoes into the trash can and tightened her grip on the knife.

"By God, I feel great," said Junior. Nova did not turn but knew he was opening the refrigerator. She heard a beer hiss open. "I feel like a damn million dollars."

"That a lot of money," said Nova. Junior laughed.

"Why do I let your smart nigger mouth get away with so much, Nova?" Junior asked. He walked around in front of her and leaned against the counter. Nova glanced up and saw how his sagging gut had stripped the buttons from his shirt.

"I don't got a clue," she said. "Maybe it ain't nothing you can help."

"Maybe," Junior said suspiciously. He sipped his cold beer, loved the way it foamed up onto his palate. "Tell me something, Nova. You ever done it with a white man?"

"Miss Ada dog better now," said Nova, glancing up sharply at Junior. It would be so easy, a lunge straight into his demon heart. But she could not do it, not like this. "I give him water and feed."

"I don't give a damn about that dog," said Junior. "I'm going to shoot him anyway." Nova stopped peeling potatoes and held the knife up and pointed it at Junior.

"Don' you kill Miss Ada dog," she said angrily, waving the knife. Junior's shoulders started shaking as he grinned and chuckled.

"You're crazy as hell," said Junior. His grin made Nova think of grease.

"Yeah, I may be," said Nova, nodding and still holding the knife up. She went back to peeling potatoes.

"You may be," chuckled Junior. "You never answered me about doing it with a white man. Come on, Nova." Junior started laughing again, and he drank the rest of his beer in two huge frothy gulps, tossing the can toward the trash can into which Nova peeled potatoes. It hit the rim, scattering remnant suds all over Nova's lap. She was looking down at the flecks of foam and gripping the knife tighter when the phone rang. Junior let it ring three times before he lumbered over and answered it.

"Speaking," he said in high good humor. Nova watched him with the predatory alertness of a hawk. "Yes. Yes." Junior sagged visibly and his eyes went round. Nova came off her stool and felt her skin grow cold. "Oh my God in heaven." Junior groaned, and the phone trembled in his hand. Nova fleetingly thought the receiver looked just like a dog bone. "Oh my God in heaven. Yeah, I know where it is. Oh my God. How could this have happened? What was she doing down there? Oh no, oh no." Huge tears rolled down Junior's fat cheeks. "You're damn right. We'll all be down there in forty minutes. Lights and everything. That son of a bitch lays a hand on her I'll rip his throat out with my own hands. Yeah. I know. We'll be along." Junior hung the phone up and sagged against the wall.

"What wrong?" asked Nova.

"Truly," croaked Junior. "She's been kidnapped." Nova dropped the knife and screamed. The knife stuck in the linoleum with a thud. Junior felt as if his brain would explode. Nova Jernigan screamed again for no reason.

+ + +

Early in the afternoon, Ada had briefly lost both reason and control. She had felt it coming for days. Throwing all her paintings out the window was merely a prologue. She had not come down for lunch, had instead heaved herself into a roaring mood of violence. She had taken all the tubes of Grumbacher oils and started squeezing them out, watching them squirt from the tubes in thick streams of red and crimson and green and yellow. She began to squirt them on the immaculate walls of her studio, which had been Junior's bedroom when he was a boy, a room cursed forever with that man's stench, Ada thought. She shouted and cried and smeared the paint with her hands all over the walls until they looked like a child's finger paints, the bright colors changing to mud except for brief lines of light that remained.

By the middle of the afternoon, she sat in her nightgown, hands creosote-colored, her rage and fear having worn itself out like a thunderstorm. She cried for an hour and realized suddenly that this life was not life at all, that in every pore, this house exuded only crass evil and death. She had taken her large can of turpentine into the bathroom and poured the fluid over her hands and washed them repeatedly, first with turpentine, then with soap, turpentine, then soap. Her hands turned a raw sienna.

She had dressed and put on a pair of old white gloves and sat before the window. She would leave all this, move back to her childhood neighborhood and start over. It was never too late to start again. She was sitting there sweating when she heard Junior coming up the stairs. She did not move when he opened the door and saw her there.

"Baby, something horrible has happened," he choked. Ada could not remember Junior speaking with this much fear. She stood and turned and looked at him, and what she saw was not a man; it was nothing, a messenger from another world.

"What?" Ada asked.

"It's Truly," said Junior. "Lord, it's Truly." He shook his head heavily. So, thought Ada. This is what has happened.

"She's dead," said Ada. "How did it happen?"

"No, no," said Junior. He came toward Ada but stopped when she began to back into the corner. "She's been kidnapped. And it's worse. She's been taken by a boy named Ripley, and Monk Reubens says they got fingerprint evidence he's the one killed all them folks."

"Christ Jesus," said Ada. Junior turned away from her slightly.

"I'm going down with the Citizens' Committee now," he said, clearing his throat. "The bastard's took off into the woods behind his house, Monk thinks." He didn't tell Ada about the torn cloth and the blood. "I'll get her back, baby. You trust me, I'll get her back."

"You'll get her back?" said Ada. She turned and walked to the window. Her shoulders were shaking and Junior came to her and turned her around to say it again. When he did, he saw that she was laughing, that her eyes had narrowed into slits.

+ + +

The pine woods filled with hot light. Snake moved ahead with Leslie and Truly just behind, burrowing through a cave of dense air, farther into the trees. Leslie whistled some joyous unknown song. They had walked hard for half an hour before they struggled up the crest of a hill overlooking a creek path that cut below them in a sinuous twist. The creek was dry. Snake was moving on adrenaline and instinct, not knowing where he was going or why. Something was perilously close to breaking in his heart.

"I got to sit a spell," said Snake as they came to the dry

creek. Ferns bobbed as they passed, wizened fronds of the deepest green. A huge fallen tree almost black with moisture and fringed with emerald moss thrust out before them, and Snake sat on it and dropped the canteen. "I got shot again."

"Let me see," said Truly. Snake pulled his shirt back and Truly could see three black pellets beneath his translucent skin like ripe berries ready to break into their own juicy season. Blood ran down them as if they were merely thorn pricks, a crown of blood upon his shoulder. "Look at that. The pellets are still in there."

"You're cut, too," said Snake, pointing at Truly's back. She did not try to feel it or look. She knew where it had torn, how the barbs had felt ripping along her flesh.

"Yes," she said. Snake started breathing hard, hyperventilating. "What are you doing?" Snake kept breathing deeper, not talking, and then he captured his breath, and his face contorted as he reached down and tried to pull the pellets up to the surface of his skin. Blood blossomed everywhere. Snake's right hand trembled violently, but he could not get the lead out of his flesh. He took his hand away. The shot was too deep; it would have to be cut out. Snake stared hopelessly at the dry creek bed. "I could bite them out."

"Get away from me," gasped Snake. "Just get away."

"Oh, I'm here for you, darling," smiled Truly. "Sort of like Bonnie and Clyde."

"God," said Snake. "What are you doing out here?"

"Does it make your blood boil?" asked Truly.

"You're crazy as a shithouse rat," said Snake. They sat in silence for a moment, their bodies slickening with sweat. "Where's Leslie?" Snake stood, feeling mildly faint, and looked through the woods. "Leslie!" His voice was thick and dead in the heavy air. "Leslie!" Snake turned around and around. "Dammit. Leslie!"

They heard it before they saw anything, a chanting like something from a monastery, over and over, then suddenly louder as Leslie came floating down the creek bed from somewhere to their right.

"There is no death, there is no death, there is no death," Leslie chanted. His arms were out to his side, and Snake thought he was pretending to be an airplane; when they had been small boys they had played Air Force, holding their arms out and bombing each other. Leslie kept chanting. When he got closer, Snake could see he was holding the claw hammer at arm's length.

"Leslie, please hush," pleaded Snake. He struggled to his feet and took a sip of the water and handed the canteen to Truly. She licked her full lips and wrapped them around the canteen and swallowed. Leslie came up to them, smiling.

"There is no death, Ghostbrother!" said Leslie.

"Cut that stuff out," said Snake. "Why don't you go on back to the house. Just get away from me. Truly, take him back to the house."

"I'm not leaving you," laughed Truly.

"Entreat me not to leave you," blurted Leslie, who looked confused about what the words meant. Snake offered the canteen to him, but he refused it. "I cannot drink your vinegar."

"It's water," said Snake. They were staring at each other. Snake began to feel a little light-headed from the loss of blood, and his shoulder felt as if it had been stung by thousands of wasps. Snake heard something. "Sssshhhh."

"What?" asked Truly.

"Shut up and listen," whispered Snake fiercely. The sound of heavy, sliding footsteps could be heard at the top of the hill. Snake stood and looked up there. At first he could see nothing, but then the outline coalesced out of the fabric of a rising mist or fog: Harry standing up there holding a pistol at arm's length, looking as horrible, as terrifying, as anything Snake ever saw.

"Our father," said Leslie. "Up there in heaven! Our father!"

"Hush up!" Snake said, and he moved straight off into the dry creek bed. They crept down it, bent over like a secretive caravan of hunchbacks, moving down a hundred yards, and then climbing back up the creek bank. A hot wind caught the tops of the pines, and they swayed back and forth. Snake kept looking back up the way, but he had lost sight of his father. Harry was clearly crazy, had killed all those people, and here they were in the woods, the blind leading the blind. The wind stirred three crows, who cried above them and flapped away. Snake led them up the pine-needle-covered slope past an area littered with granite boulders the size of horses. He and Leslie had camped here several times when they were boys, building huge fires to ward off the phantoms of the dark woods. Snake always said that the night did not frighten him, but it was mostly bravado for his brother, who could not bear the cave of night deep in the woods. "Stop a minute."

Truly was glad she had worn her Reeboks. They were good for walking and did not rub on her heels. Of all her adventures this was the strongest and the one from which she had the least fear: she had been born to run with blood into the night. She belonged here, if only for these blessed moments. Snake craned his neck and listened. For a moment they heard only the groaning and creaking of the trees. Then the steady drumming of footsteps in the leaves and needles.

"Come on," said Snake.

"Where are we going?" asked Truly.

"Hell," said Snake. He did not see that Leslie's smile had turned to a deep frown or that moments later as they struggled up the slope, his brother's cheeks were wet with tears.

14

HARRY COULD NOT believe his luck.

Snake was merely following the old paths that had been there for years, wandering off them a few yards, but heading toward the swamp along the inevitable track of his own youth. The terrain conspired to make this the traveled trail. Back years before, Harry had tracked a whitetail for three days in these woods and down into the swamp. As he walked, he felt the sweat of that chase in his heart.

His breathing was ragged, but his chest did not hurt much. Harry thought of the deer as he tramped after Snake and the others. He had been lolling one late autumn day among the pines when the flash of white had drawn his eye, and when he wheeled he saw the animal staring at him, eye to eye. Harry raised his old rifle and shot with the instinctive gauge of a born hunter, but the shot had not even buckled the deer's legs, though it drew blood along its shoulders. Yes, Harry thought. He smiled. It was just along this area of boulders that he had seen the first blood.

He could hike for miles then, break down the will of any living thing he wanted to hunt. Sometimes the crimson trail nearly faded out, but as the deer's heart kept pumping out its blood, Harry kept right after it, saying later that he could smell the blood. Harry always said that a true hunter could smell blood like a dog smells rabbits. In the swamp, six miles from the house, Harry had finally cornered the animal, which had given up, quivering and exhausted. It sank to its knees, and just as Harry had drawn a bead the animal had shivered and fallen over, dead. Harry had cursed and cried at this foul luck. But he had slung the carcass over his back and carried it home, more than one hundred pounds of meat for the table. Harry smiled. He was a man then.

But his smile faded and his jaw became grim. In a few hours it would be dark and what then? Should he keep after Henry or go ahead and kill himself? He knew: his older son must die with him and pay for the destruction of *his* life. Harry knew how it felt to kill now, and it was nothing. You pull a trigger and someone falls and blood leaks out of them. Life was not so very far from death.

The pine trees had faces. Some snarled at Harry as they bobbed about in the hot wind, and others seemed ready to break down and cry. The boulders had faces. One looked for all the world like Theodore Roosevelt, spectacles and all. Harry could hear them all muttering, babbling in words no human could understand. The trees were like fisted hands, threatening.

Harry followed their trail easily, exulting in the pretty

tread of Truly's sneakers. He walked steadily, stopping sometimes to listen: Harry Ripley's hearing was still as acute as it
had been on the troop ship, where he had often been brought
on deck to listen to the waves for anything unusual. Harry
would do his duty, terrified of the swelling waves, of their
ponderous immensity and depth. If he fell in out here in the
Pacific Ocean, how long would it take for him to hit bottom?
Harry listened now and heard the deliberate steps, three sets
of them cracking small windblown pine limbs. He kept his
eyes on the next hill.

And he thought of his childhood, the misery of poverty
and the photos his uncle had taken that day he was playing
Army under the house. He had come running out and hit his
head on the sill, bringing bright blood down his crying face.
That picture was still in the attic somewhere. Tender thoughts
crowded Harry's mind, but he became more scornful with
each step.

"Shit," he said. "Nothing but death. The worst damn luck
a man ever had, to be born when I was." Harry began to think
strange things.

He felt as if lizards were crawling inside the skin of his
arms.

He thought for a moment that he was wild game cooking
inside a stifling oven.

Each footstep seemed to reach almost to the ground but
not quite, so that he was gliding on a carpet of dank air.

But Harry took a deep, painful breath and drew the anger
back into focus. Whenever things became unclear, you
healed them with hate. Harry started to feel better, and his
feet hit the ground firmly. Everyone loves this goddamn
county so much, Harry thought. No one knows that it's held
together with hate.

Harry came up the hill past the boulders. It was only a matter of time before they stopped for the night. Harry had stayed in a running battle with Archie Holmes of Jersey City on the troop ship, and once Archie had hit Harry in the back of the head with a hammer. Harry remembered the stun, how it felt. How much would a self-inflicted gunshot wound resemble the pain of that hammer blow?

He would do it. Then there would be nothing. Another carcass on the forest floor.

+ + +

Junior Crawford felt sick. It had not taken forty minutes for sixty members of the Rockton Citizens' Committee to gather at the Ripley house: it had taken less than twenty. Junior loved the feel of his .38 in its taut leather holster, but all he could think to do now was to kill this Ripley kid. If he harmed Truly, Junior would rip his throat out bare-handed.

Bud Gilhooly and Junior stood by the fence looking at the police cars. Neither had ever seen so many in one place. They counted twelve state patrol cars, all three sheriff's cars, the five from the City of Rockton, a couple that were obviously SBI, and sheriff's cars from two adjoining counties. Men were crawling all over the place. Bud had known Junior since boyhood. They had never been friends, but Junior enjoyed Bud, who had not finished eighth grade and raised hogs now. Junior enjoyed anyone he could easily dominate.

"I'm just as sick as I can be about you girl," said Bud.

"He hurts her, I'll rip his throat out," said Junior. "Don't care if I go to the electric chair. I'd kill the son of a bitch in a heartbeat."

"Hell yes, you would," said Bud. "I would, too." Junior could scarcely stand Bud's stench; he smelled like pigs. "And

I tell you, there's not a man in Rockton County would convict you. Wouldn't even come to trial." The men were milling around, holding rifles, handguns, shotguns. Junior, by dint of his wealth and the horror of the kidnapping, was now more than the nominal leader of the Citizens' Committee: he was its heart and soul. The others were almost in awe of his impending loss. His only child, and a daughter at that. Nothing worse for a man than losing his only girl. Junior stood and stared at Monk Reubens, who talked forever to some man in a sweat-stained white shirt and black tie. Finally, Monk started walking slowly toward Junior. The other men were assembling. Something was about to happen.

Junior felt strong. If he could only kill something. Monk looked pale and weary as he came toward the men. It was nearly six-thirty by now, and the thin clouds that had blown in earlier gave way to a few heavy, late-afternoon cumulus and dry flashes of heat lightning.

The lawmen were assembling, obviously ready to head off into the woods toward Black Swamp, but toward what? Monk came up and touched Junior lightly on the sleeve and walked aside, past Truly's car, past the workout barn. Everyone watched them. Junior had the most to lose or gain.

"We're ready, Monk," said Junior, holding his enormous stomach above his belt for one moment and then letting it go. Monk nodded.

"Junior, you reckon Truly knew this boy at all?" asked Monk softly. The sheriff wasn't sure what to think. If Truly had been kidnapped, why was her car here? You don't kidnap somebody in a car.

"What in the hell are you asking me?" said Junior sharply. "She stopped for some gas at the garage, and that's when he took her." Junior's face began to quiver. "She's a beautiful girl and . . ." His shoulders shook with unspilled tears, but he fought them back. "Hell, it's a small town. She probably knew him from school." Junior drew as close to Monk as a conspirator. Monk could hardly bear his closeness, but the power of his loss and his gaze kept Monk pinned and sweating. "I see him, I'm going to blow his damn head off."

"I know how you feel," said Monk, "but you can't. You talk like that, you can stay here." His words were soft and firm, and Junior realized how best to play this.

"Well, not actually kill him," said Junior, looking off toward the woods. "It's just that I'd like to."

"We'll let the law handle it," said Monk. "We don't even really know it was him."

"Hell, you believe it was, though, don't you?" asked Junior.

"Yes," Monk said after a long time. "I do." Monk walked away and stood in front of the Citizens' Committee. No gun was even to be drawn except in self-defense. They would fan out in flanks, Junior and his men moving off to the left, all the lawmen up toward the right. Junior would carry a walkie-talkie to stay in touch with Monk. The sheriff did not say it, but he believed Snake had gone up toward the east, cutting through the woods back over to the road. Why would anyone deliberately go toward Black Swamp? "I don't have to tell you this man's armed and dangerous. Greg here's followed spatters of blood up to the middle of the field, where they peter out, so we know somebody bleeding was up that way. The state crime-lab folks will be here soon and type the blood, start putting stuff together. Chances are we won't find anything, but we got to look." Monk glanced at Junior's pink, sweating face and wondered if his presence was a colossal mistake. But a man had a right to look for his own daughter. Monk thought about the boy he'd never had.

"Let's get after it, then," said Monk. "Don't get too far, and let's don't stay out all night." The men on the Citizens' Committee glared and grumbled, flashlights dangling from their belts, guns on hips and in hand. Christ Jesus, thought Monk, look at all this firepower. "Junior, you see a thing, you call me. Is that clear? One spot of blood, one piece of torn cloth, a footprint, anything, you get on the horn and call me." They'll wander around for a few hours and feel good, thought Monk.

"Right," said Junior, and he thought, *hell no I won't call you.* As they crossed the fence and went into the pasture, Monk Reubens felt something was strange, even sinister. What was it? Yes. No one was making a sound. No one spoke a single word.

+ + +

Ada sat in the kitchen sipping her third glass of Harveys Bristol Cream, trembling as its sweet fire scalded her tongue and throat. She had cried for an hour, but no more. She did not know why she had laughed when Junior had told her of their only child, but something was perfect about it, inevitable.

"Do you know what makes a true artist?" Ada asked Nova, who sat in a chair beside her, sipping her third cold beer and feeling miserable and thick with sweat.

"No'm, I don't have no idea," said Nova. Ada opened her book of Van Gogh's letters, setting her cigarette down in the heavy crystal ashtray.

"Listen," she said. " 'I feel that my work lies in the heart of the people, that I must grasp life to the quick.' " Ada gently set the book on the table. "Do you understand what that means, Nova?"

"No'm, I reckon I don't," Nova admitted.

"The deepest part of life," said Ada. "It means being a person who loves better than anything else. Who loves his wife with such unending passion and devotion that she would never stray, that each day would be like an unfolding flower. Great artists have great loves. Fools love like fools."

Nova did not know she was going to say it, much less that Ada would agree. "Mist' Junior, he a fool," she said sadly.

"A damn fool," nodded Ada. "He doesn't know how I feel, and he doesn't care. It's this house and everything in it, the history of the place. It stinks with history, doesn't it, Nova?"

"Yes'm, it do that," said Nova. "Wouldn't never be my house."

"Or mine," said Ada fiercely. "I just wish . . ." Her voice broke, and then she thought of Van Gogh and held her head high. Even if she were the last one on earth with noble thoughts, she would act on them. "I just wish I could have done better with Truly. I don't really know what happened. I should have been stronger." Nova thought of Truly's white-hot lips and trembled with lust and horror.

"Miss Truly run everything her way," said Nova. "She get anything she want. Not a man or woman can make her do a thing she don't want to do. It take some kind of beast to make her change, I reckon."

"Her father's some kind of beast," said Ada, her face furrowed in fear, eyes wide. "My God, he's nothing but some kind of animal. What is it that makes a human being turn into an animal, Nova?"

"Maybe it forgetting all the rules," said Nova. "It thinking anything okay to do in this world you feel like."

"It's worse," said Ada, tears flowing again. "It's much worse, Nova. It's denying that love exists or that it saves everything. Love is the only thing that saves us, and it's died in this town. At least, it's dead for me. And we all just stood back and watched it die, and we didn't do a thing about it."

"Love something I don't know much about," said Nova. "About all I know about's surviving. I try to look past all this, keep my eyes on the Lord, but He's done left this town, too, Miss Ada. I didn't know the Lord'd leave a town. This town done flowed over to the Devil."

"I'm married to the Devil," said Ada, shocked at her words. She drained the Harveys Bristol Cream and felt choked, sure that she would leave soon whether Truly was alive or not.

"You sure is," said Nova, not caring what happened. The room was silent as Ada sucked the smoke from her cigarette. "How come you's to throw all them pictures out you window, Miss Ada?"

"Pictures," laughed Ada bitterly. "What are flowers worth in a town like this?"

"Most everybody flowers dead from the weather," said Nova. "Except Miss Buford. She water them flower like she baptizing something." Nova drained her beer and went to the refrigerator and got another one. "How come Rockton got so many little old lady?"

"Because it doesn't have men who live long," Ada said. "A town this corrupt makes its men go quick."

"I don' know," admitted Nova.

"Do you remember when you were a little girl, Nova?" asked Ada, not really listening to Nova's confusion. "Remember how you thought that the world always looked like it does on Easter Sunday morning, fresh and starched and full of hope? That people loved one another and lived full lives and then died surrounded by their friends and loved ones? Do you ever recall feeling that, Nova?"

"Maybe once or twice," said Nova. "I remember the sound of folks crying. My daddy dying, I remember that, Miss Ada. But I know what you mean. It was always the spring feeling made us whole, I reckon. That things-is-growing feeling you got after winter went away."

"I never really believed in evil up there in Memphis," said Ada, her eyes losing their focal point. Nova thought Ada might just drift up to the ceiling and float along the old plaster. "I was the apple of my daddy's eye. Everything was crisp and beautiful. We would sit around the table and our maid, Annie, would have set the places perfectly with our Wedgwood. And I would sit there and look at those lovely blue patterns. There were Chinese houses on the plates and waterfalls and bridges. The more I ate, the farther I went into the story I made up. A beautiful princess lived in the house, and she would walk out onto the arched bridge and wait for her lover. He was in the navy and, oh my Lord Jesus, was he handsome. When I finished my plate, they would be standing there, and she would be looking into his eyes and he into hers, and the setting sun would be on their faces, and she would turn her face up to his. . . ." Ada's voice trailed off into silence as she held a cigarette in one hand, the empty glass of sherry in the other, and stared at a spot on the table.

She looked up at Nova, tears flowing down her cheeks. "I wonder what ever happened to them?"

Nova also began to cry. She got up and walked around the table and leaned over Ada and put her walnut-colored arms around Ada's heaving shoulders and hugged her.

"I done always loved you," choked Nova. Ada waited for only a moment, sensing them again, the handsome naval officer and the lovely princess, and then she buried her face against Nova's thin chest and wept for a lost world.

Butch had gnawed half the rope and then quit, content to sit in the shade and sip the water that Nova had brought him. His long pink tongue trailed bubbles of foam into the grass. He turned his head from side to side and stared across the sunburned lawn at the kitchen windows. He could hear the small murmur of friendly voices in there. His injured foot ached, so he held it over the good paw, shifting occasionally to ease the pain. The paw had hurt since he had been run over as a small puppy. Butch began to whimper as he listened to the distant sounds of crying, and he stood and began to limp back and forth on his frayed rope like a lion gone neurotic in a cage that was too small. He licked and gulped. Halfway across his restless pacing, he saw the rope and grabbed it like a living thing, a snake in the dusty yard, and he began once again to gnaw on it, the low growling scratching the edges of the still, sodden air.

They stood at the crest of the hill. Below them, the land dissolved into the dark edges of the swamp. The light was already starting to pull back toward the tops of the thick oaks and pines. Lightning bugs lilted below them into the gloom.

"We're going into *that?*" asked Truly. She was drenched with sweat and becoming bored with the entire escapade. "I always heard of that swamp. How come we're going in there?"

"I'm going to lay low until I can get the hell out of here," said Snake. "I don't give a damn what you do."

"I've never laid low before," said Truly. "I just hope I don't get bit on the ass by a possum."

"Probably the only thing in the county hasn't bit you on the ass," said Snake. Truly grinned. As they came down the hill, Leslie laughed terribly. Snake realized right away that something was changed: instead of the sodden muck that had always been there, the floor of the swamp was dried and hard. Chips of mud turned up on their edges. He had never seen it this way. But he knew the path deeper into the swamp unerringly. It was a small hump of clay worn by deer and bobcats, wild dogs, and the occasional human who wandered in here for no good reason.

Snake remembered when he had gotten lost. He was twelve years old and had been following a red-winged blackbird with his first gun, a .22 long rifle with an oiled walnut stock and a blued barrel. God, he loved that gun, still had it in the gun case. Deep into the swamp, he realized that he was lost, got turned around and wound up coming out on the other side, near Rockton. He had gone to a farmhouse and called Harry, who picked him up. He had taken Snake home and beaten his legs with a thin stick, raising blood blisters that looked like a mountain range on a topographic map. Leslie had stood by and shouted, "Don't kill my brother!" but Harry had shoved him out of the way.

A dank, sulfurous odor arose as they walked farther. The dried mud gave way to damp earth and then a thin film of water with a patina like a swirling rainbow. The swamp was deep and threatening as the smell increased.

"It smells like something's dead," said Snake.

"It smells like everything's dead," grimaced Truly, holding her hand to her nose.

"There is no death!" said Leslie. They moved on, and Leslie hung back, then caught up, extended his arms like wings and moved just into the muck and then back. They had to jump across two turgid, tea-colored streams that bent back and forth in the gloom. Birds cried with increasing volume and vines twisted and flowed down into the water.

Filaments of blood trailed down inside Snake's shirt. Truly watched the muscles of his back as he walked, and wondered how strong he really was. Could he crush someone's head between his hands? He could kill. Would he kill anyone else?

"Maybe we should sing a song to pass the time," said Truly.

"You're crazy as shit," said Snake. "It's around here somewhere." He and Leslie had camped in the swamp three or four times on a swollen lump of land that overlooked the juncture of two small creeks. It could be close. The light above them suddenly began to go out, and Snake snapped on the flashlight, but not before the air began to fill with lightning bugs. They made a necklace around the trees. To Leslie they looked like Christmas tree lights, so he began to sing "Santa Claus Is Coming to Town" in his soft, choirboy voice. Truly giggled.

"Cut that out, Leslie." He stopped singing and they

moved down the path close together, Snake following the beam of the flashlight. Snake was looking down when he felt as if his knees were buckling, and he realized he was walking uphill. He swung the light up and saw it. "Hot damn!"

It was a level piece of ground, a plateau raised above the swamp by twelve or fifteen feet, some sixty feet long and forty feet across. Solid oaks hung above them, and the plateau was bearded with ferns.

"We're going to camp here?" asked Truly. Snake turned and shone the light on her. Leslie was not behind her.

"Where is Leslie?" Snake asked.

"He was right behind me," said Truly. "I don't know where he is." Snake cursed, and they had walked back down the trail a hundred yards when there was a sloshing sound off to their right. Snake turned the light, and Leslie was standing at the foot of a large, dead tree, hugging it. He still gripped the claw hammer tightly in his right hand.

"Leslie!" shouted Snake. His voice died in the leaden air. No sound went very far in this swamp. But it was enough to turn Leslie toward them, and he stood back from the tree and smiled and waved. He was knee-deep in water. "Leslie, you're gonna drown! Get back up here!" Leslie slogged back toward them and Snake pulled him out. He was smiling broadly.

"I thought I had found the place, Brother," said Leslie. Snake just shook his head. Leslie knew that he was going to be a hero now, that he would be the one to save them, save their immortal souls by his act. He had never felt better in his life.

"You never will," said Snake. He went back to the plateau, and they climbed back up the slope and gathered limbs, and soon Snake had a fire crackling in the middle of what seemed to them an island. The light scarcely made it to the edge of the plateau, much less into the swamp, which seemed to be moving around them. They drank from the canteen, and then Snake found two huge logs and put them on the fire. When there was more light, they felt safer. Snake got up and walked to the edge of the plateau and looked into the gloom, wondering if anyone was out there. Hell, he thought, nobody with any sense would be out there. He sat back down close to Truly. Leslie cried and jumped up and ran to the foot of an old tree.

He wept and kissed the tree.

"Oh, Leslie," said Snake, shaking his head.

Truly laughed softly. Leslie did not care. He did not see a tree there in the shadows of flame. He saw above him something so wonderful that it took his heart. It was not a tree. It was the Old Rugged Cross. Leslie wept for joy.

+ + +

Harry was having another heart attack.

He sat at the base of a tree in the sudden gloom and clenched his teeth, trying to fight off the deep pain in his chest. He hugged himself and his arms trembled, the flaccid flesh wavering, his eyes shut in fear. He did not mind dying, but he had not yet killed Henry, and dying without taking that blood back would leave his journey unfulfilled. He did not know where he was for a moment, and then saw by the faint light of the rising moon that he was on the edge of Black Swamp on the old dog trail. The moon hovered in front of his eyes and then clouds gathered on wings of lightning.

It had come on suddenly. Harry had been feeling fine

when it had slammed into his sternum with the anguish of bad news, buckling his knees and bringing him down. But he had never passed out, and now the pain was starting to ease slightly. Harry held his gun and flashlight between his legs. If the pain got too bad, he was going to blow his brains out, but now it was easing and his breath, though full of strange wheezings and squeaks, began to slow perceptibly. Great streams of sweat slithered down his chest. Then Harry slept.

When he awoke, the pain was gone, and he did not know that only thirty minutes had passed. He sat up on the cracked mud and flicked on his light, waving it around. The beam caught something fluorescent, two glowing pools, and Harry came back to it and stopped, his hand trembling. The light froze the buck, which had been foraging for grass at the edge of the swamp. Harry saw the great spreading rack, wider than anything he'd ever seen shot in Rockton County. How old would such an animal be? Harry held the light on the deer and got his .45. It was so heavy he could barely hold it up. When he fired, Harry realized the stupidity of his act, real- ized that he had missed by yards as the deer bounded off, that his shot had shattered a low-hanging limb.

A mile away, Snake thought he heard a gunshot, but Truly convinced him it was only thunder. A mile the other way, Junior Crawford and the Rockton Citizens' Committee knew better.

"I'm the biggest damn fool ever lived," said Harry. He got to his knees and smelled the acrid stench of cordite, and then he was sick. When he sat back up, he felt better, and so he pulled himself up the trunk of the tree and stood on wobbly knees, peering down the trail and into the swamp. It was full of strange birds and exotic flowers.

Harry stuffed the gun back into his sagging trousers and began to totter after the flashlight beam. His feet instinctively knew the trail, knew how to stay on it. He shuffled and sang old songs from the military very softly. He closed his eyes briefly, then opened them, closed them, opened them. He felt his feet edging into water and knew that he was off the path, but when he shone the light down, he could see nothing but the rancid flow of water around rotting stumps.

"Oh, Lord," whispered Harry, stopping and looking around. Thousands of frogs began to drum for the darkness. The sound was as heavy and deep as an approaching storm. Harry walked about a hundred feet and found himself on the edge of a nameless creek, a chunk of water that heaved itself along without banks. "Oh, Lord." The water was knee-deep. Harry shone the light up the twisting creek and saw something floating toward him, an *S* that appeared to be in pain, writhing. Then Harry could see that it was a cottonmouth, swirling in the water, something as evil as a man had ever seen. "Oh, Lord!" Harry stood transfixed as the snake came toward him and then seemed to hang, suspended in the water, its eyes glowing coals. Harry stepped back when he saw the snake's awful head, its heavy diamond-shape rising briefly from the flow as if to speak. Harry shuddered and then the snake turned and swam with the water, heading to a deeper part of the swamp.

Harry turned completely around three times, like a beacon on some forlorn coast. Bats descended from the treetops and banked and swooped around him. The air was full of bats. Harry slogged straight ahead and fell to his knees in the black water, his face not three inches from a bloated frog that shrieked, bug-eyed, for the rain. Harry pulled the gun up and put it against the frog's face, holding it there for a moment before he realized the animal was gone. Where had it gone? How could things disappear so fast in this swamp?

He stood and walked straight ahead, grunting and groaning. Vines grabbed at his shoulders, and great whorls of briers tore the thin flesh of his legs. A bobcat's angry screech came from somewhere to his left, so he turned right. The water was suddenly thigh-deep, and Harry felt white lights revolving in his brain, messages from another world. He watched another snake swim past. Two more followed it. Harry began to feel his chest hurt again. The next one, he knew, would be the last. He took a deep breath and walked straight ahead. Once, he fell in the water, but he scrambled right up. His face was bleeding from Snake's bullet, but it felt no different from the mud or water.

"Oh Lord!" Harry shouted. "Oh Lord!" He fell again, and his cheek pressed on a mound of hard-packed clay. He held the light out and saw that it was the path, the path after all, so Harry crawled up on it, laughing and then crying and then laughing again. He sat up and saw that the swamp was moving, that everything was moving in no direction at all, in circles, in swirls, looking for something to kill or some carcass to devour.

Harry Ripley stood, feeling his heart pumping once again, stood and headed deeper into the black stillness.

15

SERGEANT LOWELL PALMER of the Mississippi State Patrol sat in the living room with Ada Crawford, holding a sweating glass of tea. He was a short, compact man with gray just beginning to shade his temples, and his nose was aquiline. Ada looked at his hands, and they were strong yet sensitive. Nova had brought a fan into the room, and now it blew across them on the couch.

"You'll have to forgive this couch," said Ada, cutting her eyes at the protruding tufts of stuffing. "My dog sort of went on a rampage the other night." She laughed girlishly and moistened her lips. Sergeant Palmer sipped the tea and looked the couch over.

"Don't apologize, ma'am," he said. "I know you weren't expecting company. This is just an awful thing."

"I appreciate your kindness, Sergeant," said Ada.

"Lowell," he said, nodding. She smiled vaguely. "So what kind is it?"

"Pardon?"

"What kind of dog is it?" he asked.

"Oh," she laughed, "he's a Doberman." The mere word strangled her as she thought of dogs. "They have a reputation, you know. But he's really sweet."

"What's his name, ma'am?" he asked.

"Ada," she whispered. "My name is Ada."

"Ada," he repeated. It sounded to her almost like a vow, their repeating each other's names. "His name is Butch."

"Butch," nodded Sergeant Palmer. "I got a Boston terrier. Well, actually, it's my girl's. I hate it. Its name is Tippy. My little girl named it that because its toenails tip on the linoleum. Tippy. What a name for a dog."

"Oh, it's a fine name," said Ada. "So you have a little girl, Lowell? Where do you live?"

"Just outside of Oxford," he said. "Yeah, we have a girl, or rather my ex-wife, Clare, does. I see her on weekends. Name's Honey. I mean her real name. Clare loved that Bobby Goldsboro song? I wanted to name her Louisa after my mother, but Clare was stubborn, the stubbornest woman I ever saw." He sipped his tea and nodded as if he had made some point.

"How old is she?" asked Ada.

"She's eight now, be nine in December," said Sergeant Palmer. "Growing right up. She'll be courting before you know it." He laughed and shook his head, but when he looked up at Ada, he saw that she was staring vacantly across the room at an old clock that was clacking away on the mantel. "Oh, God, I'm sorry, Mrs., uh, Ada. Don't worry. They'll get her back."

"Oh, goodness," said Ada. "Would you like something to eat? I've asked Nova to stay over for a few hours. She makes the best apple turnovers you ever tasted. Dusted in cinnamon. My manners are not what they ought to be." She looked at her gloved hands and wished she had died before she had smeared the room with paint earlier that day.

"Oh, I don't think so," Sergeant Palmer said.

"Oh, it's no bother," said Ada. "Nova! Nova!" She waited for a few moments in the heavy silence before Nova came slowly into the room, now very drunk and trying with her tongue to bring wetness back to her lips. "Nova, make Sergeant Palmer some of those apple turnovers, would you?"

"Apple turnover?" asked Nova, narrowing her eyes.

"Yes, Nova," Ada said, looking nervously at Lowell.

"You girl done been took by a monster, and you want me makin' apple turnover?" asked Nova.

"Now, Nova," said Ada. "My husband is down there attending to things with the Rockton Citizens' Committee. With the help of all those lawmen, they'll have Truly back here in a few hours, I'm sure. You need a little faith in my husband."

"Faith, hope, and charity," giggled Nova, leaning against the wall.

"Now, Nova, you get a grip on yourself and go cook us some apple turnovers," said Ada.

"I'm really not all that hungry," said Sergeant Palmer helpfully.

"Oh, tosh," said Ada. "We always have something for visitors. Especially men in uniform. We always honor men in uniform in this house."

"Oh, is your husband a veteran?" asked Sergeant Palmer.

Ada's lips shaped the word while Nova slid down the wall laughing silently. Nova got up and stumbled back into the kitchen and got out the flour and took five red Delicious apples from the bowl on the table.

"Well, not actually," said Ada. "You'll have to forgive Nova. She's been very upset by all this. People react differently to such things. I mean, people tell the awfulest jokes when something bad happens."

"They do," nodded Sergeant Palmer. He shifted on the sofa.

"Would you be so kind as to excuse me for a moment?" asked Ada.

"Of course," he said. "I'll go check in with the radio in the car. See if they've heard anything."

"I'd be most grateful," Ada said. She drifted through the dining room and into the kitchen, where Nova had turned on the radio to a rock station. Nova held the small paring knife in her thin fingers and turned it around an apple so that the skin came off in one piece and fell into the trash can.

"Miss Ada, I sorry," Nova said. "I don't mean nothing. I never knowed how to act." Ada looked at her and shook her head gently.

"I don't mind," said Ada. She smiled. "I really don't. Why is that? All I ever wanted was a family to hold and love, and I got this. Why did I get this, Nova? Why did God do this to me? What did I do to deserve Junior and Truly?"

"Don't nobody never do nothing," said Nova. "It just what number you draw. Ailene say God got a big book with you name in it, and he done already got you life mapped out, saying everything you gone do, if you get love, everything. I'd be scared of God if I ever seen him."

"I'm afraid of him," said Ada.

On the radio, some man said it might rain at any time.

The men poured through the woods, following their flashlights. Soft mumblings melted together with the clank of key chains and limb-cracking boots. They held their guns up and looked back and forth, eyes narrowed. Monk Reubens and the lawmen had moved off to the right since no one could follow the trail of blood. Even dogs had lost the scent in the fecund odors of field and bog. Monk was covered in sweat, and he was now wondering if this night search had been a mistake after all. They could have gone anywhere.

Monk thought of Mona, thought as he often did that their names had the same letters but one, that she was not beautiful, but the way she looked when she saw his face was beautiful. The woods came to the crest of a hill covered in pines. They stopped and listened, walked on, then stopped again. None of them spoke. They could hear thunder far off.

+ + +

Junior Crawford was swaggering big-bellied down the last hill of the woods and toward the swamp. All his life he had heard of Black Swamp but only seen it once, when he'd come with the Boy Scouts and his troop's old scoutmaster, a man named Toole, who had been killed when Robert Whitsun's laundry boiler exploded in 1952.

"This place stinks like the end of the earth," said Bud Gilhooly. "I went to the Okefenokee onct on my way to Daytona, and it stunk too. How come swamps to stink, Junior?"

"Who in the hell knows?" asked Junior. He halted the men, who were spread out a hundred feet through the woods. There was no visible way to get into the swamp, and Junior took out his Swiss army knife and cut a large chunk out of a small tulip poplar that sprouted near him.

"That's gone kill that tree," said Gilhooly, to Junior's disgust.

"Go to hell, Bud," said Junior. He held the light up to his own face so Bud could see the furrows and the anger. The men crowded around, sweeping the trees and shadowed rocks with their flashlights. The scene was terrible to Junior, faces nothing but hollowed cheeks and eye sockets, shuffling men, turning and bobbing men everywhere. A bobcat cried in the swamp, and they all went silent.

"Jesus Christ, listen to that," said Wink Walker. Wink worked at the cotton mill. "It's a damn cougar."

"Bobcat," said Bud Gilhooly. "You tie up with a bobcat, you'll wish you had a cougar. Meanest animal God ever put on this earth. I heard of a man over in Sparks had his arm pulled off by a bobcat."

"Hell," said Wink.

"God's my witness," said Bud.

"Just shut up," said Junior. Some of the men mumbled on, opening foil bags of Red Man for a chew as they waited for Junior to speak. None of them seemed to think it was odd that Junior had taken over the group so quickly. "Everybody come on up here. Fred. Jake. Y'all come on." They gathered on the side of the hill. Junior looked terrible and awesome in the light, his face pale and sweating, hugely fat. "My baby girl's somewhere in there with that monster. I don't know about y'all but I'm going in after her. I can't ask all of you to go with me, but are there ten men, brave and strong, who will go with me?"

"I heard that in a TV program," said Wink. "That 'brave and strong' thing."

"Shut up, Wink," said Junior.

"Well, them woods is full of snakes and shit," said Bud Gilhooly, looking around. "I'm more afraid of a snake than a nigger with a brain." A few laughs cracked around the edges of the light.

"I'm going," said Junior.

"Shit, let's get at it," said Norman Wright. No one said much else. Birds sang. In the pine woods, the moon was strong, but the light died away into the swamp. Junior turned and let his weight carry him down the hill, going faster and faster until he was out of control, grabbing at limbs and falling face first into a clump of dried ferns. He climbed up, cursing, having scraped the top of his head.

"I'm okay," he called, feeling like an idiot. He leaned against a tree. He looked down and saw the chips of mud and walked straight ahead until the mud began to get sticky, and then he was sloshing in a thin film of water, feeling the blood trail down to his lips. The men came after him, lights swaying back and forth. Guns were drawn. The water began to get deeper. A vine grabbed Junior and threw him down into the water.

"You okay?" asked Bud Gilhooly.

"Get away from me," said Junior. "Just get the hell away from me." Junior was leaning against a tree, his mouth open, ready to kill something, anything. A shout came from off to the right. Men started drifting that way, and Junior stood almost alone in the darkness. "What is it?" he called.

"A path!" someone shouted. Junior slogged toward the cluster of muted lights, and Bud Gilhooly was leaning down looking at something, and when Junior came past the other men, he saw that it was a small piece of blue fabric clinging to a brier bush.

+   +   +

The fire had fallen to a sullen popping. Truly danced around the plateau, singing. This was the best thing that had happened to her all summer, life full of the intensity she craved. If only they had thought to bring a bottle of bourbon or wine—hell, anything. Truly danced and sang.

Snake's wounds had clotted, and he sat in front of the fire wondering why his life had fallen apart. A few days before, he had been only frustrated and unhappy; now his blood and his life were leaking out here with Truly and Leslie. What had brought him here? What had he done wrong? Leslie was clearing limbs out from around the tree and singing hymns under his breath.

"You could get killed a hundred ways out here," said Truly as she sat down very close to Snake. "You're going to let the fire go out?"

"What am I doing here?" asked Snake of no one in particular. "How did I wind up out here? I didn't plan to do this with my life."

"Oh Christ, don't go gloomy on me," said Truly. "You'll ruin all the fun." She snuggled up to Snake and put her arm around his shoulder. "Don't you think this is really fun?"

"What in the hell is wrong with me?" asked Snake. "And you? You're probably going to rot in jail. Somebody's going to kill me, and you're going to rot in jail, and you're so happy."

"Jail?" laughed Truly. "What are you talking about?"

"Agnes Longley?" said Snake. "Remember her? The old lady we killed?"

"Oh, honey, I never killed a thing in my life," said Truly. "I don't know what you're talking about."

"Right," said Snake.

"Well, it's true," Truly said, sitting up. "Why would anybody kill all those people? You really did do it, didn't you? I mean, I promise I won't ever tell anybody, but you really did kill Dr. Smith and all those people, didn't you?" Snake pushed her hard into the brush and stood up, trembling.

"I shot Agnes Longley in self-defense!" he screamed. "That was all. Dammit, you are the stupidest bitch ever lived." Truly got up and came to him. Snake did not know what to do when she put her face close to his.

"Come on," she said. "Did they squeal when you were about to shoot them?" Snake's face twisted into a silent fury, and he hit Truly as hard as he could with the back of his hand. She staggered and fell face down and did not move. *What have I done?* thought Snake. *Oh Lord God*, and he kneeled down and turned her over and blood was trickling from the corner of her mouth, and Truly Crawford was laughing. Her eyes were bright and she was laughing. "You fool." She laughed more. Then she scrambled past him and ran down the edge of the plateau and into the darkness of the swamp, out of the weak firelight. Snake went back to the fire. Leslie was walking around the tree singing "Shall We Gather at the River."

"I'm not coming after you," said Snake. "I can't stand this."

"Stand what?" called Truly. The sound of her body falling into the water echoed across the plateau, and Snake turned and looked. He cursed ever meeting her, and then took his flashlight and waved it over the swamp and saw nothing.

"Where in the hell are you?" asked Snake. "You're going to get killed in there."

"Stand what?" asked Truly. She lay in the fetid water with only her face showing. She sat up, dripping slime. The frogs around her had gone silent. She was laughing when she stood and walked back up the slope toward Snake; filaments of gooey weeds clung to her neck, and her nipples were visible through the wet fabric of her shirt. "Who's dead?" Snake looked at her in the thin light and could not believe anyone such as Truly had ever lived. She came toward him, arms out, blood dripping from the corner of her mouth and all over her wet shirt. When she got to the top, she took the tube top off and stood before him, her breasts shimmering with water, sweat, and blood. Snake looked at her breasts and felt the familiar tug of lust. She smiled, was smiling when Snake pulled her to him, smelling the odor of death, of swamps. He kissed her and tasted blood.

Truly knew she had Snake now. She knew she could have anyone she wanted.

+   +   +

Harry staggered forward toward the uncertain beam of his flashlight. His mouth was open, and he gulped in the dank air. If this was hell, he was spinning deeper into it. Harry's shoelaces flapped against the underbrush.

He stoked his anger like a furnace, and now it was nearing the intensity of light, going from red to white. Harry fed off the anger, always had. When he was a boy, it was the size of his fists that had cleared the paths before him. And in the war, too. He had flattened anyone who had not broken before him, and they all stayed flattened, by God, except for Henry.

Hadn't he taught him to box? He had given the kid all the tools. Henry had won Golden Gloves titles, hadn't he? I did that for him, Harry thought. He never loved me. That boy never loved me. Harry began to cry.

Leslie loved me, but what is Leslie? Don't have a damn idea. Started out just like anybody else, and then it was watching a car slip on ice. He started to get foggy, and by the time he was fifteen, he was wandering off. Hell yes, he was. Lost two days' business at the garage, and they found him in the 4-H camp carving napkin holders. Hell, that was fourteen miles away, and he'd walked the entire way. I don't know what in the hell Leslie really is. Some stuffed animal come to life.

Harry's breath came in ragged gasps. His stride became a stagger. A wisp of bramble brushed his shoe, and he fell off the mound of clay and into the water. The flashlight was waving light underneath the canopy of limbs, and then it went out. Harry was in profound darkness. He sat up and felt first for the .45; it was still tucked heavily in his pants. Then he felt for the flashlight in the water. Harry began to cry and his nose ran, and he cursed as he splashed around, feeling for the light and imagining the sinuous glide of serpents. He was suddenly afraid and leapt up and fell again into the water, stood and finally found the heaped path and got up onto it.

He lay there for a long time. Birds were shrieking, and frogs by the millions drummed from the trees. Harry groaned. He was afraid. He got to his knees and began to crawl down the path, drooling and babbling, finally making random noises that blended with the moving screech of the swamp. *"The Lord,"* he said out loud. He wept and crawled, tearing the frail skin of his hands on briers, ripping his knees.

"The Lord is my shepherd, I shall not want," said Harry. "I shall not want . . . anything *but to kill Henry Junior.* The Lord is the thing to kill Henry Junior. He leadeth me beside the still . . . swamp, he leadeth me beside . . . what in the hell does he lead me beside . . . yea, though I walk through . . . the valley of death, I will . . . be afraid of no . . . oh Christ."

He stopped. He almost thought he could hear voices against the eternal racket of Black Swamp. He sat up.

"Ssshhhhh!" Harry said. He looked around him and saw nothing yet, but glimmerings were starting to filter from the moon above the thick branches. "Sshhhhh!" Harry laughed. Who in the hell was he shushing? He stared through a bush. A creek cut through the darkness, and light from a break in the trees illuminated it, painted it gold and glowing. Harry listened again, and he could hear it, the sound of a faint voice.

He thought about Truly Crawford. Harry felt faint now, wondered if he was about to die, but his chest did not hurt at the moment and he could move slowly along the path toward something. If it was a path, it had to lead to something. Hell, hadn't he been the first one to really know this swamp? Hadn't he hunted its deer and rabbits, wandered away from the stench of poverty when he was a boy? Hadn't he brought meat for the table?

Harry began to claw his way along the path. He stood finally and walked on the sides of his blistered feet. Bats filled his eyes, his ears, his mouth. His eyes went black with the darkness of hell.

When he stopped to swat the bats away, he could hear the voices again. Now, he was very close.

+ + +

Truly and Snake had done it standing up against a tree, and now they were both pulling their pants back up. Snake hefted the gun and walked back to the dying fire. He threw several black limbs on the dull glow, and it was popping angrily in a couple of minutes. They could hear Leslie crashing around on the other end of the plateau. Snake sat and stared into the flames.

"It wasn't you," said Truly.

"You think the hell I don't know that?" asked Snake.

"It's just like an urge I have all the time, like an itch needs scratching," she said.

"I done my share of scratching it," said Snake. Truly laughed and stretched. She felt so good. She wondered if someone would come and get her soon.

"I'd like to say I loved you," said Truly. She could still taste the blood, but it was hardening. The side of her mouth was swollen, turning dark. "But the fact is I don't love anything. Never learned how." She sat down not far from Snake. They could hear Leslie singing a hymn.

"I learned how, but didn't nobody ever care," Snake said. "My daddy's the meanest man ever lived on God's earth. Ruined my whole life."

"My daddy ruined my life, too," said Truly. They were silent for a moment.

"What are we doing here?" asked Snake to the fire. Leslie

came by them humming happily, and had taken a few steps past the fire when he gasped with delight.

"Our Father!" Leslie cried. "Our Father, who art in heaven!" Snake jumped up and swung the gun around in time to see Harry standing not forty feet away at the edge of the plateau.

"Get the hell out of here, Leslie!" screamed Snake. Leslie, suspended between his brother and his father, backed slowly to one side, still holding his claw hammer. Harry was holding his .45 up straight at Snake's head. He wanted to shoot Snake in the head.

"You lost, son?" cackled Harry. He began to cough violently, but he never took his eyes or the barrel off Snake's head. His chest was hurting again. "What you doing out here in the middle of this swamp?"

"What *are* you?" asked Snake. They stood pointing their guns at each other, waiting.

"I'm *you*," said Harry, beginning to grin. "I'm everything you ever were, everything you'll turn into. Except I'm turning you into a corpse now." Harry's chest was torn in half by a spasm of pain, and his face contorted terribly.

"No," said Snake, beginning to cry. "Damn you. No." Harry suddenly could not breathe at all. He stumbled forward two steps, his face white as ivory, dark sweating circles under his eyes. Harry fired twice, both times hitting limbs far over Snake's head. At the same instant Harry fired the last time, Snake pulled the trigger. A burst of gunfire blazed into Harry's chest, into the heart that had already stopped beating.

Harry hung still for a moment. The noises of the swamp became deafening. Harry's mouth was open, and blood was pouring out. He dropped his gun, but the hand hung out toward Snake for a moment. Harry fell forward heavily and curled into a fetal position, groaning and writhing for less than five seconds before he was still. Truly had hidden behind a tree and was watching Leslie, who had come stumbling out now, looking back and forth from Snake to their father, disbelieving, begging with his eyes that it be some strange dream.

Snake fell to his knees as Leslie ran to Harry and rolled him over. He was covered with blood, and his eyes were open and staring, pupils dilated and fixed. Leslie tried to say "Father," but the word would not come out, and he instead kept making fine bursts of some unknown *F* sound. Truly felt her heart beating wildly. She came to Leslie and pulled him back from the corpse and took him over to the fire, which was starting to grow dim again. Snake had not moved.

"Well, now you've done it," said Truly. Snake turned and looked at her. She was shaking.

"What *are* you?" whispered Snake. "Did you fly up from hell to make all this happen?"

"You're going to scare Leslie," Truly said. "And you ought to know where I'm from, John Henry Ripley. I'm from Wentworth Street in Rockton, Mississippi. I'm from good stock. My ancestors helped settle this county." She shuddered again. "Leslie, you sit down and catch your breath."

Leslie sat. Snake stared at Truly and felt his mind going numb, felt himself fading into the murky darkness. He stood and walked over to Harry, who was stone dead and lying on his back. His eyes were already glazing over and his veins sinking.

"We should bury him," choked Snake.

"Let's go home," said Truly. Leslie held both his hands

up near his face and started looking at them, both sides, over and over.

"You get the hell out of here anytime you want to," said Snake. "Go on!" He stood and came toward Truly. "Get up, you damn bitch! Just get up!" Truly felt better now and stood. She wondered if Snake would hit her again. She hoped he would. She hoped he would break her skull wide open and spill her brains all over a rock.

"You are white trash," Truly said, leaning close to Snake. "Just plain trash." Snake's eyes went wide, and he started gathering every limb in sight, throwing them on the fire, more and more, until the flames leapt twenty feet into the air. He turned his face to the sky and screamed. He raised the gun over his head and fired it three times.

Snake danced around the fire like an Indian. If there were lawmen out looking, he'd bring them on, go ahead and end this horror, take Truly to jail with him. The hell with killing her. Snake chanted and sang and danced.

Leslie saw Snake's arms out and realized his brother would soon turn into a hawk and fly up to heaven with Harry. He would be the last one left in the family. He ran to Snake and tried to hold his wings down so he would not flap again.

"Don't leave me," cried Leslie. He ran to Truly and stood in her face. "Don't let him leave me! He's going to fly up to heaven!" Snake felt a deep tenderness for his brother, but it could not last.

Snake screamed and screamed and screamed.

+ + +

The limbs nearby were creaking. The first drops of rain hit like gunshots on Ada Crawford's back steps, where Nova sat in disbelief. Nova had made five fresh apple turnovers and dusted them with cinnamon. Then she had made coffee and put it in a silver pot, cream and sugar in their own silver containers. Sergeant Lowell Palmer of the Mississippi State Patrol was hungry, and he and Ada ate the pastries and talked about their families. Ada said that Truly was her darling, and then she wept several tasteful tears before going on to other things. Nova had listened to them talk in the dining room, eavesdropping.

Truly. Nova was thinking of her again and crying. Why hadn't Truly loved her? It was what this house was all about. She could see Ada slowly tearing herself away from it all. *I could do that*, Nova thought. *I could be strong. You can start over any day if you are strong, just walk away from the heat of hell into the light.*

The rain began to blow. The lightning was still far to the north, but it forked and broke like a deep groan. Nova walked out into the rain. It was amazing. This was not rainfall; it was separate, heavy drops that assaulted anything unprotected. Nova's dress began to get wet, but she did not move from the rain. She looked up and saw dark, roiling clouds in each flash of lightning. She had seen these clouds in a picture, but which one was it?

Twenty yards in front of her, Butch ran back and forth, tongue out, excited beyond measure at the coolness of the rain. When Nova finally saw him, she thought he might be a demon. That was when she remembered the clouds: in her Bible, on the day Jesus died, those black clouds had come over the whole earth. Something sacred was dying, Nova thought. She fell to her knees and prayed to God with all her might to show her the way.

Inside, Ada Ripley was giggling, her gloved left hand on Sergeant Palmer's knee. She leaned forward slightly, remembering to keep her lips moist.

"And you remember the car with the hundred-gallon gas tank?" asked Ada. "That was one of my favorites."

"Allen Funt was so funny," said Sergeant Palmer. "We used to watch that, my wife and I, when we were first married. I wonder what ever happened to that show?"

Ada started to answer, when she heard the sound of rain.

"My word, Lowell, isn't that rain?" she said. They listened and could hear it clearly, hitting on the front hedges.

"I believe it is," he said turning. He set his coffee cup down on the coffee table.

"You eat that last turnover now," Ada said. She picked it up with her gloved hand, and when Lowell shook his head and smiled, Ada stared at the jewels of cinnamon that clung to the pastry as if the turnover were the most terrible thing she'd ever seen. "Well, my husband will eat it."

"It's starting to come down out there," said Sergeant Palmer. "I didn't think it would ever rain again."

"Shall we sit in the porch swing?" asked Ada. He was already tired of this, tired of baby-sitting this wretched woman who was trying to please him with such painful desperation. "I've always loved the cool breezes when a thunderstorm comes. I've never been afraid of storms."

"Fine," said Sergeant Palmer. They went out to the front porch and sat in the swing, which was turned to give them a view of the fine gardens and the rain. Palmer was afraid the swing would break under their weight.

"Don't you just love a stormy night?" Ada exulted. "It

makes me feel like I'm in a Rembrandt painting. Don't you just love art, Lowell?"

"I don't know much about that, Miz Crawford," Sergeant Palmer said.

"Ada," she said.

"Ada," he repeated.

"Well, great artists knew how to love well, Lowell," she said. "That was what separated them from the others, not their talent with a brush. Lordy, lots of people can paint. But great artists love well. Except those that are queers." She brought her hand to her mouth and giggled. "That was just awful, wasn't it?"

"Kind of comes with the turf," said Sergeant Palmer.

"My husband," said Ada, and then she stopped and looked out at the rain, not remembering exactly what she was going to say or why. "Lots of wrecks in weather like this."

"And it won't help the search," said Sergeant Palmer. "That's not good."

"What search is that?" asked Ada, leaning a little closer to him.

"Your daughter, ma'am," said Sergeant Palmer.

"Oh," she laughed. "I almost forgot. My husband will find her. That's what I was going to say. My husband will find her and bring her home. You can count on that." Ada began to tremble. Lowell Palmer turned to her and saw that she was shaking.

"You okay, Miz Crawford?" he asked.

"I told you to call me Ada," she said. She began to tremble violently. She stood and wrapped her arms around herself and felt the hopelessness of this place, the utter horror.

"I'm sorry," he said. "I'll go check back on the radio." Ada turned and tried to smile at him.

"Oh, tosh, it's pouring, Lowell," she said.

"I really need to," he said. He walked out into the rain, and when he got inside the car he radioed the dispatcher at the Ripley house.

"This is Grady, go ahead," a voice said.

"Y'all got anything?" asked Sergeant Palmer. "This woman's really coming unglued."

"Not a word," said Grady. "Not a blessed word."

Ada walked into the house and straight upstairs to her room. She took a large suitcase from the closet and laid it on the bed. She began to stuff it with dresses, underwear and bras, cold creams and depilatories. Rain came in the windows. She turned sharply and cried out.

The house was breathing. *The whole goddamn house was breathing.*

16

THE MEN WERE running single file down the path deeper into the swamp, Junior Crawford out front wheezing and panting. The gunshots and screaming were not far away. Junior held his gun in his fat fist, and he felt the tissue of his sanity breaking. He desperately wanted to kill something, anything.

When they had heard the shots, Bud Gilhooly had turned to Junior sharply.

"Call Monk, Junior," Bud had said, gesturing toward the walkie-talkie. "Get them other boys over here."

"Right," Junior had said, trembling. The members of the Rockton Citizens' Committee were pouring over the edge of the trail, a few afraid but most ready to start shooting. "Search One, this is Search Two, come in." Junior waited two seconds, knowing damn well there would be no response be-

cause the volume was turned off. Then he cursed and started
trotting forward, gun in one hand, flashlight in the other.

Now he was gasping for breath, panting like a dog almost, mouth open. The screaming was closer. It was the
most terrible thing Bud Gilhooly had ever heard. Suddenly
the screaming was close. Junior stopped, and Bud Gilhooly
ran into him full steam, knocking him flat into a bush of
brambles.

"You stupid . . ." hissed Junior, pushing him away and
trying to get up. Junior rolled off the path and into the black
water, making a terrible noise. He climbed up, slapping Bud
with the back of his hand.

"It was a accident," begged Bud.

"Shut your mouth," said Junior angrily. "Listen." The
men behind him toned down their trembling voices at his
command. He felt the power of command surge through his
fingers. He thought: *God, I am a natural leader of men, I
should have been in the war, could have been a captain, maybe
even a major.*

"God, that sound makes me sick," said Jimbo Fischer.
They listened for another second.

"Look yonder!" cried Elmo Waters. Elmo worked at John
Blankenship's Chevy dealership as a grease monkey and was
under five feet and had only seven teeth. "Over 'ar!" They all
turned to the right and saw through the murk a dull flame of
orange a hundred yards away, like someone had struck a
match against the night.

"Come on," said Junior. "And keep quiet, goddammit."
They moved slowly along the trail. Junior thought: *I am a
leader of men, an example to all of them, and wherever I go,
they will follow.*

Snake was bleeding profusely from the wounds on his shoulder. Gouts of blood pumped out and down his chest. He kept screaming as he began to run back and forth. Harry had always taught him to think of boxing like a hundred-yard dash. Always pace yourself like you are running from home to the store and back. And remember that the last three rounds are like the final heat before a race.

"Final heat!" Snake screamed. Truly Crawford was immensely entertained. She clapped rhythmically, and then she stopped with an idea. She screamed at the breaking point of her heart. Leslie was climbing the tree now into that spot where the branches forked, knowing his time on this earth had come to an end. Already, his brother was turning into the hawk that would fly with their father up into heaven. Leslie's blond hair was stuck to his face with sweat. He got to the crotch of the tree and grasped the hammer tightly in his right hand. First, before he did it, he would have to pray. He held on to the limb and closed his eyes.

"God bless Henry Junior and Daddy, God bless little Leslie and the hawks that rise above us. God bless Truly. Amen."

When Truly screamed, Junior's skin turned to ice. Men cursed, and they all ran faster and faster. The trail curved, and suddenly they were only forty yards away from this high spot along the dark path. Snake heard them coming.

Junior saw Snake running back and forth around the fire. Truly heard the sounds of men talking, of splashing in the turgid waters of the swamp. Her heart raced. She stood and ran to the edge of the plateau.

"Help me!" she screamed. "God help me!"

"Don't hit her!" Junior screamed. "Fan out around them."

As if he were George Patton, the men obeyed, slogging around the plateau, surrounding it as Snake ran from one corner to another. Leslie could see them out in the swamp. They were devils. He must save his friends before the devils came up to steal them to the minions of hell.

"Come on and get me!" chanted Snake. Truly screamed, her hands around her face like a heroine from a silent movie. Men splashed all around them.

"Truly, come on!" Junior screamed. She turned toward the sound.

"Daddy?" she cried. "Oh God, Daddy, come help me!" She made herself start to cry. Junior felt his heart cringe and bleed. This was more than a man could stand. Hell, even Monk Reubens would understand that. It was too much.

Men had their guns leveled at Snake. The fire was at its height, blazing angrily, and Snake knew that this was what he had been born for, to live in misery, die in misery, to pay for the weak blackness of his father's words.

"Leslie," he said, turning to his brother. Then he raised the gun and pointed it at Truly Crawford.

When he did, the men began to fire. Junior emptied his gun. Snake was hit more than twenty times as Truly fell to her stomach and found herself face to face with the swelling corpse of Harry Ripley, who seemed to be smiling at her, saying, Look, here is what the world is all about. To Snake, it felt like getting hit by several good body blows. He knew for ten seconds that he was going to die. He propped himself up on one elbow and looked at Leslie. He wanted to say he loved him. He made a word that started with an *L*, then a 30.06 bullet hit the back of his head.

Truly saw his head explode. He fell face down, twitching

for a moment. Junior ran up onto the plateau and others followed, slogging up out of the mire.

"Baby! Baby!" cried Junior. Truly thought her father looked ridiculous in the firelight, his huge stomach folded out from his shirt and over his pants. She came to him, and he enfolded her in his fat arms, pecking small kisses across the crown of her head. "It's okay, baby, Daddy's here. I saved you." The words were like a bracing gulp of brandy, so Junior Crawford said them again: "I saved you."

"Look up in that tree!" a man shouted, and they all turned to see Leslie standing in the crotch of the tree, smiling at them.

"Don't shoot him!" screamed Truly. "He's off his rocker. Snake made him crazy." Leslie saw them all there below him. He felt a chill glaze his skin and knew that he, not Snake, was the Son of Man. This was all his, the people of his heart and hands. And he must do this thing for all of them.

Leslie held his arms out wide.

"Father forgive them," said Leslie. With a swiftness that surprised them all, Leslie reached into his pocket and took out a twenty-penny nail and knelt and put the point of it on the top of his left foot, which was bare and flat against the tree. "Remember that I did this for you."

Leslie drove the nail through his foot in three swift strokes.

"Christ God Almighty, look at that," said Bud Gilhooly. Another man, surveying the carnage and seeing Leslie's act, stumbled to the edge of the plateau and got sick.

"Oh, my God," cried Truly.

"You all right, sweetness?" asked Junior, turning her from Leslie's act. "Did he hurt you?"

"He beat me and raped me," said Truly. "I'll go to the hospital to confirm the rape, of course. Oh, Daddy, get me out of here."

For a moment, he thought her words odd, but Truly was always saying strange things.

Leslie's face was twisted in pain. He had no idea it would hurt this much. Blood poured from the nail in his foot, but he took another nail in his trembling fingers and placed its point on the top of his right foot. He drove the nail through his foot and into the tree in one great arc of hammer through the gloom. Men cried and fell back in horror from the spectacle. Leslie stood in the crotch of the tree on his broken feet and spread his arms out in a rough cross and thought of hawks soaring through the summer air, of a place where they were all happy and together, Harry, Snake, and Leslie.

"He's gone die up there," cried a man. Leslie looked wearily down upon the man and shook his head.

"*There is no death,*" Leslie whispered. He hung suspended for a moment in the tree and then, feeling faint, he turned and hugged the limb. This was his moment. He just knew it.

Nova Jernigan wandered through the house, feeling its mass loom over her: a silver tray, crystal goblets in the china cabinet, the ticking clock Junior's grandfather had brought back from Europe, the creaking of her feet on the floorboards. Ailene and Lena would be worried about her by now, probably thinking she was dead. If that man really took Truly, there was nothing to fear in this house.

Then why was she terrified? Why did the high ceilings

and the debris of the Crawford family bring her down so far? At least the rains had come. A cool breeze blew through the house as Nova wandered around with a bottle of Miller Lite in her soft palm. A sound percolated upstairs. The sound of crying.

Miss Ada crying, thought Nova. She walked up two steps, listening to them creak. The house almost moaned from the wind and rain. When she got to the top of the stairs, Nova walked slowly down the hall to Ada's room and then went inside. Ada was finishing with her suitcase, closing it and snapping it shut. When she turned and saw Nova, Ada started moving faster.

"I'm getting out of here," said Ada.

"What about your daughter?" asked Nova.

"I never had a daughter," said Ada. "That thing sprang straight from Junior Crawford's loins. It never was mine, never was about me at all." Ada busied around the room, picking up things and looking at them, a ginger jar, a silk scarf, gold and diamond earrings from the bureau.

"She from the Devil," said Nova, who came in and sat on the edge of the bed and watched Ada scurry around with her long white gloves.

"Right as rain," said Ada. "She is the Devil. If there's a God, she and Junior will kill each other some day." She moved faster and faster from object to object.

"Maybe you need a Valium or something," said Nova.

"Don't you talk to me like that, you stupid little nigger!" Ada shouted. She stamped her foot at Nova and then began to cry, immediately aghast at what she had said. "Oh God, Nova, I'm sorry. I didn't mean it. I'm just going crazy. Everything's crazy."

"It don't mean nothing to me," Nova said. "I been called worse than a nigger."

"Don't say that!" shouted Ada, putting her hands over her ears. "Nobody with a soul would ever say that word. This is a beautiful world. This is a world made for love and art. Say that with me, Nova. *This is a beautiful world made for love and art.*"

"This a beautiful world for love and art," mumbled Nova.

"Yes," said Ada. "That's better. That's much better. Don't you feel better now?"

"No'm, I don't reckon I do, but I don't hardly know nothing about art," Nova said. "I don't hardly know nothing about nothing."

"Why sure you do," Ada said, still scurrying from object to object, wondering what she should take with her. "Tell me what you know about love, Nova. You can tell me that."

"Well, God loved this world so much he give his son to save us all from the Devil," said Nova. Ada stopped in her manic whirl and stared at Nova for a moment and burst out laughing. Then she slammed the suitcase shut and pulled it off the bed and started out the door, into the hall, and down the stairs. Sergeant Lowell Palmer of the Mississippi State Patrol was standing at the bottom of the stairs, smiling.

"Miz Crawford, they've rescued your daughter!" Sergeant Palmer shouted up at her as Ada struggled down the stairs. "They killed the guy who murdered all those people. Your husband got your daughter back himself! They just got back out of that swamp, back to the house. That boy'd killed his own father! Said it looked like the old man had gone out to look for them, and the boy killed his own father. But your daughter is fine."

Ada stopped on the stairs, Nova beside her. Neither of them smiled at all. They stared at Lowell Palmer with fierce blankness. Then they started together down the stairs without saying a thing. When they got to Sergeant Palmer, they brushed past him and headed through the dining room, toward the kitchen. Completely puzzled, he followed, repeating what he had said about Truly.

"Leave me alone," said Ada. "They deserve each other."

"Are you going somewhere?" asked Sergeant Palmer. Ada turned and looked at him, wondering if his little girl was sweet, if she hugged him before she went to bed. Then she remembered that he and his wife were divorced.

"Yes," said Ada. "I damn well am going somewhere." Ada opened the back door and went outside, Nova right behind her. The rain had almost stopped, but the air was full of night sounds, and a wind had come up. The leaves in the treetops swished. Sergeant Palmer stood on the top doorstep and watched as Ada put the heavy suitcase in the backseat. She stared at Butch, and with a shiver, thought of taking him with her. But she knew that dark vision was retreating now. She got in her car, then Nova walked around and got in.

"How about dropping me by my house, Miss Ada?" said Nova.

"Yes, I will," said Ada. When she turned on the car, they both saw, in the headlights, the silent marbled eyes of the dog beneath the tree. Ada drove around the house and swerved to plow down three or four boxwoods before she came over the curb, flinging sparks from the tail pipe. It wasn't so far to Memphis.

+ + +

Leslie Ripley had never in his life seen so many lights. They turned, blue and red, around his house, dancing on the walls of the barn and into the trees, into the clouds that were now starting to spatter the dusty earth with rain. Ambulances and police cars seemed to be everywhere. Television cameramen and reporters were grabbing everyone in sight for a comment. Monk Reubens had already talked with Truly for half an hour, and she told how she had stopped at the Ripley Garage for a Coke, how Snake had taken her back to his house and then fled when the lawmen arrived, how brutally he had assaulted her. Junior had sat at her side with his face in his hands, groaning and crying.

Monk felt strange about the whole thing, as if it were part of some charade, a play with an inevitable yet inconclusive ending. When he got home, he could talk to Mona about it and see what had happened more clearly. But he was glad that it was over. It would all be wrapped up quickly. They were treating the younger boy in the ambulance before they headed to the hospital.

Monk climbed into the back of the ambulance and crawled up beside Leslie's face. He seemed confused but alert. They'd bandaged his feet, and an IV twisted into the inside of his elbow. An attendant was wiping the sweat off his face.

"Is he stable?" asked Monk.

"Seems to be," said the attendant, who was fat and soft.

"Leave us alone for a minute," said Monk.

"Sure thing, General," said the attendant, and he crawled past Leslie and got out. Monk took Leslie's hand and held it, smiled at him. Leslie smiled back.

"You're going to be all right, son," said Monk softly. "There are people who will take care of you."

"They will?" said Leslie. He looked away from Monk. Something was forming in his head or his heart. Perhaps it was light or the sound of rain. He seemed to know something he had forgotten. Jesus had gone to a better place, but men kept killing each other. His feet began to hurt terribly. He trembled. "Oh, it hurts!"

Monk squeezed his hand tighter. Leslie's eyes filled, and he looked up at Monk. Each was surprised to see the other crying.

A TV reporter from New Orleans was interviewing Junior about how he had saved his own daughter and killed the maniac who had ravaged Rockton. Junior swelled with pride, his face starting to drip with rain. The ambulances carrying Snake and Harry pulled out of the yard, red lights drumming against the darkness, sirens off.

"Do you feel like a hero?" the woman asked. Junior smiled and thought of the Crawford family, and he was already nodding.

"I guess I do," he said, his voice rising. "Now that you said it, I guess I do. I didn't say it. But I guess if the hat fits . . ." Junior coughed and laughed.

"Did you think you were going to be able to save her when you got out there?" a newspaperman asked. Junior was staring at the TV reporter, who had long black hair and blue eyes. The newspaperman repeated the question.

"Well, me and my men are a disciplined outfit," Junior said. Monk Reubens, standing nearby, felt for the first time as if he would be sick. "I thought that once we had them out there, we could take over unless Truly was tied up or something." While he talked, Truly wandered out of the lights and into the barn. The single light bulb was still on, and Snake's gym equipment was unmoved from several hours before, flecks of blood on the wall from where he had been hitting the heavy bag. Truly touched one spot of blood on the wall.

"Did you ever lose hope?" the TV reporter asked.

"Hope? Hell, sugar, I invented that," Junior said. His laughter echoed across the pasture, out into the silence, the night.

+   +   +

Truly and Junior got home just before midnight. Sergeant Lowell Palmer of the state patrol had long been gone, and the house was silent, lights on everywhere.

"You call Mama?" asked Truly, yawning. Junior had refused permission for Truly to be examined at the hospital, and since Snake Ripley was dead, the matter of rape was unimportant. Junior snapped his fat fingers just as he put the car into park.

"Damned if I didn't," he grinned. "Wait till she hears what happened. This is what she's been waiting to hear for so long. She's never got over the fact I don't have a regular job. Wait till she finds out I'm a hero."

They went together up the steps. Truly had left her car at the Ripley house. Monk said they would bring it on home later, after the state crime-lab boys looked it over. The house was still as a tomb.

"Baby!" called Junior. He swaggered through the house looking for Ada as Truly sat at the kitchen table and sipped a cold beer she had gotten from the refrigerator. Junior climbed the stairs and looked in their bedroom, calling her name. The room was suffocatingly hot. The rain had stopped an hour before, and the cool breeze was gone. The heat had come back.

Junior lumbered downstairs into the kitchen and saw Truly drinking a beer.

"That looks good," Junior said. "I reckon your mama's out driving around in that damn air-conditioned car. All this and she's just out driving around. You'd think she'd of waited." Junior got a beer from the refrigerator.

"I knew she didn't love me," said Truly. "I always knew that."

"She just loves paintings," shrugged Junior. "She never did love anything that was real. A painting. Hell, that's nothing but marks on a sheet of canvas. Who in the hell would fall in love with something like that?"

"I couldn't guess," said Truly.

"God, it's hot in here," said Junior. "Let's go back outside. Let's go sit on the back steps. It's usually cooler out there." Junior thought about Snake Ripley raping his only daughter and wanted to tear some living thing apart. They walked outside.

"I want to sit in the grass," said Truly. "Let's go sit where it's cool and wet in the grass."

"Okay, sweetness," said Junior. They went out to the spacious back lawn and sat in the wetness. The stars were lost in the rainless black clouds. They sat, side by side, and sipped the beer.

"Life," laughed Truly, looking up and seeing nothing.

"Hell of a thing," said Junior Crawford. The wind came up again, and a few miles away, thunder boiled up like the firing of cannons. They did not notice, when the lightning briefly swayed over them, that a leash lay frayed and empty against the water oak.

They did not notice the curled lip of the dog that was nearly upon them or see the coiled muscles taut and ready to spring. They did not hear the first growl erupt.

Junior was just reaching out for his daughter's hand.

About the Author

PHILIP LEE WILLIAMS lives near Athens, Georgia. This is his sixth published novel.